MOLLY THYNNE
THE CRIME AT THE 'NOAH'S ARK'

MARY 'MOLLY' THYNNE was born in 1881, a member of the aristocracy, and related, on her mother's side, to the painter James McNeil Whistler. She grew up in Kensington and at a young age met literary figures like Rudyard Kipling and Henry James.

Her first novel, *An Uncertain Glory*, was published in 1914, but she did not turn to crime fiction until *The Draycott Murder Mystery*, the first of six golden age mysteries she wrote and published in as many years, between 1928 and 1933. The last three of these featured Dr. Constantine, chess master and amateur sleuth *par excellence*.

Molly Thynne never married. She enjoyed travelling abroad, but spent most of her life in the village of Bovey Tracey, Devon, where she was finally laid to rest in 1950.

D1282145

BY MOLLY THYNNE

MOLLY THYNNE

THE CRIME AT THE 'NOAH'S ARK'

With an introduction by
Curtis Evans

DEAN STREET PRESS

INTRODUCTION

ALTHOUGH British Golden Age detective novels are known for their depictions of between-the-wars aristocratic life, few British mystery writers of the era could have claimed (had they been so inclined) aristocratic lineage. There is no doubt, however, about the gilded ancestry of Mary "Molly" Harriet Thynne (1881-1950), author of a half-dozen detective novels published between 1928 and 1933. Through her father Molly Thynne was descended from a panoply of titled ancestors, including Thomas Thynne, 2nd Marquess of Bath; William Bagot, 1st Baron Bagot; George Villiers, 4th Earl of Jersey; and William Bentinck, 2nd Duke of Portland. In 1923, five years before Molly Thynne published her first detective novel, the future crime writer's lovely second cousin (once removed), Lady Mary Thynne, a daughter of the fifth Marquess of Bath and habitué of society pages in both the United Kingdom and the United States, served as one of the bridesmaids at the wedding of the Duke of York and his bride (the future King George VI and Queen Elizabeth). Longleat, the grand ancestral estate of the marquesses of Bath, remains under the ownership of the Thynne family today, although the estate has long been open to the public, complete with its famed safari park, which likely was the inspiration for the setting of *A Pride of Heroes* (1969) (in the US, *The Old English Peep-Show*), an acclaimed, whimsical detective novel by the late British author Peter Dickinson.

Molly Thynne's matrilineal descent is of note as well, for through her mother, Anne "Annie" Harriet Haden, she possessed blood ties to the English etcher Sir Francis Seymour Haden (1818-1910), her maternal grandfather, and the American artist James McNeill Whistler (1834-1903), a great-uncle, who is still renowned today for his enduringly evocative *Arrangement in Grey and Black no. 1* (aka "Whistler's Mother"). As a child Annie Haden, fourteen years younger than her brilliant Uncle James, was the subject of some of the artist's earliest etchings. Whistler's relationship with the Hadens later ruptured when his brother-in-law Seymour Haden became critical of what he deemed the younger artist's dissolute lifestyle. (Among other things Whistler had taken an artists' model as his mistress.) The conflict between the two men culminated in

Whistler knocking Haden through a plate glass window during an altercation in Paris, after which the two men never spoke to one another again.

Molly Thynne grew up in privileged circumstances in Kensington, London, where her father, Charles Edward Thynne, a grandson of the second Marquess of Bath, held the position of Assistant Solicitor to His Majesty's Customs. According to the 1901 English census the needs of the Thynne family of four--consisting of Molly, her parents and her younger brother, Roger--were attended to by a staff of five domestics: a cook, parlourmaid, housemaid, under-housemaid and lady's maid. As an adolescent Molly spent much of her time visiting her Grandfather Haden's workroom, where she met a menagerie of artistic and literary lions, including authors Rudyard Kipling and Henry James.

Molly Thynne--the current Marquess has dropped the "e" from the surname to emphasize that it is pronounced "thin"--exhibited literary leanings of her own, publishing journal articles in her twenties and a novel, *The Uncertain Glory* (1914), when she was 33. *Glory*, described in one notice as concerning the "vicissitudes and love affairs of a young artist" in London and Munich, clearly must have drawn on Molly's family background, though one reviewer reassured potentially censorious middle-class readers that the author had "not over-accentuated Bohemian atmosphere" and in fact had "very cleverly diverted" sympathy away from "the brilliant-hued coquette who holds the stage at the commencement" of the novel toward "the plain-featured girl of noble character."

Despite good reviews for *The Uncertain Glory*, Molly Thynne appears not to have published another novel until she commenced her brief crime fiction career fourteen years later in 1928. Then for a short time she followed in the footsteps of such earlier heralded British women crime writers as Agatha Christie, Dorothy L. Sayers, Margaret Cole, Annie Haynes (also reprinted by Dean Street Press), Anthony Gilbert and A. Fielding. Between 1928 and 1933 there appeared from Thynne's hand six detective novels: *The Red Dwarf* (1928: in the US, *The Draycott Murder Mystery*), *The Murder on the "Enriqueta"* (1929: in the US, *The Strangler*), *The Case of Sir Adam Braid* (1930), *The Crime at the "Noah's Ark"* (1931), *Murder in the*

Dentist's Chair (1932: in the US, *Murder in the Dentist Chair*) and *He Dies and Makes No Sign* (1933).

Three of Thynne's half-dozen mystery novels were published in the United States as well as in the United Kingdom, but none of them were reprinted in paperback in either country and the books rapidly fell out of public memory after Thynne ceased writing detective fiction in 1933, despite the fact that a 1930 notice speculated that "[Molly Thynne] is perhaps the best woman-writer of detective stories we know." The highly discerning author and crime fiction reviewer Charles Williams, a friend of C.S. Lewis and J.R.R. Tolkien and editor of Oxford University Press, also held Thynne in high regard, opining that Dr. Constantine, the "chess-playing amateur detective" in the author's *Murder in the Dentist's Chair*, "deserves to be known with the Frenches and the Fortunes" (this a reference to the series detectives of two of the then most highly-esteemed British mystery writers, Freeman Wills Crofts and H.C. Bailey). For its part the magazine *Punch* drolly cast its praise for Thynne's *The Murder on the "Enriqueta"* in poetic form.

> *The Murder on the "Enriqueta"* is a recent thriller by
>   Miss Molly Thynne,
> A book I don't advise you, if you're busy, to begin.
> It opens very nicely with a strangling on a liner
> Of a shady sort of passenger, an out-bound
>   Argentiner.
> And, unless I'm much mistaken, you will find
>   yourself unwilling
> To lay aside a yarn so crammed with situations
>   thrilling.
> (To say nothing of a villain with a gruesome taste
>   in killing.)

There are seven more lines, but readers will get the amusing gist of the piece from the quoted excerpt. More prosaic yet no less praiseful was a review of *Enriqueta* in *The Outlook*, an American journal, which promised "excitement for the reader in this very well written detective story … with an unusual twist to the plot which adds to the thrills."

Despite such praise, the independently wealthy Molly Thynne in 1933 published her last known detective novel (the third of three consecutive novels concerning the cases of Dr. Constantine) and appears thereupon to have retired from authorship. Having proudly dubbed herself a "spinster" in print as early as 1905, when she was but 24, Thynne never married. When not traveling in Europe (she seems to have particularly enjoyed Rome, where her brother for two decades after the First World War served as Secretary of His Majesty's Legation to the Holy See), Thynne resided at Crewys House, located in the small Devon town of Bovey Tracey, the so-called "Gateway to the Moor." She passed away in 1950 at the age of 68 and was laid to rest after services at Bovey Tracey's Catholic Church of the Holy Spirit. Now, over sixty-five years later, Molly Thynne's literary legacy happily can be enjoyed by a new generation of vintage mystery fans.

Curtis Evans

CHAPTER I

THE SNOW HAD begun in the second week of December. It was hailed with joy by the entire infant population of the country; by the Press, which had already exhausted such time-worn copy as is to be culled from November fogs, and was at a loss to fill the hiatus that lies between "Collisions in the Channel" and "Christmas Shopping," and by those inveterate sentimentalists who care not how bitter the weather may be, provided it is "seasonable."

A white Christmas was predicted. Winter-sport enthusiasts routed their skis out from the attics where they had lain hidden for a twelvemonth, and less fortunate people, who had never set eyes on a Swiss mountain, spent happy hours fitting runners on to soap boxes, pessimistically aware that at any moment the snow might turn to sleet, and the fair, untrodden fields of virgin white to black slush. But for once it seemed that they were to be pleasantly disappointed. Day after day they woke to see the snow-flakes drifting slowly past the windows; and day after day the drifts rose higher and higher in the country lanes, until even the children grew tired of snowballing and turned to the contemplation of their chilblains, and the adult population of the country began to look upon "seasonable weather" as a rather grim joke.

And then it got beyond a joke. Conditions reached a point at which they ceased to be funny and became merely irksome and annoying. Posts were late; the milk did not arrive in the morning; gutters and drains got stopped up in the evening, when it was too dark to see to clear them; and even the most confirmed among the sentimentalists began to grumble.

And still the snow went on. And, inevitably, the slow-moving but irrepressible sense of humour of the English reasserted itself, the absurdity of the situation caught their fancy, and the whole business became a joke once more. Within five days of Christmas the roads showed signs of becoming so blocked that it was doubtful whether the holiday-makers would reach their destinations, while the holly and turkeys destined for the delectation of those who had wisely elected to stay at home seemed unlikely to reach London at all. In spite of which, transport, though difficult, had not yet become impossible, and "going away for Christmas" had merely taken on the proportions of a gigantic game, in which the would-be holiday-maker pitted himself gleefully enough against Nature, and usually managed to win out in the end.

It was in this spirit that Angus Stuart set out to spend Christmas at Redsands. Indeed, it would have taken more than a snowfall to abash him, for he had only lately achieved a condition of serene content that would probably never again be his in this life. Love might come to him and possibly fame, but once only can a man taste success in the full tide of his youth and vigour; once only, after a period of sordid poverty, can he watch his bank balance swell in a few months to proportions he had never dared dream of; once only, and, when one is twenty-three this is perhaps the greatest bliss of all, can he prove himself right in the face of his disapproving elders.

Small wonder that Stuart was a little fey that morning when, in defiance of the ominous list of blocked roads which had issued from his (brand-new) loud speaker the night before, he climbed into the car that had been his for barely a month and set out for the most expensive pleasure resort on the map of England. Whether he succeeded in reaching it or not was, on the whole, immaterial to him. Less than a year ago he would have had his expenses scheduled to the last farthing, and any hitch on his journey, if it entailed the added cost of a night's lodging, would have curtailed his Christmas holiday proportionately. Now, for the first time, he was realizing the power of money. He would put up anywhere he chose, no matter how expensive the hotel, and even should he wreck the car on the road, the disaster would be one he would be able to face financially. For, with a suddenness that even now took his breath away, he had become that most fortunate of mortals—the author of a best seller.

Three years before, in the face of the strident disapproval of an apoplectically-inclined father, a mother whose capacity for tears had been a weapon that until then had never failed her, two aunts, the one gloomy, the other acid, and an abominably level-headed and capable elder brother, he had thrown up a job which would in all probability have ended in a partnership. When, as an excuse for this act of wanton folly and ingratitude, he had explained that his first novel was already in the hands of a publisher, and that he proposed to become a writer of books, there had ensued a scene which he was still trying in vain to forget.

Six hours later he was in London with only twenty pounds and the problematical royalties of an as yet unpublished novel between him and starvation. For two years he had scratched a living out of the bare husk which, in his innocence, he had once glorified by the name of Art; but in the meagre hours snatched jealously from the hack work he did not dare refuse, he had managed to produce two more novels, and with the second his luck had turned. As in a dream he had watched the editions multiply; had sold the film rights for what had seemed to him then an incredible sum; had dealt graciously with editors who but a few months before had been known to him only by the slight variations in the wording of their printed rejection slips; and, at last, still dazed with the magnitude of his own success, had found himself blinking inanely across the footlights at an enthusiastic audience on the first night of the dramatization of his book.

And now he was on his way to Redsands, an expedition which, as he quite realized, was only another manifestation of that slight inebriation from which he had been suffering of late. He had never broken with his people, though during the lean years he had avoided seeing them, and when his mother had written, taking it for granted that he would accept his father's belated suggestion that he should spend Christmas at home, he could not quite stifle a feeling of resentment. Conceit had never been one of his failings, but he was human enough to feel that the invitation had followed a little too closely on the heels of his success. It was no doubt some unconscious reaction that had made him choose Redsands—the latest, most exclusive and expensive of coast resorts—as an alternative to the fatted calf at home. In his present state of elation he took no account of the fact that he was by nature shy, and inclined to be awkward in the presence of strangers. And among strangers he would certainly find himself, for not only had he no acquaintances there, but he had never at any period of his life mixed with the kind of people who go to such places as a matter of course.

It was not until his thoughts had begun to turn towards lunch that it dawned on him that he had taken close on three hours to travel less than fifty miles. Also, it was snowing more heavily than when he had started, and the roads were becoming noticeably worse. For some time driving had been not only difficult, but actually dangerous, and twice he had narrowly escaped ditching the car. The strain and the cold were beginning to tell on him, and he realized that, unless the snow stopped soon, the roads would become almost impassable.

He had already made up his mind to put up at the first decent inn he came to, when he arrived at the hill that was destined during the next few days to prove the undoing of many a better car than his.

His attention was first drawn to its possibilities the forlorn little group which had parked itself at the bottom. Three of the cars had obviously shirked the ascent. A lorry, now firmly lodged in the snow-filled ditch, had had a shot at it, and a big Rolls, slued half way across the road, had evidently only escaped a similar fate by backing into the lorry. A very aged person, with a sack round his shoulders, was observing the wreckage with a certain dour satisfaction.

"You'd better bide where you be, sir," he piped planting himself in the path of Stuart's car, "or she'll be on top of 'ee. Oy, there she come!"

His voice rose to an exultant squeak, and Stuart became aware of a large touring car majestically pursuing its inexorable way backwards down the hill towards them. It was gathering momentum with every yard, and Stuart, with a hasty glance behind him prepared to back out of harm's way. But the wearer of the sack seemed quite prepared to deal with the situation. Planted in the middle of the road, he addressed the chauffeur, whose anxious face could just be seen peering from the driver's seat. He was doing his best to keep the car straight, but, with the wheels locked and the car gathering speed each moment as it skidded down the steep incline, he was finding it a difficult business.

"Turn 'er into the ditch there, just ahead o' tha' lurry, I tell 'ee. Turn 'er in, or you'll smash, for sure. Turn 'er in, I tell 'ee!" he piped vociferously.

And the chauffeur, seeing nothing else for it, turned her in. There was a thud as the luggage carrier met the bonnet of the Rolls, then the two cars settled down side by side in the snow, and the tension was over.

The chauffeur climbed out and opened the door of the car. After a short and apparently animated discussion he carefully handed out an old lady.

She was short and plump and evidently badly shaken. The chauffeur, who looked himself as if a stiff drink would do him no harm, was obviously at a loss as to what to do with her now that he had got her out into the snow. She was clinging to him with both hands, staring helplessly in the direction of Stuart and the aged yokel, and looked as if at any moment she might collapse in a heap at his feet.

Stuart, remembering the flask he had thrust into his pocket just before leaving, got out of his car and started up the hill towards them. He arrived just as the head of another, rather younger, lady was thrust through the still open door.

"Pull yourself together, Connie!" said the owner sharply. "By the mercy of Providence we are none of us any the worse. Let us be thankful!"

The first old lady continued to stare helplessly at Stuart.

"Eh?" she queried vaguely.

"Trumpet!" ejaculated her companion, with almost vicious intensity.

Stuart, not unreasonably mistaking the word for one not usually employed by old ladies in polite society, stood aghast, his offer of assistance frozen on his lips. Then his eyes fell on the black satin cornucopia dangling from the plump lady's wrist, and he understood.

At the same moment the chauffeur, rising to the occasion, gently disengaged the hand that was clutching his shoulder and placed the ear-trumpet in it. Mechanically the old lady raised it to her ear.

"Eh?" she repeated.

Her companion bent forward.

"Move away, Connie, and let me get out," she exclaimed, her voice shrill with suppressed exasperation. "I can't do anything while you stand there!"

"Move? Where?" murmured the owner of the ear-trumpet helplessly.

Stuart stepped forward and took her gently by the arm. With a start the old lady swung the trumpet violently in his direction, hitting him hard on the mouth.

"If you'll let me help you," he shouted valiantly down the orifice, his eyes watering with the pain of the impact. "We'll try to get a little farther away from the door."

She allowed him to support her for a few steps, while the other old lady climbed nimbly down into the snow and immediately took charge of the situation.

"Sit here," she said briskly, brushing the snow off the running board of the car. "This gentleman will help you, I'm sure, and you'll feel quite all right in a minute. My sister is a little shaken," she explained to Stuart as, between them, they managed to get her seated. "But she'll be quite herself after a short rest. She's not so young as she was, and I must say it was an alarming experience."

Fortunately the snow had almost ceased, though there was obviously more to come in the near future.

Stuart proffered his flask.

"If she's feeling faint—" he suggested awkwardly.

"Most kind of you, if I can only persuade her to touch it. Connie, this gentleman is offering you some brandy," she shouted into the wavering ear-trumpet. "Take a little drop—it will do you good."

"Eh?"

"A little drop of brandy—it will do you *good!*" reiterated the younger lady.

Then, in despair—

"I think if you would pour it out I might get her to drink it."

Stuart poured a stiff dose into the metal cup. Even if it did go to her head, he felt it could hardly make her more helpless.

"Now, drink it, dear, and sit quiet for a moment. Then you'll feel better," said her sister, bending over her.

Stuart tactfully withdrew and joined the chauffeur, who was investigating the damage to the back of the car.

"You wouldn't be any the worse for a drink yourself, I expect," he said, by way of an opening. "You'll have to take it straight from the flask, however."

The man accepted the offer gratefully.

"It did give me a bit of a turn when she began to skid," he admitted. "With the two old ladies inside and all."

"Lucky it wasn't worse," agreed Stuart. "I'm going to have a try at it all the same. I don't see the fun of staying here all night."

The chauffeur cocked an eye in the direction of Stuart's car.

"You'll likely do it all right in a light car," he said. "Another few yards and I'd have got her over the top. We'd never have made Redsands, though. There's two hills worse than this, and I'll bet there's not a car got up them to-day."

"There's one thing," he went on, as he handed back the flask to Stuart, "the luggage ain't damaged, and I can get it off all right. I'll have to cart it up to the inn and then get on to my owners."

"Hired, eh?"

"That's right, sir. The boss didn't want to let her out, seeing what the roads were like, but the old ladies had taken their rooms at Redsands for Christmas, and were so set on getting there that he gave in to them; but I'll lay he won't be surprised when I get through to him. Lucky for them that the old 'Noah's Ark' is close and handy."

"What's that? An inn?" asked Stuart.

The chauffeur nodded.

"If you turn up the lane at the top of the hill you'll come to it. It used to be one of them coaching inns, but it caters mostly for hunting gentlemen nowadays. Even now, the landlord was telling me, they get a bit of custom. Mostly cyclists and that. It's not new-fangled enough for motorists, but there was a party I was driving a couple of months ago stayed the night there, and I hadn't got no fault to find with the way they treated me."

How far on is it? It looks as if I'd better put up there myself, if what you say about the Redsands road is true."

"You can take my word for it, sir, you won't make it to-night. The snow's stopped, but by the look of things there's plenty more to come. You'll find the inn about three-quarters of a mile up the lane, and pretty bad going at that, I expect. How the old ladies are to get there, beats me. They'll find it a stiff walk, I'm thinking."

Stuart cast a calculating eye over the luggage.

"If I can make the hill I'll take them on," he said. "I can manage this stuff as well, I think, if you'll cart it to the top. Meanwhile, I'd better go and see about having a shot at it."

He returned to the two old ladies. The elder had apparently recovered herself, and they now stood, forlorn and utterly at a loss, gazing pathetically at their derelict hireling.

"Your chauffeur tells me that there's quite a good inn just round the corner," he said. "I'm going to try to get my car up the hill, and, if I succeed, I can give you a lift. It'll be rather a crush, I'm afraid, with the luggage, but better than a walk in this snow."

He waited while his proposal was conveyed to the elder of the two ladies through the medium of the ear-trumpet, and then, having received their almost tearful thanks, returned to his car.

His faith in her was justified, and he reached the top of the hill without mishap, to find the old ladies pluckily following in his wake, clinging to each other and giving little breathless cries of alternate warning and encouragement. The chauffeur followed, carrying their smaller luggage.

"There's a party down there that's turning back to Rushton," he said. "They'll give me a lift, and I can get on to my owners and send some one to salvage the car. They'll have to send down from the 'Noah's Ark' for the trunk."

"And we must stay on at this inn until he can come and fetch us," said the younger of the two ladies. "There's nothing else for us to do, I'm afraid, though it is annoying to feel that our rooms are waiting for us at Redsands all the time. However, we're very lucky to have fallen in with such a kind Samaritan," she finished gratefully.

"I feel for you," answered Stuart, who was busy making room for their luggage. "I've got a room at Redsands eating its head off, too. We'll hope that, with luck, we shall get there before Christmas, however."

"Surely we shall not have to stay long at this dreadful inn," whispered a husky voice at his elbow.

He turned, with a start, and realized that this was the first coherent sentence that had emanated from the sister with the ear-trumpet. Her little round face, blue and streaked with cold, was upturned to his, the trumpet inclined at an inviting angle in the direction of his mouth. He thought he had never seen anything so pathetically helpless.

"Not more than a night or two, I expect," he assured her, his habitual shyness forgotten. "And it will probably turn out to be quite comfortable. Things will look more hopeful, you know, when you've had a good warm and some food. If you can manage to squeeze in here beside the luggage, I'll run you and your sister up to the inn in no time."

He helped her in and tucked a spare rug round her. When he had finished, she peered over the top of it at him with the confiding trustfulness of a child.

Her sister was of stouter fibre, and as she climbed into the front seat beside him, with an agility that belied her years, her tongue wagged unceasingly.

"Most kind of you, I'm sure. In fact, I do not know what would have become of us if you had not taken compassion on us. Still, it is all in the nature of an adventure, isn't it? And we lead such quiet, uneventful lives at Tunbridge Wells, that when something unusual does happen, it's almost a relief. My sister, of course, doesn't feel like that, but one can hardly expect it, what with her deafness and everything. Such a trial to her—"

And so she prattled on, until Stuart found himself hoping that, if he ever did reach Redsands, it would not be to discover the two ladies established at the same hotel as himself.

He found the lane and turned into it. The snow had been cleared the day before, but it was, as the chauffeur had predicted, bad going, and his attention was fully occupied with the car. When he was able to attend to his passenger once more, he discovered that she was introducing herself.

"The least we can do is to tell you our names, after all your kindness," she was saying, in her bright little voice. "I am Miss Amy Adderley, and my sister is Miss Adderley. If you are ever in Tunbridge Wells, I hope you will call on us. What did you say, Connie dear?"

Miss Connie's husky whisper had barely made itself heard behind her. It reached Stuart, though, as she leaned forward and, with an effort, raised her voice.

"Leave him to his driving, Amy, and don't talk so much!"

There ensued an embarrassing silence, during which Stuart gazed ahead with a face of preternatural seriousness. But Miss Amy Adderley did not open her lips again till a bend in the lane brought them within sight of a scattered village.

"At least there will be a post office," she exclaimed. "We can get in touch with somebody. We must send a telegram to Agnes, Connie, and tell her not to forward any letters till she hears from us. Such a nuisance when one's letters go astray, isn't it?"

Stuart agreed with her.

"I'm afraid I never introduced myself," he went on shyly. "My name is Stuart, and I'm most awfully glad to have been of service to you. Anyway, we can make sure of having a roof over our heads to-night. There's the inn."

It stood four-square to the village street, reassuring in its rambling spaciousness. Unless half the rooms had fallen into disuse, there should be more than enough space for unexpected guests. The flickering light of a heaped-up fire shone on the uncurtained windows of the taproom, and a wide arch, to the right of the main building, led into a yard that, so far as Stuart could see, was large enough to house a dozen cars. It was easy to picture the cheerful bustle that must have prevailed when the mail arrived in the old coaching days. A signboard hung from the old-fashioned porch, and Stuart glanced at it as he climbed stiffly from the car.

"The 'Noah's Ark,'" he said, extending a helpful hand to Miss Amy. "It sounds a bit antediluvian, but there's something cheery about the place all the same."

The landlord himself came out to meet them. He was a spare, elderly man, whose face showed the rather wizened shrewdness of one who has dealt with horses all his life. Stuart was to discover later that he had been coachman to the family that owned most of the property in that part of the world, and that the old inn had been left to him by his late master as a tribute to long and faithful service. Also that the "Noah's Ark" was not quite such a back number as it seemed. It was well known to hunting men, and, but for the heavy fall of snow, would have been filled to capacity at this time of year.

As it was, he could accommodate them easily, the landlord assured them, and would have fires burning in their rooms by the time they had warmed themselves and finished the lunch which was just being served in the coffee-room. He turned the old ladies over to a capable-looking maid, while Stuart established good relations over a drink in the bar.

"I can put up your machine all right, sir," said the landlord. "We've a good-sized barn back of the stables there, though it's 'orses I cater for mostly, even in these days."

"It's been a bad season for you so far, I'm afraid," sympathized Stuart.

"And looked as if it was goin' to get worse. But there's some good in all things evil, as they say, and it seems as if this 'ere snow was goin' to bring custom, instead of drivin' it away. If it had been a frost now, I should have had the place empty on my hands."

"Well, I hope we bring you luck," said Stuart pleasantly.

The landlord laughed.

"Oh, you're not the first by any means, sir! That hill's fair put the fear o' God into the motorists. There's three lots turned up before you, and I'm thinking there'll be more before nightfall. If I've read the signs right, there's another heavy fall to come."

"You'll have us here over Christmas, if this goes on," said Stuart rather ruefully.

"And welcome, sir, as far as I'm concerned," was the landlord's hearty rejoinder.

As he spoke a dark shadow fell across his face, and Stuart, looking round in surprise, realized that twilight had fallen suddenly on the wide, low-ceilinged room. Then, in a second, the blight was lifted, as the huge motor coach that had caused it ceased to block the long window and drew up in front of the door of the inn.

The landlord hurried to the door.

"What did I say, sir?" he exclaimed over his shoulder. "Here's another of 'em! Looks to be one of them coaches this time. We shall get a bit of all sorts at this rate."

With unashamed curiosity, Stuart gulped down what was left of his drink and followed him into the passage. As he did so it occurred to him that, should he be held up indefinitely, the "Noah's Ark," with its involuntary and heterogeneous cargo, might prove a more entertaining place in which to spend Christmas than the magnificent hostelry that awaited him at Redsands.

CHAPTER II

STUART'S SENSE of well-being increased considerably as he made his first detailed inspection of the interior of the "Noah's Ark." He had glanced casually round him on his first arrival, and had decided that the place seemed clean and comfortable; but now he realized how completely even successive generations of local painters and paperers had failed to mar its beauty. The roomy passage, which ran from the front door to the foot of the stairs, and which had been turned into a miniature lounge, was panelled to the height of a man's shoulder, and the wide staircase possessed an oak balustrade that many a London dealer had tried to buy in vain. Above the panelling was, needless to say, the inevitable, abominable Victorian wall-paper, and the wood itself had been painted and repainted a nauseous chocolate; but the paper had faded until it had become so neutral as to be hardly noticeable, and nothing could alter the graceful proportions of a house that had been built in less hurried and more spacious days.

At the foot of the staircase was a table littered with newspapers. Stuart seated himself at it and, under cover of a dog's-eared magazine, settled down to observe the new-comers, realizing with some amusement as he did so that he was already adopting the superior attitude that the established guest invariably takes towards a new arrival.

At the sight of the first person to enter the lounge he decided that his critical attitude was more than justified. Everything about the young man who strolled, with an air of ineffable languor, through the front door, was an offence to one who, with all the care in the world, had never been able to control the crease in his trousers or the vagaries of his ties. For this favoured individual, whose delicately tinted felt hat was just a fraction wider in the brim, his frieze coat a trifle rougher in texture, its upturned collar a shade higher than is usual, had emerged from what must have been a singularly trying journey looking as though he had just stepped out of a Hollywood dressing-room. The bitter cold had failed to do more than add an interesting pallor to features which even Stuart felt bound to admit were faultless in their regularity.

The next arrival offered a distinct relief, for he was as completely undistinguished as his predecessor had been spectacular. A shabby young man this, tightly buttoned into an overcoat manifestly too thin for the time of year. From the folds of a gaudily striped muffler emerged the tip of an upturned nose, blue with cold, and a pair of grey eyes which, as Stuart was to learn later, were capable of an impish humour. At present they were clouded with an anxiety which Stuart, in view of his own recent past, had no difficulty in interpreting. He was probably summoning up his courage to ask for the cheapest room in the inn, and wondering how much even that would cost him.'

Then the third, and last, occupant of the motor coach entered, and Stuart's interest in the other two passengers evaporated completely. For the old man who stood for a moment in the doorway, his keen eyes taking stock of his surroundings, was endowed with the two subtlest of human qualities—charm and personality. He gave the impression that, in whatever company he might find himself, he would be at his ease, and at the same time, without being in the least incongruous, strike quite a definite note. No longer young, his clothes good but inconspicuous, scrupulously neat, from his little pointed white beard to his brilliantly polished square-toed black shoes, he filled the stage, as it were, from the moment he stepped on to it. He had removed his hat on entering, revealing a magnificent crop of white hair, so thick and virile that it stood up almost *en brosse*, an effective setting to the observant black eyes and clear olive skin below.

Stuart observed that he had fallen instinctively into the role of spokesman to the little party, which had now advanced to within earshot of the table at which he sat. He also noticed that the old man inquired first after the cheapest accommodation, and that it was not until the boy in the shabby overcoat had been catered for that he engaged a large front room for himself.

The landlord conducted them upstairs. On his way down, a few minutes later, he paused at Stuart's table.

"Luncheon will be served in a few minutes now, sir," he said. "You'll find the coffee-room on the right there."

"You've got a mixed bag this time," remarked Stuart, with a smile. "Who's the old gentleman with the white hair?"

"Name of Constantine. It sounds foreign to me, but he speaks English all right. Very pleasant gentleman to deal with."

"Constantine!" repeated Stuart. "I've seen that name somewhere! I remember wondering whether it was Greek, but I can't get the connection at the moment."

He was still worrying over it as he entered the coffee-room five minutes later, and it was not till he was eating his soup that he remembered where he had seen it. He thrust his hand into his pocket and brought out the elaborately got up pamphlet issued by the syndicate that was responsible for the magic transformation of the obscure little fishing village of Redsands. It had certainly left no stone unturned in its efforts to cater for the various tastes of its guests. Among the less frivolous of the entertainments arranged for Christmas week was a chess tournament, and among the names of the various champions who had been persuaded to take part was that of Luke Constantine.

Lunch had already begun when Stuart took his seat at the table, and he had had little time in which to observe his neighbours. He was tucking the little book away in his pocket when the man on his right addressed him.

"I see you're one of the lucky ones," he remarked genially.

Stuart failed to get his meaning, and, as was his way when caught at a disadvantage, immediately became absurdly shy.

"I'm afraid—" he stammered.

"Bound for Paradise like the rest of them," explained his neighbour. "Except for those two waiters there, I believe I'm the only poor devil in this room that isn't, or rather wasn't, going to Redsands for Christmas. When I saw you come in I had a kind of hope that you might be just an ordinary human being like myself. Then I looked round and there you were, complete with book and all!"

There was something disarming in the man's friendliness; something engaging, too, in the rueful voice with its Cockney twang. It dissolved Stuart's shyness, and, in the reaction, he was moved to candour.

"To tell you the truth, this is my first visit to Redsands," he said. "I've never been able to afford anything of the sort before, and I don't suppose I ever shall again. But I thought I'd like to see what it was like."

"And you'll pay through the nose for it by the time you're through. And what's more, you'll get just about the same sort of thing that you'd find at Blackpool, if you waited till next August, only served with a gold spoon, as it were."

Stuart laughed.

"At this rate it doesn't look much as if I was going to get anything at all," he said. "It'll be a queer Christmas if we're hung up here."

"Queerer for me than for you," was his neighbour's gloomy rejoinder. "You'll melt in all right after a day or so, but I see myself sitting alone in the bar. Have you cast an eye on that crowd over there?"

He jerked his head in the direction of a smaller table placed in the bow window overlooking the street. Stuart glanced at it, and with difficulty suppressed a chuckle, for a more inaccessible little group of people he had seldom seen.

At one end of the table he recognized the two Misses Adderley. But they had become very different beings from the shivering derelicts he had picked up in the snow. He could only imagine that they had reverted to their Tunbridge Wells manner. Very erect, and icily unconscious of the other occupants of the coffee-room, they were silently lunching. If they had been able to converse in low refined voices they no doubt would have done so, but Miss Connie's inevitable ear-trumpet made this impossible.

Before he had time to remove his eyes, Miss Amy saw him and treated him to a bow, so graciously distant that it was all he could do to keep his countenance. He turned his attention hastily to the other occupant of the table. He was seated by himself, facing Miss Connie Adderley, but apparently completely unconscious of her existence. A middle-aged man, whose muscle had run to fat, with a bull neck and an obstinate jaw. He wore a regimental tie, but it was difficult to imagine his slack, bulky figure in uniform.

"There's a worse crowd upstairs," vouchsafed Stuart's neighbour, with relish. "But they're so blooming proud that they have their meals in their own sitting-room. Name of Romsey. There's the old boy and his son and two daughters. And that's the lot, so far. But it doesn't look as if we were in for one of those old-world Christmases—parlour games, hunt the slipper, snap dragon, and that sort of thing! Can't you see them at it?"

Stuart laughed in spite of himself. He was easily disconcerted, and was already beginning to feel out of things himself, and there was something refreshing about the man's good-tempered vulgarity.

"Who's the fat man, do you know?" he asked.

His companion snorted.

"A proper bounder, if you ask me. Major Carew, he signs himself. A War major, I'm willing to bet, demobbed in 1918 and stuck to his rank ever since. He's the sort that would. Come to that, I could call myself Captain Soames, if I cared to, but I leave that to the regulars. I don't know who the old ladies are. They've only just come, but they don't seem what you might call pally, exactly."

"Their name's Adderley," said Stuart. "I'm afraid I'm responsible for them. I picked them up in the snow, and brought them along. They're harmless enough, really."

"All I can say is that you must have a nerve! I'd as soon pick up a nettle! I'm not complaining, and I'm not one to push in where I'm not wanted, but if I've got to be here over Christmas, I'd like to find some one I can talk to. I hope this snow lets up and we can get away, that's all."

"We shall get off all right. It can't go on like this for ever. Anyway, we're not going to be dependent on them for company. A motor bus came in just now with a load of three. Two of them look decent enough." Soames gave a groan.

"Good lord, only two? What's the matter with the third?"

"I'll leave you to judge," answered Stuart, as the door opened to admit the occupants of the motor coach.

He waited with glee for his companion's first trenchant comment, as the young exquisite, even more beautifully tailored than before, now that he had shed his outer garments, strolled up to their table. But none came. He glanced at his neighbour. Soames's face had lost its habitual look of cheerful effrontery, and there was an expression almost of awe in his eyes as he watched the oldest member of the little party take his seat on the opposite side of the table at which they sat.

For a while they ate in silence. Then suddenly, as though he could contain himself no longer, Soames leaned forward.

"I beg your pardon, sir," he said. "But aren't you Dr. Constantine?"

"That is my name," answered the older man, with a ready courtesy that relieved Stuart. He realized suddenly how much he would have disliked to see his neighbour snubbed.

"I knew you as soon as you came in," went on Soames eagerly. "That was a great game you played against Zilitzky at the Caxton Hall, if you'll allow me to say so."

The old man's eyes lit up with interest.

"If I had dreamed that I was going to meet a chess enthusiast I should have taken my misfortunes more philosophically," he said. "You play, of course?"

Soames's jolly face grew a shade redder.

"I'm no match for any tournament player, sir," he answered. "It's just a hobby with me, as it were, and being always on the road, I don't get much chance of playing. There's a little chess club I belong to, but it isn't often I manage to get down there."

The old man gave a sigh of relief.

"Then two of us, at least, are independent of the weather," he announced with conviction. "It may go on snowing till doomsday for all I care. That is to say, if you will take pity on a marooned chess maniac and play with me!"

Soames's face was a study in pleasure and gratification.

"I should count it an honour, sir," he stammered; and thus it was that two of the most incongruous figures in that mixed caravanserai entered into a partnership that was to outlast all the strange happenings of that Christmas week.

After that the conversation became general. Gradually each member of the party revealed himself. The genial Soames was, as Stuart had suspected, a commercial traveller, bound for the Station Hotel at Thorley, a house of call much more to his liking than the one in which he found himself. The shy boy, a chartered accountant's clerk, had been on his way to a village some twenty miles off, where he had intended to spend his brief holiday.

Stuart noticed that it was the old man, Constantine, who deftly evoked these particulars. His interest and sympathy seemed so genuine as to rob the questions that dropped from him casually in the course of conversation, of all offence.

As they rose from the table he made a characteristic suggestion.

"I have a suspicion," he said, "that we are only the forerunners of quite a procession of refugees. Also, it is beginning to look as if we should be obliged to spend several days, at least, in their company. Look at that!"

He pointed to the window, through which the snow could be seen falling heavily.

"That being the case," he went on, "I propose to take up my position as near as possible to that very pleasant fire in the lounge, and gratify my insatiable curiosity by watching the rest of the party arrive. Incidentally, there seems nothing else to do!"

Stuart was only too ready to join him. Soames and the boy, Trevor, disappeared to their rooms.

"Talking of curiosity," remarked Constantine, as he settled himself as comfortably as was consistent with the vagaries of his rather battered wicker chair, "I am afraid I have been pumping the landlord! He told me your name, and, unless I am mistaken, you are a very fortunate person. What is a vice in me is a sacred duty to you. Observation, which after all is only another name for curiosity, is your trade. You *are* the Angus Stuart who wrote *The Appian Way?*"

Stuart blushed.

"I'm afraid I must plead guilty," he answered.

"Why? It is a very good book. Rather a remarkable book for a man of your age. It is a great thing to have learned so much, without bitterness, in so short a time. All of which speaks well for curiosity," he concluded, with an infectious twinkle in his dark eyes.

Upon which, as he had no doubt intended, Stuart promptly told him all about himself.

"Well, you are in luck's way," was the old man's comment when he had finished. "By nightfall this inn should be teeming with material for a novelist, and it may be that we shall be as completely isolated from the outside world as the inhabitants of the original Noah's Ark. You will have your copy thrust at you, so to speak. I was once snowed up for a fortnight in Canada, years ago, and it is a very curious experience, I can assure you. Men become very primitive when they are bored, and with the exception of ourselves and our friend Soames, who I hope is going to play chess with me, everybody is going to be bored to extinction."

Stuart laughed.

"If the worst comes to the worst, I've got a pile of proofs with me. I may as well correct them here as at Redsands."

Soames rejoined them, and Constantine immediately began to draw out all that was best and most interesting in the commercial traveller. It was part of Soames's job to gauge the psychological reactions of his customers, and he was an expert in his own line. His shrewd comments on men and things showed him in quite a new light, and Stuart, as he sat and listened to the two older men, felt in little danger of succumbing to boredom.

They had been talking for nearly an hour when an icy blast from the front door heralded the arrival of a fresh batch of derelicts.

Now we shall see," murmured Constantine contentedly, settling himself deeper in his chair.

This time the predominating note of the party that entered was unmistakably that of affluence. It was easy to imagine the type of car which had discharged the litter of Bond Street gilt and lizard skin that was being borne by a chauffeur in the wake of a large, perfectly upholstered lady, whose voice immediately proclaimed her American origin. She was followed by a fair, quietly dressed girl—evidently a dependent of some sort—and an obvious lady's-maid, carrying a green morocco dressing-case.

As she threw open the front of her perfectly matched sable coat and drew off her gloves, she positively burst into scintillation. Stuart was irresistibly reminded of a newly-lit chandelier. Emeralds flashed on her plump white hands, and a bevy of little brooches, dotted here and there over her expansive bosom, vied with the diamonds in her ears. A more incongruous figure had probably never before graced the dingy lounge of the old inn.

"Well, I guess we'll just have to make the best of it!" was her comment, as her disparaging glance swept her surroundings, and, coming to rest on the little group at the foot of the stairs, dismissed them as completely negligible.

"And we'll just have to make the best of you," murmured the irrepressible Soames, as she swept upstairs, followed by her retinue.

"Curiously enough," remarked Constantine when she was out of hearing, "I can tell you a good deal about that lady. She has been pointed out to me several times. She is a Mrs. van Dolen, the widow of a rich American banker, and is chiefly remarkable for two things: the number of husbands she has tried and found wanting, and a certain emerald girdle that forms part of the regalia—I gather there is no other word for it—that she has been amassing for the last twenty years."

"It must be an uncommonly large girdle," was Soames's irreverent comment.

"I am told that it has increased with the years," Constantine informed him gravely. "Every stone in weight that she has put on has cost her thousands of pounds. As you may have guessed from my name, I am half Greek, and the Greeks of London are not only lovers but connoisseurs of precious stones. I have heard that girdle exhaustively discussed in the Greek colony, and from all accounts it is a very lovely piece of workmanship. The emeralds are linked together by a narrow, very flexible, gold and platinum band. An Italian firm in Paris made it."

An excited monologue broke out at the head of the stairs. Soames, whose seat was the only one that commanded a complete view of the staircase, grinned delightedly.

"I can tell you what that is," he announced. "Your American friend has clicked with the noble lord!"

"Hence the paean of triumph," murmured Constantine. The chances are that she has sat on some charitable committee with him, and has never relinquished her grasp on him since. I am told that her pertinacity is amazing."

"Does she live in England?" asked Stuart.

"She lives in hotels—anywhere—provided the hotel is expensive enough. During the London season she takes a furnished house and entertains lavishly. From all accounts she is an amazing creature. The story goes that her first husband took her from behind the bar of a public-house in Deptford, and that she has only acquired her American accent of late years. Her enemies say that she is apt to revert to Cockney in moments of stress."

He shifted his seat and peered round the corner of the oak stair-rail, only to give a gasp of dismay.

"Lord Romsey!" he exclaimed. "I know him, and, what's more unfortunate still, he knows me."

Stuart, following his example, caught a vision of a portly figure; above it, a pale, expressionless face, surmounting a massive double chin, and then Lord Romsey was upon them.

"Ha, Constantine!" he exclaimed, advancing with ponderous affability. "On your way to Redsands, of course!"

"I suppose you may call it that," admitted Constantine. "Though it seems a somewhat optimistic way of putting it."

Lord Romsey's pale, rather protruding eyes fastened themselves suspiciously on Constantine's face. He did not like jokes, and he had a dim idea that the older man had endeavoured to perpetrate one.

"Ah, the weather," he ejaculated, his seriousness unmarred. "We can only hope it may mend. As a matter of fact, I came downstairs to see if there was any possibility of a short stroll before tea. Our sitting-room is a little cramped. Do you feel inclined to come with me?"

Constantine smiled and shook his head.

"I detest exercise for its own sake," he said. "And I have at last reached an age at which I dare say so; besides which, it is still snowing very heavily."

Lord Romsey's heavy face looked slightly perturbed.

"My son and daughter are out in it," he said. "I was thinking of joining them."

He strolled through the open door into the coffee-room. They watched him, a dark, majestic figure, standing by the window, gazing out into the falling snow.

Constantine smiled.

"The greatest bore in Christendom," he murmured. "And it has paid him well. They gave him a Colonial appointment to get him out of the House of Commons, but he made such a hash of that that they simply had to recall him. Then he wormed his way back into the House, and was so insufferable there that they made him Baron Romsey of Romsey and sent him to the House of Lords."

"Do you mean to say they couldn't freeze him out any other way?" demanded the astonished Soames.

Constantine shrugged his shoulders.

"He's got the hide of a rhinoceros and he's one of the richest men in England. He's never recognized either a joke or a snub in his life. What could they do? Men like that are invulnerable. And the curious thing is that his son is quite a normal, decent fellow, and the younger daughter is charming."

An abrupt silence fell upon the party as the subject of their conversation reappeared in the doorway of the coffee-room.

"I am happy to say that they have had the sense to return," he announced.

The front door burst open and two figures, the one tall, the other short and slim, plunged into the lounge. They were so completely enveloped in snow that it was difficult at first to determine even their sex, and one of them, at least, was speechless with laughter.

Lord Romsey stood looking at them in silent disapproval.

"Angela fell into a snow-drift about ten feet deep, and it was all I could do to get her out," announced the taller of the two, shaking himself like a dog.

They pulled off their hats and revealed themselves. Three years ago, Angela Ford had been quoted as the prettiest debutante of her season, and her portrait had hardly ever been out of the illustrated papers since. Stuart noted, with mingled relief and appreciation, that she bore no resemblance to her father, and that no photograph he had seen, so far, had done anything like justice to her vivid beauty. Geoffrey Ford, her stepbrother, and her senior by sixteen years, had inherited Lord Romsey's heaviness of build, but he struck Stuart as sedate rather than pompous, and the grave smile with which he was looking down into his sister's glowing face was very pleasant and human.

Lord Romsey did not share his children's mirth.

"I should suggest your going to your rooms at once," he said frigidly. "You are making the lounge in a disgusting mess. A most foolish expedition altogether."

His daughter caught sight of Constantine, who had risen at her entrance. She came forward with outstretched hand.

"Mr. Constantine! How nice! Am I too wet to shake hands with?"

"Your father was just about to join you when you appeared," said Constantine, with a malicious twinkle in his eye. "I was trying to persuade him not to brave the weather."

"Pshaw!" ejaculated Lord Romsey, to the delight of Stuart, who until then had never believed that the word existed outside the dictionary.

"There's a car coming up the lane," announced Miss Ford. "We saw it from the corner. It looks as if we were to have more companions in misfortune."

Soames had picked up a magazine and was apparently absorbed in its contents. These people, his manner proclaimed, were not for him. But his attitude had not escaped the keen eyes of Constantine.

"May I introduce Mr. Soames," he said suavely, "and Mr. Angus Stuart, whose books you have no doubt read?"

"Not *the* Angus Stuart?" she exclaimed.

"*The* Angus Stuart," assented Constantine imperturbably; while Stuart, his face a rich brick-red, was still trying in vain to frame a suitable answer.

He was saved by the opportune arrival of the latest, and, as it afterwards turned out, the ultimate addition to the oddly mixed company.

At the sight of her Stuart realized that, no matter how sorry a trick the weather might play him, he was to receive some compensation. For, if the snow did not abate, he would spend Christmas under the same roof with two of the most attractive women he had ever met.

The new-comer was a good ten years older than the girl to whom he had just been introduced, but was of the type that gains, rather than loses, by maturity. One had but to look at her to know that she would be beautiful even in old age, and she was possessed of that subtle charm that some women carry with them to the grave.

As she stood there making her arrangements with the landlord, the eyes of every man in the lounge, down to the elderly waiter who stood peering out of the coffee-room, were upon her. Stuart could see even Lord Romsey straighten himself and give a thoughtful touch to his tie.

She had reached the foot of the staircase before she noticed her companions in misfortune. Until then her mind had been fully occupied by the landlord, who was explaining that her car would have to go on to the wheelwright's in the village, the hotel barn being already full to overflowing. The last lady to arrive had sent her car there, he assured her, and her chauffeur had been quite satisfied with the accommodation. She need have no fear as to its safety.

She acquiesced with a smile.

"Will you see that some one shows my man the way? And when he has finished with the car, I should like to see him," she said. "You can put him up, I suppose?"

As she spoke she cast an idle glance at the little group round the table.

As she did so, her whole body seemed to stiffen. For a moment she stared blindly, while the colour drained slowly from her face, leaving it as white as the drifting snow outside.

Then, with an obvious effort of will, she mastered her emotion, her grip on the balustrade relaxed, and she turned and went swiftly up the broad staircase.

But not before Stuart had had time to follow the direction of her eyes. Lord Romsey was standing as he had seen him last, pompous and unperturbed, with, if anything, a faint look of complacency on his heavy features.

CHAPTER III

THE DAY WORE ON and still it snowed. The Romsey clan retired to its self-imposed isolation, and the three men stayed chatting by the fire until the elderly waiter brought them tea, after which Constantine and Soames disappeared upstairs to the former's bedroom to indulge their passion for chess.

Stuart sat for a time smoking and trying to interest himself in an ancient magazine. There were no further arrivals, a walk was out of the question, and he began to realize that the boredom prophesied by Constantine might turn out to be a very real thing. There was, literally, nothing to do; and at last, in despair, he was driven to avail himself of the old man's invitation and visit him in his room. But the sight of two figures wrapt in contemplation over a chess-board did not prove inspiring.

Fortunately snow induces sleep, and he ended by relapsing into dreamless slumber on his bed.

Dinner proved uneventful, except for a rather stilted little chat with Miss Amy Adderley in the lounge afterwards. She announced that she and her sister were "exceedingly comfortable," and vouchsafed the information that Mr. Girling, the landlord, had been head coachman at the Abbey; that the house-party included Lord Romsey and the Honourable Victoria, Angela, and Geoffrey Ford, his son and two daughters, and finished up with a not very charitable commentary on "that vulgar American woman that arrived this afternoon."

"Fortunately there are two quite good sitting-rooms," she concluded, "so one will not be obliged to spend all one's time in one's room. The landlord has just shown them to us. A large billiard-room on the third floor for the gentlemen, and a comfortable little drawing-room for the non-smokers. Mr. Girling only moved some of the furniture in to-day. I must say he *is* doing his best to make us comfortable!"

Later in the evening Stuart sampled the billiard-room. It covered the whole depth and half the frontage of the old house, and was so vast that the billiard-table, tucked away at one end, looked small in comparison. It was a comfort to feel that here, at least, he need not be for ever treading on the toes of the rest of the company.

After a desultory game of billiards, he and Soames joined the landlord in his little den behind the bar, and collected data concerning the afternoon's arrivals.

The entire party, Girling informed them, now consisted of themselves, Constantine, Lord Romsey and his family, Melnotte, the ineffable young man, who, Stuart afterwards discovered, was a *gigolo* engaged by the management of the hotel at Redsands to which he himself had been bound, Mrs. van Dolen, Major Carew, the Misses Adderley, and Miss Hamilton, Mrs. van Dolen's secretary. The attractive lady who had been the last to arrive was a Mrs. Orkney Cloude.

"It's been a job fitting them in, too," concluded Girling. "It's not the rooms. As far as the house goes, we could put up double the number. It's the service. The American lady wanted her meals in her room, same as Lord Romsey and his party, but I had to tell her it couldn't be done. And now there's a chauffeur just come in. Takin' his master's car to Redsands, he is. Well, he's down with lumbago, poor devil. We had to all but lift him out of the car when he got here, and it was all he could do to get himself to bed. He's got to be looked after, and that means an extra tray at every meal, and me with only the two waiters, and the chambermaids run off their legs already. And the weather forecast isn't any too cheerful. But it's all grist to my mill, so I suppose I oughtn't to complain."

"The weather forecast! Then you've got a wireless?" exclaimed Soames.

"There's a small one I had put up in the bar. We get the National Programme, but nothing much else. From all accounts the roads will be blocked to-morrow, if this snow doesn't let off. I'll do my best for you, gentlemen, but you mustn't blame me if the service isn't what you're accustomed to."

"I've no complaints," said Soames heartily, rising and stretching himself. "All I need now is my bed, and, from the look of it, it'll be a comfortable one."

"I'm ready for mine," agreed Stuart. "This snow makes one sleepy. You might tell your maid to go on knocking till I answer to-morrow, Air. Girling. It takes an earthquake to wake me!"

Stuart made his way up to his bedroom on the second floor, leaving Soames turning over the magazines in the lounge in search of something to read. The staircase ran up the centre of the house—wide passages on either side of it, on both the first and second floors, leading to the sleeping quarters.

Stuart was wearing house shoes, and his feet made little or no noise on the carpeted stairs. He had almost reached the top of the first flight when he became aware of two people, apparently in urgent conversation, in the passage to the right of the stairs.

"I wish to God you *could* get away!"

The voice, that of a man, was so urgent that it captured Stuart's attention, and before he had time to make his presence known, he had overheard the answer.

"You've got to get me away somehow! I don't dare stay here! Goodness knows what will happen if I do!"

To do the eavesdropper justice, his fit of coughing had begun before the woman, for a woman it was, had reached the middle of her last sentence. Stuart heard a low exclamation from the man, then silence; but he was so near the head of the stairs that, though the passage was empty when he reached it, he heard the click of the latch as the second door on the right was hastily closed.

He went on up the next flight, smiling to himself as he remembered Constantine's specious argument concerning the legitimate curiosity of novelists. This was no concern of his, he told himself, but in spite of his efforts, he had already, almost subconsciously, connected the little episode with the look he had surprised on Mrs. Orkney Cloude's face as she paused on her way upstairs that afternoon. He had had a strong impression at the time that if she could have turned and fled from the place then and there, she would have done so.

His own room was the first on the left, at the head of the stairs, and there were two more doors beyond his before the passage turned. As in so many old houses, the floors were not all on the same level, and there was a short flight of steps leading to other bedrooms beyond, opposite the last door in the passage.

As he went into his room he glanced at the two doors on his left, wondering who his neighbours might be. The sight of two pairs of small, square-toed shoes left him in little doubt. They were so neat, yet so manifestly built for comfort, that they brought the Misses Adderley and Tunbridge Wells irresistibly to his mind. Well, they would be quiet neighbours, at any rate.

His head had no sooner touched the pillow than he fell into a deep, dreamless sleep that would, in normal circumstances, no doubt have lasted till morning. As it turned out, he opened his eyes abruptly, sometime in the small hours of the morning, on to a pall of pitch darkness; and lay blinking, vaguely aware that something definite had awakened him, and quite at sea as to his whereabouts.

Then a faint but persistent knocking brought him to a sense of his surroundings. He switched on the light, tumbled out of bed, and opened the door.

He was confronted by a fantastic figure, which, after a moment of sheer bewilderment, he recognized as that of the younger Miss Adderley. She was clad in a red dressing-gown of some woolly material, and wore round her head and fastened under her chin that knitted abomination which, for some obscure reason, is known as a fascinator. Certain curious projections in the region of her forehead suggested curl-papers beneath.

She was carrying a small kettle, and Stuart could see that the hand that held it was trembling. She stared at him, her eyes wide with apprehension.

"I'm so sorry to disturb you, Mr. Stuart," she whispered, with a terrified glance over her shoulder, "but I do feel that some one ought to know that there's a man in a mask in the passage!"

Stuart stared at her in bewilderment.

"A man in a mask?" he repeated stupidly. "Impossible!"

She nodded.

"That's what it seemed to me. So strange! You see, my sister couldn't sleep, and so I got up to re-fill her hot bottle. I lighted the little spirit-lamp without which we never travel, and went over to the bathroom to fetch some hot water. That was when I saw him. He was standing near the stairs, looking at me, with a mask over his face!"

She blinked suddenly and averted her eyes, and Stuart, looking down, became conscious of his own undress. He went back into his room and caught up his dressing-gown.

"I'll go and see," he said. "You say it was near the stairs that you saw him?"

She clutched at his arm with a shaking hand.

"You surely won't go without some sort of weapon. He wouldn't wear a mask if he wasn't dangerous."

Stuart smiled in spite of himself.

"I'm afraid I haven't got any weapons, Miss Adderley," he said.

"Wait," she announced impressively. "Don't move until I come back."

She disappeared into the room next door, and came out almost immediately bearing a small black poker, which she pressed into his hand.

"There!" she exclaimed. "You can hit him hard with that."

Stuart, feeling distinctly foolish, started along the passage, armed with the poker, Miss Adderley following at an ever-increasing distance in his rear.

They had not gone more than half a dozen paces when there was a click, and the entire passage was plunged into darkness. Stuart stopped dead, and Miss Adderley gave vent to a little squeal of terror and, literally, threw herself upon him.

"I saw his hand," she whimpered frenziedly. "He was on the stairs all the time."

He disengaged himself gently.

"You go back to your room and wait there," he whispered. "I'll try to get to the switch."

Grasping the poker firmly, he felt his way carefully along the wall, expecting every moment to come in contact with a warm, yielding body. But nothing happened, and, after some difficulty, he managed to find the switch, which was placed just at the head of the stairs.

He turned it on, blinking for a moment at the sudden transition from darkness to the light which flooded not only the passage but the stairs below.

There was no one to be seen. The intruder had seized his opportunity and made his escape in the darkness.

Stuart hesitated. He realized that it was useless to pursue his quarry down the stairs. If there had been any means of escape that way, the man would have taken it. The very fact that he had risked the turning out of the light showed that he had been unable to reach his objective without crossing the landing on which Stuart and Miss Adderley stood. It was therefore pretty obvious that he had gone to one of the upper floors, and, Stuart concluded, had probably used the little staircase at the opposite end of the passage which corresponded with the one outside Miss Adderley's room. He felt fairly certain that no one had passed him in the darkness, though he had a vague idea that both flights of steps led to the servants' quarters. To reach the billiard-room he had used a small back staircase which ran from behind Girling's office on the ground floor. This was about as far as his knowledge of the lay of the house extended, and he realized that it would be useless to attempt the exploration of such an unknown territory by himself.

He jumped involuntarily as something brushed his elbow. It was Miss Adderley, who had crept silently to his side.

"He may be *anywhere!*" she whispered fearfully voicing his own thoughts.

"He may. And it's not going to be easy to find him now, I'm afraid. Look here, Miss Adderley, you trot back to your own room and lock the door. You'll be quite safe there. I'll go and knock up the landlord and see if we can find any trace of the fellow."

Then, as she hesitated: "I'll come with you to your door, though I'm sure he's nowhere near that end of the passage."

He conducted her to her room, and, after a slight delay occasioned by the fact that her sister had firmly locked the door after her departure and, owing to her deafness, could not be made to understand that a murderer was not lurking on the other side, managed to deposit her there.

Then, still grasping the ridiculous poker, he made his way past the head of the stairs to Constantine's room. Where Soames was sleeping he did not know, though he had an idea that he was somewhere on the same floor as himself.

He had some difficulty in waking the old man, but, when he did come to the door, tying the cord of his black silk dressing-gown round his waist, his thick white hair on end, and his dark eyes bright with vitality, he looked equal to dealing with any situation.

"What is it? Fire?" he demanded.

Stuart reassured him, and described Miss Adderley's vision.

"If it hadn't been for that business of the light, I should have been inclined to think that she had imagined the whole thing," he finished.

Constantine nodded.

"Thank God it isn't fire," he exclaimed. "It's a thing I'm always afraid of in an old house like this. But this is delicious! A masked man in a snow-bound hotel! You realize he could hardly have come from outside on a night like this?"

"The question is, how are we to get hold of the landlord?" said Stuart, who was beginning to feel chilly, and did not quite share his companion's obvious enjoyment of the situation.

"You might knock up Soames, to begin with. His knowledge of hotels and their ways is positively uncanny. His is the first door on the right at the top of the flight of steps at the end of this passage. If the man slipped round this way he must have passed both our rooms."

Stuart routed out Soames, who proved sleepy, but helpful.

"The servants' quarters are all at the back there," he informed them. "I heard them moving about after I got to bed. You cut round and up the stairs at your end, and I'll go this way and try to get old Girling on the way. We're bound to meet somewhere, and, if the beggar is lurking in the back regions, we ought to head him off. But you may bet he's gone to earth by now. I like your little poker," he added appreciatively.

"That's really Miss Adderley's contribution. Will you keep an eye on the stairs here, sir?" said Stuart, turning to Constantine.

"I will look after this end to the best of my ability," he assured them, with a twinkle in his eye that brought the absurdity of the whole expedition home to Stuart. "Though I must warn you that my fighting days are over."

Soames was as good as his word, and, when Stuart eventually ran him to earth in what seemed a labyrinth of narrow passages, all equipped with unexpected little steps designed to trip up the unwary, he was already in conversation with Girling, who showed himself frankly sceptical about the whole occurrence.

"In all the years I've been 'ere," he was saying, "there's never been so much as a pin stolen, and if there's any one up to mischief, it isn't any of my little lot, that I can vouch for. Those that haven't been with me for years are from the village, folks as I've known all their lives. And I'd like to see the burglar as'd come from outside on a night like this."

He was sufficiently impressed, however, to rouse the boots, and, together, the four men made the round of the whole house, to find that not only was everything undisturbed, but that all the windows and doors were as securely fastened as they had been when the household retired to bed.

It was not until they had worked their way round to the lounge, and were hailed by Constantine from the top of the first flight of stairs, that Stuart, to his relief, was able in some degree to substantiate his story.

Constantine was standing on the stairs, by a small window close to the landing.

"I haven't seen a soul," he informed them, "but this looks as if it might have some bearing on the matter."

He pointed to the carpet immediately under the window. A couple of handfuls of snow, evidently dislodged from the outside sill of the window, and now fast dissolving into a pool of water, were lying there, and, through the window, the bottom of which was open some ten inches, the flakes were drifting in and settling in a thin layer on the inside sill.

"Did you find that there window open, sir?" asked Girling. "I latched it myself last thing."

"It was just as you see it," answered Constantine. "I only got here a minute ago."

Girling threw open the window and peered out into the darkness, and Stuart, looking over his shoulder, discovered that it gave on to a balcony, though how far this extended he could not see.

Girling, who had been leaning far out of the window, heaved himself back on to the staircase. His head and shoulders were thickly powdered with snow.

"Here, you, Joe," he said. "Hop down to the office and fetch that torch of mine. You know where to find it.

"Can't see a thing out there," he went on. "But even if the chap did get in that way, which I find it hard to believe, he wouldn't leave no trace. This snow'd cover anything in five minutes."

"How far does that balcony run?" asked Stuart.

"Right past the two bedrooms on that side. But it's a tidy way up from the ground, and I wouldn't care to do it, even with a ladder, in weather like this."

"Who is occupying those rooms?" asked Constantine.

"The American lady comes first, then that Mrs. Orkney Cloude that arrived this evening. They're big rooms; that's why there are only two on this floor to three on the floor above. The American lady would be just under you, sir. You didn't hear anything, I. suppose?"

"Nothing," answered Constantine. "But I was fast asleep when Mr. Stuart knocked at my door. All the same, I think it might be as well to see tint she's all right, though I don't fancy she's been disturbed."

Girling disappeared round the angle of the passage, and they heard him knock softly at Mrs. van Dolen's door. Stuart looked at Constantine.

"You're thinking of the emeralds," he said. "But surely she couldn't be such a fool as to have them here."

"If all I've heard of the lady is true," answered the old man, "she's certain to have them with her. And you may be pretty certain that Girling doesn't boast a safe, so she won't have left them with him. But, if she was the objective, I fancy she's escaped this time. Whoever opened that window was getting out, not in."

"How do you make that out?" asked Stuart, staring at him.

For answer Constantine shut down the window.

"If you wait a moment I'll show you," he said. "But you can see for yourself that there isn't a sign of damp on the carpet, except where the snow has fallen from the window ledge. No human being could have got in from outside without leaving a wet trail behind him. And another thing. I'll admit it never does to generalize, but you must see that the cat burglar theory hardly holds water. By to-morrow we shall be as completely isolated as the original Noah's Ark on its waste of waters. Even if we accept the amazing theory that a burglar, knowing all about Mrs. van Dolen's emeralds, happened to find himself in the village tonight, we have still to explain how he proposed to get away with his booty."

"He might have followed her from London, meaning to have a try for the girdle at Redsands," suggested Stuart, "and then have found himself hung up by the snow here."

"In which case he's in this hotel and this is an inside job," retorted Constantine. "He's far safer here than lodging at some cottage in the village. If I know anything of these small country places, no stranger is likely to escape notice for more than twelve hours."

He bent forward and threw the window open. The snow had had time to collect once more on the outside ledge of the sash, and as he raised it a goodish lump detached itself and fell on the carpet at his feet.

"It isn't necessary to come in through the window to bring the snow with you," he pointed. "Miss Adderley must have disturbed our friend in the nick of time. Why he was such a fool as to show himself, remains to be seen."

He was interrupted by the reappearance of Girling.

"Mrs. van Dolen hasn't heard anything," he said. "And I've had a look at her window. It's one of those French ones, with an ordinary catch and no shutters. Easy enough to force, if any one wanted to; but it hasn't been touched, and the snow outside doesn't show anything. I went out to look, but that's no proof on a night like this."

He turned sharply at a sound on the stairs, but it was only Joe returning with the torch.

"It's no good bothering about the balcony. We shan't get anything there. You get a coat on, Joe, and take the torch with you. And the key of the barn. Go right round the outside and keep a sharp look-out to see if there's any sign of any one's having got in anywhere. And have a peep into the barn and see if there's a ladder missing. If you don't want to go alone, wake Hawkins. He'll go with you."

"I ain't afraid o' nothin'," stated Joe stolidly, as he plodded heavily down the stairs. "The snow's what I minds."

"And he'll get it, poor chap," remarked Girling. "Well, he's a long sight younger than I am, and it won't hurt him."

"I'm afraid he's wasting his time," said Constantine, and proceeded to propound his theory.

As he did so the hard-bitten lines on Girling's face deepened.

"I don't like it, sit," he said frankly, when Constantine had finished. "I don't like it at all. If I'd known of the quantity of jewellery that there lady's got with her, I'd have made it very plain in the beginning that I wouldn't hold myself responsible for anything that might happen. We haven't got no safe here, never had any call to have one, and what valuables I've got goes in a box under my bed. It fair took my breath away when she told me just now what she's got in that room there. It isn't right nor fair to travel with all that stuff, and I told her so straight. All she says is, that she's never been robbed yet."

"Well, I shouldn't brood over it. You may be sure it's all insured, and, even if it wasn't, she can afford to lose it. Don't waste your anxiety on a silly woman," rejoined Constantine consolingly.

"And now you tell me that I'm harbouring a thief in my house," went on Girling. "And, what with the chauffeurs and such these gentry have brought with them, I'm willing enough to believe you. I'm ready to answer for every man and woman on my own staff, but what do I know about the lot we've got here to-night? I tell you, sir, I'll be glad to see the back of that American lady, and that's the truth."

"Did she happen to tell you whether she is in the habit of locking her door at night?" asked Soames, who, Stuart realized, had been unwontedly silent since the discovery of the open window.

Girling nodded.

"Always locks her door, she says, and I'm glad of it. They're old, heavy doors, with good locks, and they'd take some getting through."

"Whereas the windows are modern, flimsy contrivances with the usual slip-up catch, I suppose?" put in Constantine.

Girling stared at him.

"That's right, sir. Meaning, I suppose, that if any one wanted to get into one of those rooms, he'd choose the window rather than the door. Likely you're right."

He sighed heavily.

"Looks as if there's nothing for it but to go to bed," he said. "It's not likely he'll try again to-night, and we've done the best we can. I'll pass the word to Tom Bates, the constable, to-morrow, and, if there's any strangers in the village, he'll get on to them quick enough. I don't see what more we can do."

He took himself off, a badly worried man, while the others followed more slowly up the stairs to their own floor.

"I wish the fellow had got on to the balcony," said Soames. "With that amount of snow on his shoes we could have followed his tracks on this carpet anyway. As it is, who knows where he may have gone to earth! I suppose that Miss Adderley didn't give any sort of description of him?"

Stuart smiled involuntarily at the mention of her name.

"The fact that he wore a mask was enough for her," he answered. "Besides, she only saw him for a second."

"That's the most puzzling element in the whole business," remarked Constantine reflectively. "Why, when the man had got the window open and was, we suppose, about to get out, should he have gone out of his way to go on to the landing and show himself in the passage? He must, presumably, have heard Miss Adderley moving while he was in the act of opening the window. The last thing one would expect him to do would be to go in the direction of the sound he had heard."

"You're sure she didn't say whether he was short or tall?" pursued Soames, obviously following up a train of thought of his own.

"I can ask her if you like, but I'm sure she was incapable of noticing anything, once she had seen that mask," answered Stuart.

"You've got an idea, eh?"

The question came sharply from Constantine, whose keen eyes were on Soames's shrewd if rather heavy face. They had reached their own landing and had halted to finish their conversation.

Soames hesitated.

"I can't say that," he said slowly, "but one rather funny thing happened when I was making the round of the passages after I had knocked up Girling. If Miss Adderley had said that her man was tall I'd have been inclined to think I knew who he was, only the idea seems so preposterous."

"Out with it, man," urged Constantine impatiently.

"Well, Girling was getting into some clothes and said he'd follow on, so I went ahead and worked my way round to the floor under this. I suppose I must have made a bit more noise than I thought, because a door opened just as I was passing it and a chap stuck his head out. It was that tall fellow, Lord Romsey's son. He asked if anything was the matter, and I told him. He said he'd get some clothes on and join us, but he's been a precious long time about it."

As though in answer to the criticism a voice hailed them softly from the landing below. Stuart swung round. A tall figure, clad in a dressing-gown, below which showed a pair of pyjama trousers, was standing looking up at them.

"Talk of the devil," murmured Soames.

"Is everything all right up there?" came softly from below.

Constantine answered him.

"Perfectly," he said. "We've drawn a blank and we're on our way to bed."

"Right. Let me know if you need me."

The figure disappeared. Soames grunted.

"What is his name, anyway?" he asked morosely.

"Officially, he's the Honourable Geoffrey Ford," Constantine informed him, his eyes twinkling with amusement. "Why this disapproval? He really is a very excellent young man."

"He may be the President of the Y.M.C.A. for all I care," was Soames's answer. "But I'd give something to know why, when he says he's going to dress, he goes and gets into pyjamas and vice versa."

Constantine stared at him, his bushy eyebrows raised in interrogation.

"When he opened his door," went on Soames doggedly, "he took jolly good care not to open it too wide, but I saw him, all the same. He'd got a dressing-gown on all right, but he was wearing his dress trousers underneath it. If he'd been to bed at all, I'll eat my hat."

A sudden recollection came to Stuart.

"Where is his room?" he asked sharply.

"At the top of the little flight of steps opposite the room next to Mrs. van Dolen's," answered Soames.

Stuart relapsed into silence. The door next to Mrs. van Dolen's was the one that had closed so softly, immediately after the conversation he had overheard on his way up to bed that night. And the landlord had said that Mrs. Orkney Cloude was sleeping there. He looked up to meet Constantine's quizzical gaze.

"So some one else has got an idea," remarked the old man softly. "We are getting on. Who is it this time?"

But Stuart was not to be drawn. He grinned and shook his head.

"Nothing doing," he said. "I must go and reassure my old ladies; then I'm going to bed, and all the burglars in the world won't get me out of it. Good-night."

"Good-night," called Constantine after him. "We shall meet in the morning."

"And you'll pick my brains as neatly as you've picked those of everybody else in this house, and I'm blessed if I shall be able to help myself," reflected Stuart, as he knocked gently at Miss Adderley's door.

CHAPTER IV

STUART SLEPT LATE next morning. So, he gathered, did his companions in adventure, for when he eventually got up, he found them in sole possession of the coffee-room.

Soames greeted him with a grin.

"I don't know how the cold light of day affects you," he said, "but I'm beginning to have an uncomfortable feeling that we made fools of ourselves last night. Somehow this masked man business doesn't seem so convincing at breakfast."

Stuart nodded.

"I know," he answered, with an appreciative eye on the dish the waiter had just set down in front of him. "I've been feeling all kinds of an ass myself ever since I woke. It wouldn't be so bad, somehow, if it wasn't for that beastly little poker."

Soames choked into his teacup, and, from the fleeting gleam of sheer delight that lit up Constantine's face, Stuart realized that he had cut quite as comic a figure as he had ruefully suspected.

"All the same," he protested, "some one was on the prowl. Witness the lights and the window."

"One of the chauffeurs after the whisky, as likely as not," scoffed Soames.

"Which he no doubt expected to find on the balcony," put in Constantine dryly. "No, though I do admit that I find the masked man a little difficult to swallow, I am at a loss to account for the window. If it were not for that walking jeweller's shop, Mrs. van Dolen, I should dismiss even that as negligible, but the fact remains that that balcony runs across the whole of the front of the house, past her window and those of Mrs. Cloude and the Romseys, all of whom have probably got strings of pearls, even if they are too wise to travel with the bulk of their jewellery. Apart from the emeralds, there would be a good haul for any one from that balcony alone."

It struck Stuart suddenly that Dr. Constantine appeared to be remarkably well posted as to the whereabouts of his fellow-guests.

"You seem to have been studying the lie of the land, sir," he said.

Constantine's eyes twinkled.

"I see suspicion dawning already," he sighed. "But I can assure you, I haven't been planning a neat little burglary, and my climbing days are over. The fact is that I had a chat with Girling while I was waiting for my breakfast, and even went so far as to step out of the front door into the snow and have a look at the house. It wasn't worth risking rheumatism for. Whoever plastered that abominable, jerry-built balcony, with its vile French windows, on to the front of this old house ought to have been slain. I was glad to discover that it had been done before Girling's time."

"Would it be possible to reach the balcony from the ground?" asked Stuart.

"In ordinary circumstances it would be easy, but, with every foothold plastered with snow, I should imagine it impossible, even for the most accomplished cat burglar."

Soames finished his tea and pushed the cup from him.

"Well, if you are taking the thing seriously," he said, "which, mind you, I'm not inclined to do, now that I've slept on it, I can only repeat that there was only one member of this little house-party that was up and dressed, to my knowledge, and that was the Honourable Geoffrey Ford."

He leaned back and glared provocatively at Constantine, who immediately took up the challenge. Evidently these two had discussed the matter before.

"If you can give me any reason why the son of one of the wealthiest men in England should choose one of the most unsuitable nights in the year to commit burglary, I am ready to listen to you," he answered tartly. "Geoffrey Ford, to my knowledge, has always been an almost painfully correct young man. He has no expensive vices, and, incidentally, inherited a large fortune from his mother. When his father dies he will be fabulously rich. Upon my word, I can see no reason why he should wish to add Mrs. van Bolen's ill-chosen gewgaws to the Romsey collection, which, I assure you, is quite adequate and in much better taste."

He spoke with considerable asperity, and Stuart, who had seen his response to Miss Ford's greeting the day before, suspected that he had a warm spot in his heart for that young lady. For which he did not blame him.

"Do you know anything about this Mrs. Orkney Cloude?" he asked.

Constantine flashed a penetrating glance at him.

"So you noticed it too," he countered. "Except that she seems an exceptionally charming lady, and that there is some one in this hotel whom she did not expect to meet last night, I know nothing about her. What interpretation do you place on that little incident?"

"I think it was the sight of Lord Romsey that upset her," answered Stuart diffidently. "She looked as if she had seen a ghost."

Constantine nodded.

"And Romsey seemed, if anything, rather flattered by her attention," he observed. "He certainly didn't look guilty; but, even if he were caught in the act of stealing Girling's spoons, one can't imagine him doing that. If you knew the man and his colossal conceit as I do, you would realize that he is quite capable of taking the lady's emotion as a tribute to his own charms. The man's preposterous, but, to do him justice, he's utterly incapable of anything in the nature of an intrigue."

This was obviously Stuart's cue to retail the conversation he had overheard the night before, but, from an absurd feeling of loyalty to a distressed lady of whom he knew nothing and with whom he had never even exchanged a word, he could not bring himself to the point. He knew that Constantine's eyes were upon him, in the hope that there was something more up his sleeve than the little scene at the foot of the stairs, and he felt an impish joy in baffling the astute old man, much as he liked him. But this did not prevent him from drawing his own conclusions. The night before, he had suspected the male voice he had heard of belonging to Lord Romsey, incredible as such a possibility appeared, even to him. Now, he was inclined to think that the second speaker must have been Geoffrey Ford, though this brought him no nearer to the elucidation of the mystery of the open window.

Breakfast finished, they strolled into the lounge, and the first person they set eyes on was Mrs. Orkney Cloude. She was coming slowly down the broad staircase, and, at the sight of her hag-ridden face, Stuart felt glad that he had held his tongue. Whether or not the commotion in Mrs. van Dolen's room next door had disturbed her, it was evident that she had passed a sleepless night. There were dark smudges round her eyes, and the quick, penetrating glance she cast in the direction of the three men was both nervous and troubled.

She went straight to the little room Girling called his office, and stood there with her back to them. As Stuart passed behind her he could hear Girling's voice.

"I wouldn't advise you to try," he was saying. "The road's blocked between here and London. We had it on the wireless last night, and it's been snowing steady ever since. It was all the postman could do to get up the lane this morning, and, if it goes on, they say as Mr. Thornton, up at the Lodge, is going to try fetching the letters on horseback."

"What about the trains?" she asked anxiously. "I've got important business in London, and I must get up if I can."

"The nearest station's Thorley, and that's all of four miles away, and off the main road at that. And they tell me the 7.10 didn't run last night. That looks as if the line's blocked."

She gave a little gesture of despair.

"There's nothing for it but to stay here, then," she said.

Then, with a charming courtesy which Stuart guessed was characteristic of her—

"I'm not complaining of your hotel, Mr. Girling. You have made us delightfully comfortable, and I know it couldn't have been easy at such short notice. It's only that I've important business elsewhere that I ought to attend to."

"I've done my best, ma'am, and I hope if there's anything you'd like different, you'll mention it," was all Girling said; but Stuart could almost hear him apostrophizing her mentally as "a very pleasant lady."

Going back to her room she came face to face with Geoffrey Ford on his way downstairs. Stuart watched the meeting with pardonable curiosity, but Ford's expression, as he stepped aside to let her pass, was inscrutable, and neither of them gave the slightest sign that they had met before.

He also was on his way to Girling's office, and apparently bent on the same mission.

"No chance of our getting away to-day, I suppose, landlord?" he remarked carelessly, as he filled his pipe.

"None at all, I should say, sir," answered Girling. "I was just telling the lady."

He repeated his tale of woe. Ford took the news philosophically, and asked if there was a telephone within reach, as his father wanted to get through to London.

"There's one at the post office, just across the way," Girling informed him. "And the line was clear this morning. The American lady's chauffeur got through all right."

Ford thanked him, and joined the group that was hanging aimlessly round the fire.

"What was the rumpus last night?" he asked. "I gathered you were after somebody, but I'm a bit vague as to how it all ended."

Constantine told him what had happened, Soames keeping a meditative eye on the young man the while.

"Old ladies are apt to exaggerate a bit when they're startled," Ford observed when Constantine had finished. "She may very well have imagined the mask. But I'm sorry our American friend fetched up here. Half the crooks in London must have had their eye on those stones of hers for ages, and it'll be a nuisance if some one does have a shot at them while she's here. I don't suppose the village bobby's very efficient, and we're effectually cut off from any other police station."

"The whole thing was probably just a scare," put in Soames gruffly.

"I hope so. I don't want my sisters frightened."

Constantine looked amused.

"I can imagine your sister Angela welcoming a little diversion of that sort," he remarked. "I remember hearing a delightful story of the way she dealt with a navvy who threw a brick at her during the strike."

Ford laughed. He was evidently proud of his step-sister, and not ashamed to show it. Stuart began to realize that there was something likeable about this grave young man.

"The worst of Angela is that she's always in the thick of it," he said. "I don't want her knocked on the head just because a donkey of a woman chooses to travel like a Hatton Garden merchant. No, it was Victoria I was worrying about. She's not strong, and apt to be nervous at the best of times. I should be grateful if you wouldn't mention this bother to her, unless she's already heard of it."

"Mrs. van Dolen knows already, unfortunately," said Constantine, "but she doesn't seem to have taken it much to heart, so perhaps she'll keep quiet about it." Ford turned to Stuart with a friendly smile.

"The problem of the moment, according to my sister, is how to pass the time until we can get away," he said. "She asked me to find out whether you played bridge, and to say that she's discovered from the landlord that there's an old ping-pong set stowed away somewhere, and he's offered to rig up a table in one of the attics. I don't know whether you are a bridge-player, Mr. Soames? I know it's no use asking Dr. Constantine."

"It is not!" the old man assured him heartily.

"I'm afraid I'm no good to you," answered Soames. "Never could play cards. That Major Carew, now—"

"I ran into Major Carew on his way up to bed last night," said Ford dryly. "Or rather he fell into me. I think we'll give him a miss."

Soames whistled.

"So that's his little trouble, is it?" he exclaimed.

"One of them, at any rate."

His tone was venomous. It was obvious that Geoffrey Ford did not like Major Carew.

"The pretty lady looks as though she might be a bridge-player," remarked Constantine thoughtfully.

Ford turned quickly.

"The pretty lady?" he demanded.

"Mrs. Orkney Cloude, I think her name is. She arrived yesterday. You passed her on the stairs just now."

Ford hesitated.

"I don't think we can very well approach her," he said at last decisively.

"I don't mind asking her," volunteered Constantine. "I consider my white hairs a guarantee of respectability."

"My father or Victoria will make a fourth if necessary," said Ford, "though they're neither of them very keen players. Thank you all the same. As a matter of fact, Angela's set on getting up a ping-pong tournament, and her mind's probably entirely absorbed in that."

"It would be more in my line, I must admit," said Stuart, who was appalled at the thought of playing bridge in the company of Lord Romsey. "I'm a rotten bridge-player, I'm afraid."

"Then I'll give you a call when we've settled up something," concluded Ford as he turned to go.

Constantine looked after him meditatively, but he did not give voice to his thoughts. Soames showed no such reticence.

"The Romsey lot don't seem to have cottoned to Mrs. Cloude," he observed. "Yet I should have said she was more their sort than any of the rest of the crowd. What about a spot of billiards, Mr. Stuart? You're off chess for this morning, I think you said, sir?"

Constantine turned his back reluctantly on the fire.

"I'm writing letters for my sins," he said. "If the post ceases to function to-morrow, I shall count it as distinctly one of my blessings."

They found, as Soames afterwards put it, "the whole blooming Noah's Ark" in the billiard-room, and it was obvious to the meanest intelligence that at least two of the inhabitants wished themselves most heartily elsewhere.

Angela Ford, curled up in an armchair, with a book and a cigarette, was turning a determinedly deaf ear to the very audible and somewhat one-sided conversation that was going on between Mrs. van Dolen and a thin, colourless middle-aged woman whom Stuart rightly placed as Angela's step-sister, Victoria Ford. She had a book on her lap, but Mrs. van Dolen evidently had no intention of allowing her to read it. From the wild look in Miss Ford's eyes, it would seem that she had reached that acute state of boredom at which the vitality of the victim is so sapped, that she has neither the strength nor the energy to free herself. Mrs. van Dolen, on the contrary, was in her element. She was describing a house-party to which she had been, and as the names of her fellow-guests rolled unctuously off her tongue, Stuart was irresistibly reminded of the "from the left to right" inscriptions under the photographs in the *Tatler*.

Facing them, on the other side of the fireplace, was an equally ill-matched couple.

Mrs. Orkney Cloude had, unfortunately for herself, omitted to provide herself with even a book, and possessed no more adequate protection than a gold cigarette case. She was smoking furiously, and presented the pathetic spectacle of an essentially gracious and kind-hearted woman trying her hardest to be rude. Bending over her, his face rather more flushed than the heat of the room warranted, and gallantry in every curve of his somewhat billowy figure, was Major Carew.

In a chilly corner, well removed from the fire, sat the fair girl who had arrived with Mrs. van Dolen, and who presumably acted as her secretary or companion. She was reading a book with unnatural absorption, and Stuart, as he helped Soames to remove the cover from the billiard-table, noticed that ever and again her eye roamed nervously in the direction of the gallant Major.

Through the open door in the room beyond, the two Misses Adderley could be seen sitting side by side decorously knitting.

With the exception of Constantine, the shabby boy Trevor, and Melnotte the professional dancer, the house-party was complete.

Stuart was engaged in choosing a cue when he heard a voice at his side, and turned to find Angela Ford at his elbow.

"Please, may I play too?" she begged. "Unless you're going to have a really serious match. You don't know how deadly it is over there."

"Of course," he said eagerly. "We can take on Soames. He beat me hideously yesterday."

"Let's get a fourth," she suggested. "There's that pretty woman over there, Mrs. Cloude, isn't she? She looks a good sort, and she'll have screaming hysterics in a minute if some one doesn't rescue her from that awful man. She's been snubbing him steadily for the last half-hour, and it only makes him worse."

"Who's going to ask her?" asked Stuart nervously, shyness descending on him like a blanket.

"I will, if Mr. Soames doesn't mind."

Soames, appealed to, did not mind at all. He had cast more than one appreciative glance in Mrs. Orkney Cloude's direction, and was heartily of the opinion that she ought to be rescued at all costs.

"You'll have to do it, though, Miss Ford," he said. "I wouldn't go near her now if you paid me. That purple-faced bounder's given her a sickener for stout men with red faces by now, you may be sure."

Miss Ford chuckled, a delicious sound, fat and appreciative, and strolled over to the fireplace. Stuart could not hear what she said, but he saw Carew spring heavily to his feet, with the evident intention of joining the party, only to remain rooted firmly to the hearthrug where the two women left him.

"I was hideously rude to him," announced Miss Ford cheerfully. "I think I must have a talent that way. Do you think I ought to go and exercise it on Mrs. van Dolen before I settle down to enjoy myself? It would be a fine, knight-errantish thing to do."

"You saved my life, I think," Mrs. Orkney Cloude assured her. "The man's insufferable! He forced an introduction on the grounds that he knew a distant cousin of mine, and, short of going to my room, there was no way of getting rid of him."

The colour had returned to her cheeks and the brightness to her eyes, which kept returning to Angela Ford's face as though it were a lodestone she could not resist. It struck Stuart that there was something more than admiration in her gaze; an intensity he could not understand. Meanwhile he was unable, for sheer pleasure, to refrain from watching the two women; they made such admirable foils for each other.

They both put up a good game. As they played they talked intermittently, and Stuart realized for the first time the curious freemasonry that existed among these people who, even though they had never before met, had so much in common.

So interested was he that they had played two hundred up and the morning was well on its way to lunch time, when he discovered that the pertinacious Carew had transferred his attentions to Mrs. van Dolen's secretary. In his desire to stand well with Mrs. Orkney Cloude he had no doubt limited his attentions to her to the heavy gallantry peculiar to his type; but, from the hot flush on his second victim's face, it was obvious that he had not considered it necessary to show any such consideration to one so low in the social scale as a mere secretary.

"It looks as if you would have to go again to the rescue," murmured Stuart to his partner as she returned with her ball to balk, after a particularly neat winning hazard.

"I know," she answered indignantly. "I've been watching them. It's an abominable shame. She's the sort of nice girl that hasn't got a chance with a man like that, and that old pig she works for hasn't moved a finger to save her, though it's been happening under her nose for ages, if this goes on we shall have to form an Anti-Carew League. Hallo, that's torn it!"

Evidently the man had gone too far at last, for the girl had risen to her feet, her cheeks flaming, and, after a moment of hesitation, during which it looked perilously as though she were going to burst into tears, hurried from the room.

Angela Ford threw a glance at Stuart over her shoulder.

"Action postponed," she said. "But never mind, we'll get him yet!"

Stuart's was easily the most cheerful countenance at lunch that day. Indeed, he was probably the only member of the marooned house-party that did not desire actively to get away. Now that he had entered into so delightfully intimate an alliance with Angela Ford, he could afford to watch the ever-increasing snowstorm with equanimity.

He had never been for a long sea-voyage, but life at the "Noah's Ark" seemed to him very like the existence on board ship—as he read of it in books—with the billiard-room as the promenade deck. People forgathered, played games or talked, and took refuge in their rooms, only from sheer boredom to emerge and meet again. He managed to spend a fair portion of the rest of the day in the company of Angela Ford, and was even introduced to her sister, with whom he held a short and devastatingly banal conversation, in the course of which he discovered, to his astonishment, that her only interest in life was in gramophone records, of which she possessed an incredible number.

But what became more and more clear as the day wore on was the disconcerting possibility that the Anti-Carew League might of necessity become a very real thing. As Soames put it somewhere about tea-time: "The 'wine and women' stage is well under weigh already; I think we may take it we shall get the 'song' all right later."

Major Carew had started the day with the firm intention of cementing himself to the Romsey party, but his efforts so far had met with little success. Neither Lord Romsey nor his son had shown themselves for more than a few minutes at a time, and had presumably spent the greater part of the day in their rooms. Victoria Ford's frigid aloofness had proved a more effective weapon even than her sister's uncompromising rudeness, which nevertheless had actually succeeded in piercing his hide earlier in the day. Even later, when his inherent snobbery had been dissolved by frequent libations and had given place to a still more unpleasing trait, he was wary of approaching her. Before the afternoon was half over, his principal objective in life had become the unfortunate Mrs. Orkney Cloude, and by tea-time he had driven her to the seclusion of her room. Failing her, he was prepared to put up with Miss Hamilton, Mrs. van Dolen's secretary: a more defenceless if less distinguished quarry.

The three men and Angela Ford held a council of war over the fire in the lounge.

"At this rate he'll be either helpless or fighting drunk by the evening," said Constantine. "We can only pray that it will be the former."

"I'll get him to bed if I can," volunteered Soames. "I've had a bit of experience of that sort of thing. You're apt to come across it in my job."

He and Constantine had spent the afternoon over the chessboard, and had missed the spectacle of Carew's bacchanalian antics.

"Where is he now?" asked Constantine.

"In complete possession of the billiard-room," answered Angela Ford bitterly. "The pleasantest room in the house. When I went in just now I met the nice Trevor boy coming out. His face was the colour of beetroot, and that great beast was sprawling in front of the fire, muttering something about 'Twopenny excursionists in their stinking charabancs.' He'd evidently been insulting the wretched boy. I fled before he had time to see me, and wasted ten minutes on the stairs being positively fulsome to the poor Trevor thing, trying to soothe his wounded pride."

"How did you get rid of him?" asked Constantine with interest. It was not the first time he had observed Angela's methods with appreciation.

"I poked him into the little sitting-room," she informed him guilelessly. "You see, Miss Hamilton was sitting there alone, and I suggested that he might keep an eye on her and see that she didn't get into the clutches of Carew again. He was feeling frightfully manly and chivalrous; then I left him, and the door into the billiard-room was shut, so I don't suppose Carew will find them."

And now I suppose you consider that you have done your good deed for the day?" mocked Constantine.

She blinked at him through her long lashes.

"Well, they would make rather a nice little couple, don't you think?" she suggested, unabashed.

They ordered their tea in the lounge and sat on there chatting casually, till Angela Ford remembered that she had promised to read aloud to her father till dinnertime.

She had risen and was about to go upstairs, when the door opened and a man was blown in, bringing a flurry of snow with him.

"Geoff!" she cried. "You might have told me you were going out! I'd have come with you!"

He slipped out of his overcoat and shook the snow off his cap.

"It's pitch dark, and the snow's too heavy to be pleasant," he said. "Walking's impossible, but if we'd got some skis here we could have a gorgeous time. We shall have to get some exercise somehow."

His sister nodded.

"I know," she said. "Father's getting goutier every moment, and, short of taking him out snowballing, I can't think what to do with him."

Constantine chuckled openly at the thought.

"I'm going to sleep," he announced, "and if I wake with a liver it'll be no one's fault but my own."

He followed Angela up the wide staircase, but when she turned down the passage to her father's room, he did not pursue his way up to his own floor. Instead, he stood for a few minutes motionless on the landing, his hands lightly clasped behind him, his eyes fixed on the carpet at his feet. Then he glanced down the passage to his left. Angela had already disappeared, and there was nobody to watch his movements as he made his way thoughtfully along the passage to the foot of the short flight of steps which led, as he now knew, to the back stairs.

The trail of wet on the carpet, emphasized here and there by a little clot of melting snow, was easy enough to follow, and it led, as he had expected, to the foot of the steps. He turned back along the track, crossed the landing, and went on down the passage to the right of the stairs.

At the door of the room next to that of Mrs. van Dolen he paused, and bending down, passed his hand lightly over the wood of the door jamb. It came away wet. On the carpet was a little lump of snow, as though some one had brushed a sopping coat against the side of the door and knocked the snow off in the passing.

Geoffrey Ford was not the only person who had decided to brave the weather that evening! Humming a little tune softly under his breath, Dr. Constantine passed on up the stairs to his room.

Half an hour later, Stuart, finding himself nodding in front of the hot fire, decided to follow Constantine's example. He was standing near the door of his bedroom, cutting the pages of the book with which he proposed to read himself to sleep, when a sound outside his door made him pause.

There was the noise of a scuffle, then a girl's voice raised in evident distress, followed by another sound so unmistakable, that he made a plunge for the door and threw it open, feeling very little doubt as to whom he would find outside.

But swiftly as he had moved, some one else had been quicker.

The boy Trevor was already standing between Carew and the shrinking figure of Miss Hamilton, his fists clenched and his face ablaze with anger.

Then, before Stuart could interfere, Carew lurched sideways and brought his arm, with all the force of his heavy body behind it, across the boy's face, hurling him clean off his balance and against the wall behind him.

Stuart stepped neatly in between them.

"Look here," he said. "We can't have that sort of thing here, you know."

He spoke quietly, but there was an edge to his voice that penetrated Carew's drunken fury. Also the stockiness of Stuart's build and the alertness of his poise suggested that he might prove a more formidable antagonist than the boy who was already mopping a crimson nose behind him.

"What do you mean by interfering?" stormed Carew. But even now his truculence was only half-hearted.

"We've stood as much as we intend to stand from you to-day," pursued Stuart, ignoring the interruption. "And it's as well you should know it. Your room's at the other end of the passage, I believe. If you take my advice you'll go to it."

"Who are you—" began Carew angrily.

Stuart's answer was to take a step forward.

"Are you going?" he asked, without raising his voice.

Carew fell back, stood glaring at him for a moment, and then, surprisingly, collapsed like a pricked bubble.

"No offence meant," he muttered vaguely. "Was annoyed, naturally. Misunderstanding—"

His voice trailed into silence as he turned and stumbled away down the long passage.

Stuart watched him turn into his room before he transferred his attention to the couple behind him.

"So that's that," he remarked cheerfully. "Sometime or other, and not so long ago either, I fancy that chap got what he deserved from some one and he hasn't forgotten it yet. I came out of it better than you did, I'm afraid. He hasn't broken your nose, has he?"

Trevor removed the blood-stained handkerchief from his nose and felt the bridge tenderly. He looked as he felt, piteously humiliated, but he managed to achieve a rueful grin.

"No damage done," he muttered. "Afraid I made rather a fool of myself."

"You were splendid!" gasped Miss Hamilton.

She looked exceedingly pretty and very futile, Stuart thought, standing there with her hands clasped, the ready tears still wet on her long lashes.

"I don't think he'll bother you again," he said reassuringly. "If he does, let out a screech. One of us is sure to be handy."

Then, feeling that he was no longer needed, he retired, leaving Trevor to the grateful ministrations of Miss Hamilton.

Carew did not appear at dinner.

"Let's hope he's sleeping it off," concluded Stuart, after describing what had passed.

Soames took a more pessimistic view of the situation.

"I've been having a word with Girling," he said. "He's pretty sick about it, I can tell you, and he tells me that the beggar's got a couple of bottles of whisky up in his room. He sent for them this morning, and Girling had no excuse then not to let him have them."

There was no sign of him that evening, and Girling, who had made an excuse to go to his room, reported that he had found him asleep on his bed.

In spite of which, Soames's forebodings were verified.

He and Constantine had sat up late, playing chess in Constantine's room, and it was close on one o'clock when they were disturbed by a series of suggestive bumps in the passage.

Constantine got up and opened his door. He was immediately confronted with the congested profile of Carew. He was being propelled down the passage by Geoffrey Ford, whose usually sedate features were convulsed with rage.

"Where's this fellow's room, do you know?" he rasped over his shoulder.

"The last one on the right, next to Melnotte's," Constantine informed him, with an appreciative eye on the operation.

Soames slipped past them and opened the door of Carew's room.

"Want any help?" he asked, with a cheerful grin.

For answer Ford propelled his victim through the door and drew back into the passage. A heavy bump from within suggested that Carew had reached his destination on all-fours.

Transferring the key to the outside, Ford slammed the door and locked it.

"If he shouts I can't help it," he said. "There's no other way of dealing with the brute."

They stood listening, but there was no further sound from within.

"What happened?" asked Constantine, who had joined them.

Ford turned on them a face white with fury.

"The foul beast tried to get into Mrs. Orkney Cloude's room," he said shortly, and swung away down the passage.

Soames stared at his retreating back.

"What with the weather and Carew," he remarked sapiently, "there'll be blue murder here before Christmas!"

CHAPTER V

BY THE TIME Stuart reached his room, there was only one thing he desired—sleep. Not only was he feeling the effects of the night before, but the weather, combined with lack of exercise, was beginning to tell on him; and, as he sank gratefully into bed, he decided that, snow or no snow, he must somehow manage to get into the open for a couple of hours each day. His last drowsy thought before he lost consciousness was one of thankfulness that Carew's room was not at the far end of the passage, and that, should he elect to make himself objectionable during the night, Soames and Constantine would have to bear the brunt of his activities. Judging by his last view of them, they had settled down to an all-night seance over the chessboard, so that they would no doubt be up and ready to deal with any situation that might arise.

It seemed as though he had no sooner closed his eyes than he found himself involved in a wild dream. He was on the hill where he had originally encountered the Misses Adderley. They were both there, seated on the running-board of their car, clad in crimson dressing-gowns, with woollen fascinators round their heads, shrieking encouragement to Lord Romsey and Angela Ford, who were running hand and hand up the hill in pursuit of Major Carew. Miss Connie was shouting through her ear-trumpet, which had miraculously turned into a megaphone: "Stop him! He's taken the emerald girdle, and he's going to bury it in the snow!" Urged on by their cries, Stuart was trying to catch them up; but the snow, which now reached above his knees, made progress impossible, and he was engaged in one of those gigantic efforts that only occur in dreams—forcing himself to run violently against overwhelming odds and achieving no progress whatever—when a hand was laid on his shoulder, and, turning, he realized that Carew had somehow managed to outflank his pursuers and was holding him captive from behind. He made a violent effort to wrench himself free, but the grasp on his shoulder tightened ...

He opened his eyes. The first thing they fell on was the lighted bulb of the electric lamp that he had turned out on going to bed. Then he was aware of Soames's fresh-coloured countenance in close proximity to his own.

He stared up at him.

"Talk of the seven sleepers!" ejaculated Soames softly.

His brain began slowly to function. Soames was wearing his pyjamas under an overcoat, so he must have been to bed. Stuart found his voice.

"What time is it?" he asked stupidly.

"Close on three. Dr. Constantine sent me along. There's something queer happening. That chap Carew has got out of his room, and we've got to find him. Heaven knows what he may be up to. If he has another shot at Mrs. Cloude's room, I honestly believe Ford'll do him in. I never saw a man in such a murderous rage as he was last night."

Stuart climbed out of bed reluctantly. Hunting Carew in a dream was bad enough, but running him to earth at three o'clock on a winter's morning, in a house as rambling and spacious as the "Noah's Ark," was beyond a joke.

"How did he get out?" he asked. "Dr. Constantine told me that Ford had locked him in."

"That's the extraordinary part. Down a rope from his bedroom to the balcony underneath."

Stuart stared at him in amazement.

"He couldn't! It'd be a physical impossibility for a chap in his condition! Besides, he's as soft as butter, even when he's sober. Have you looked in his room?"

"Can't! The key's gone."

"Gone? Where?"

Soames suddenly lost patience.

"My dear chap, I don't know! For Heaven's sake get a move on. If he had the grit to get through that window on a dark night like this, you may be sure he was drunk; and if he's drunk, goodness knows what he may be up to. At any moment there may be an appalling shindy from one of the women. We've got to find him, and bottle him up before it's too late."

"Confound the fellow!" ejaculated Stuart, with deep feeling, as he followed Soames down the passage.

"Amen to that," was his companion's heart-felt rejoinder. "I don't feel as if I should ever be warm again."

At the head of the stairs Constantine joined them.

An idea struck Stuart.

"Look here," he exclaimed. "If he did get down on to the balcony without a smash, he'd have to get off it somehow."

"That is what is troubling us," said Constantine. "With the exception of the little window on the stairs, the only way off that balcony is through one or other of the two rooms opening on to it: Mrs. van Dolen's or Mrs. Cloude's. They'll be frightened to death if he tries to get in there."

They had reached the window on the stairs. Stuart bent over it and examined it carefully.

"This is latched on the inside, so he hasn't come in that way," he said.

He unlatched it and raised the lower sash.

"I'd better get out, I suppose," he continued reluctantly. "He may have come a cropper and be lying helpless on the balcony."

He squeezed out with some difficulty, and immediately found himself almost up to his knees in snow. Considering that his nether limbs were dad in pyjama trousers and bedroom slippers, the language that floated back through the window to Soames's appreciative ears was perhaps excusable.

Stuart ploughed his way along the balcony. This was worse—a good deal—than his dream, he decided. But at least there was no sign of the ominous black bulk he dreaded to find, hunched against the whiteness of the snow. Something brushed his face lightly, and he almost cried out, only to find that it was the end of a thin rope, dangling, presumably, from Carew's window.

He reached the end of the balcony and looked down.

He could not see the ground, but it was obvious that, unless he had fallen over, Carew could not have left the balcony that way. Chilled to the bone, and conscious that his slippers were ruined for ever, he felt his way past the French windows of the two bedrooms giving on to the balcony. Softly, so as not to arouse the inmates, he tested them. They both appeared to be securely latched on the inside.

Soames's black shadow was blocking the window. Constantine was standing behind him.

"Well?" whispered Soames.

"Nothing doing. Unless he's fallen over. I suppose we'd better go down and see. Heaven knows how you get out of this place at night, and I haven't a torch."

They got the front door unbolted, and Stuart, who was so wet already that a midnight stroll held no terrors for him, plunged once more into the snow. With the aid of a box of matches, filched from the table in the hall, he made a fairly exhaustive examination of the ground underneath the balcony.

The snow lay as it had fallen, in an unbroken layer, and it was evident that Carew's exit had not been made that way.

"I'm going to get into some clothes," announced Stuart, through his chattering teeth, when he got back into the hall. "But I'm bless-ed if I can see what we're going to do next."

"I'll hold a council of war with the doctor while you're dress-ing. He's prowling about upstairs somewhere. If the key's gone, the beggar must have got out somehow."

Stuart hurried up the stairs, leaving a wet trail behind him; but he was not to achieve comfort just yet.

For Constantine, it appeared, had been prowling to some pur-pose. He met them at the top of the first flight of stairs.

"Find anything?" he asked.

Stuart shook his head.

"He's not there."

"No traces of him?"

"So far as I could see, none. The windows on the balcony don't appear to have been tampered with, and there's certainly no sign of him on the ground below."

Constantine glanced at his sodden slippers.

"You'll have to get those things off, or we shall have you down with pneumonia," he said. "But before you change, I wish you'd have another look at that balcony. I'll get some matches."

"I've got some," admitted Stuart, with marked lack of enthusiasm, as he prepared to climb once more through the staircase window.

Lighting matches as he went, he made a second journey along the balcony. It was a loathsome job. His hands were numb and stiff with cold, and the matches, extinguished by the drifting snow, fizzled out as fast as he lighted them. But he managed to make some sort of inspection, though his own blundering progress, on his first expedition, had effectually fouled any trail there might have been. It was not till he arrived at the spot where the rope hung from Carew's window that his suspicions were aroused. The snow here was so extensively trodden down that it seemed unlikely that all the traces could be his own. Unfortunately, owing to his foot-gear, his progress had been a series of shuffles, and it was impossible to see whether his trail had been superimposed on that of some one else.

He was on his way back, and had just struck the last of his matches, when a gleam of light shone suddenly on his face, and he realized that the curtains in Mrs. Orkney Cloude's room had been parted, and that the window was being unlatched.

It opened, and the light disappeared as the curtains fell into place behind her.

"Who's there?" she called sharply.

He hastened to reassure her, though her voice sounded startled rather than panic-stricken.

"It's Angus Stuart," he said softly. "Don't be frightened. It was jolly plucky of you to open the window."

"I heard you striking matches," she whispered, "and I had to know who it was. What's the matter?"

"It's Carew," he answered. "Ford locked him into his room, and he seems to have got out through the window. You've not heard anything of him, have you?" She gave a little shudder of disgust.

"Nothing, since he made a repulsive scene outside my door quite late this evening."

"There's been no disturbance of any kind in Mrs. van Dolen's room, I suppose?"

"I've heard nothing."

Then, realizing his condition—

"You'll catch your death of cold, Mr. Stuart! Do go and get some clothes on at once, if you're really going to look for him. You're wet through."

He managed to achieve a rather crooked grin, but his teeth were chattering so violently that he could hardly speak.

"I know. I thought I'd have another look at the balcony before I changed. I'm off now."

She hesitated for a moment, then—

"You'd better come through my room, it's quicker. Wait a minute while I tidy up things a bit."

She shut the window again and he heard the latch click. In spite of his own miserable discomfort, he found himself smiling at her precaution. He hadn't, somehow, credited her with so much prudishness. It seemed a long time before she reopened the window, but then, in his present condition, he was no very good judge of time.

"I'm bringing in a good deal of snow," he apologized ruefully.

She had already produced a little spirit-lamp, and was filling a kettle.

"Nonsense! Get up to your room and change, and by that time this will be boiling. I've got a flask of brandy, fortunately. If you don't have something hot you'll be ill."

He hesitated in the doorway.

"I say, it's all right, really. I don't need anything, honestly. Please don't trouble."

The sight of her room, in all its intimate disorder, had abashed him, and his absurd shyness had descended on him once more. He was really ridiculously young for his age, and, in this moment, he realized it and hated himself for being so easily discountenanced.

She smiled at him over her shoulder, and drew her silk dressing-gown a little closer. It dawned on him, for the first time, that she was a very understanding person "Nonsense! Come to the door as soon as you have changed and I'll have it ready for you."

Her tone was so entirely maternal that he felt younger than ever; but, somehow, her smile had dissipated the spasm of self-consciousness that had made him feel both loutish and inadequate.

"It might be wiser to lock your door after I've gone," he suggested. "Carew may be somewhere about, and, if he's drunk …"

She was bending over the spirit-lamp.

"I shall be all right," she answered, almost carelessly. "Call out softly when you knock."

As he closed the door behind him he saw Constantine and Soames standing at the foot of the little flight of steps at the end of the passage. He was about to report what had happened when Constantine stopped him with a gesture.

"Have you been along here at all this evening?" he asked. "Since you've been out in the snow, I mean." Stuart shook his head.

"Some One with wet feet has been along this passage. It looks as if Carew must have made for the back stairs."

"He hasn't been near Mrs. Cloude," said Stuart. "I disturbed her, and she let me in through the window. She hasn't heard anything, and she says there's been no noise from Mrs. van Dolen's room. I've told her to keep her door locked in case Carew turns up."

"I'm beginning to wish he would," sighed Soames. "I'd give a good deal to go to bed."

Constantine placed a hand on Stuart's shoulder and propelled him gently down the passage.

"Get out of these wet things at once," he said. "I ought not to have kept you talking here. And if you find you can't get warm, go to bed and stay there. Soames and I can deal with this."

Stuart grinned.

"Mrs. Cloude has taken my welfare in hand," he announced. "She is brewing a concoction on her spirit-lamp. You needn't worry about me."

"I'm not," grumbled Soames. "Some people have all the luck!"

"I've never known a man to travel with a spirit-lamp," remarked Constantine thoughtfully. "And I've never come across a woman who travelled without one. And, over and over again, I've been grateful to them for it."

It did not take Stuart long to throw off his sopping clothes, give himself a rub down with a hard towel, and get into a thick sweater and trousers.

As he was leaving his room, the door next to his opened, and Miss Amy Adderley put her head round the edge. As before, it was discreetly shrouded in wool.

"I heard you moving about," she whispered. "Is anything the matter?"

"Nothing that you need be alarmed about," he assured her. "But it might be as well to lock your door. The truth is, Major Carew isn't quite himself to-night, and he seems to be wandering about the place somewhere. We're trying to find him."

A look of blank astonishment came over her face.

"You don't mean to say that it was Major Carew in that mask last night?"

The idea was so preposterous that Stuart laughed as he hastened to reassure her; but as he made his way down the stairs to the next floor, he began to wonder why it shouldn't have been Carew, as well as another. A middle-aged gentleman of sedentary habits who shinned down ropes on cold winter nights would be capable of anything.

He found the other two men waiting for him outside Mrs. Orkney Cloude's door. Soames looked hideously bored by the whole business, and, but for the older man, would obviously have been back in bed by now. Constantine, on the contrary, was inclined to treat the matter seriously.

"I don't understand it," he said. "And I don't like it. According to your report of the condition, of the balcony, Carew probably did get down that rope. And he must have been in a pretty queer condition even to have attempted such a thing. We've been all over the house, short of going into the servants' bedrooms, and there isn't a sign of him."

Stuart stared at him.

"I believe we've been making fools of ourselves," he cried. "We've been chasing all over the place looking for him, when in all probability he's simply gone back to his room and locked himself in!"

"How did he get back?" asked Constantine.

"Up the rope, I suppose," was Stuart's rather lame suggestion.

"Could you get up that rope on a night like this?"

"In cold blood, I couldn't, but goodness knows what I might do if I was screwed," returned Stuart; but, even as he said it, he knew that the suggestion was preposterous.

Mrs. Cloude's door opened.

"I thought I heard your voice," she said, holding out a steaming glass. "Make him drink this, please, Dr. Constantine. He's still shivering."

Stuart accepted it gratefully. He was still chilled to the bone, and the immediate effect of the hot liquid made him realize how badly he needed it. While he drank it, Constantine explained to Mrs. Cloude how matters stood.

"There seems only one thing to do now," he concluded. "We must try to rouse Carew, if he is in his room, and make sure he's all right. Once we've got him to answer, I'm going to wash my hands of him and go to bed."

She was about to answer, when the door of the room next to hers was flung open.

Mrs. van Dolen, mountainous in a wadded silk wrapper, stood on the threshold. In one hand she clutched, of all incongruous objects, a small half-eaten sponge finger.

"I don't know why you're all standing around there like a lot of sheep," she exclaimed, her naturally strident voice grim with mingled scorn and indignation. "But I'd have you know that my emerald girdle has been stolen!"

CHAPTER VI

CONSTANTINE said afterwards that Mrs. Van Dolen's attitude towards her loss was the one thing needed to add the last nightmarish touch to that fantastic night. At the moment it was unbearably aggravating.

The truth was that, for once in her life, Mrs. van Dolen was badly frightened. A woman of robust nerves, possessed of all the unreasoning obstinacy of one who, owing to her wealth, had never been crossed, she had flaunted her jewels from one hotel to another, persistently ignoring the warnings, not only of her friends, but of the police. And, until now, she could boast of having done it with impunity. So long had her immunity lasted that she had begun to trade on it, and, as time went on, had grown increasingly careless. With a curious perversity she had taken a positive pleasure in leaving her valuables lying openly about in her room, and it had even amused her to witness the distress of her maid, whose honesty she knew to be unimpeachable.

The loss of the girdle was a rude shock, though, being above all things a business woman, she had insured it to the full extent of its value; but the blow to her self-esteem, and, what touched her more nearly, her sense of security, had thrown her completely off her balance. The knowledge that some one had been in her room and had ransacked it while she slept, filled her with real terror. She had sense enough to know that, had she happened to awaken, she would possibly have paid for her obstinacy with her life, and, with the natural reaction of a strong-minded person who has been badly scared, she was now in a towering and completely unreasonable rage. Being perfectly aware that no one but herself was to blame for what had happened, it had become an actual necessity to her to find some one on whom to vent her wrath, and the discovery that, as she put it, "half the hotel" had been up and about while she was being robbed gave her her opportunity.

She literally herded the three men into her dishevelled bedroom, where, to their amused resentment, she proceeded to subject them to what was neither more nor less than a thorough scolding.

It was some time before they could get in a word edgeways, but Constantine, by dint of sheer pertinacity, did at last manage to wring from her some sort of account of what had happened.

Stuart could hardly believe his ears when she announced, quite casually, that the emeralds had been lying in their case in the top of an unlocked dispatch-box.

"What you were doing, wandering round the passages at this time of night, I don't know," she stormed. "But I do know that it's impossible to get a wink of decent sleep in this hotel. Last night I was dragged out of my warm bed by that fool of a landlord. If he thought there were thieves about, why didn't he do something about it, instead of leaving people to be robbed and murdered in their beds? And to-night, what with the talking in the passage, and the opening and shutting of doors, I might as well have been trying to sleep in a railway depot!"

"Have you any idea when you did wake?" asked Constantine suavely.

She shot him a vicious glance. Her inability to ruffle this urbane old man only served to augment her sense of grievance.

"I have not. All I know is that the noise of the door of the room next to mine, shutting, woke me."

"That would be less than half an hour ago," commented Constantine.

"I don't care when it was, but I know I couldn't get to sleep again, and at last, when I was feeling sick at my stomach from exhaustion, I got up and opened a tin of biscuits I had with me. It was then that I remembered that scare last night, and, just in case there was some reason why all you folk were astir, I thought I'd cast an eye on my emeralds. They were gone, case and all, and I'd like to know what, in the name of goodness, you people think you were doing, keeping folks out of their beds with the beastly shindy you were making, and letting the thief get away with it like that!" she finished furiously. She had thrown refinement to the winds now, and her cockney accent was plainly perceptible.

"Is the window locked?" asked Stuart.

"Shut and bolted! I looked at it first thing. But, as you're asking, I can tell you what wasn't locked! That's the door. And I locked it myself when I came in here last night. When I ran out just now I tried to turn the key, and it was then that I found out that some one had unlocked it."

Soames, who had gone in search of Girling, arrived with him at that moment. The sight of the landlord proved as infuriating as a red rag to a bull. Stuart, bored and embarrassed by the tirade that followed, slipped out into the passage, followed by Constantine. They stood and stared at one another.

"Well, she's got what she deserved at last," said Constantine. "I never pitied any one less. I'm sorry for Girling. We must get him out of that room as soon as we can, for more reasons than one."

Stuart nodded.

"It puts rather a different complexion on the Carew affair, doesn't it?" he said. "We ought to be doing something, I suppose, but I'm hanged if I know what."

"We've been all over the house once," Constantine reminded him. "There are the servants' bedrooms, of course, but unless the thief is the woman's own chauffeur, who, one presumes, must know her habits fairly well, it seems unlikely that we shall run any one to earth in them. It looks to me as if this were a professional job. There's only one thing to do—get to the other end of that rope from Carew's window."

Stuart was assailed by a wild suspicion.

"You don't suppose he's been shamming all this time?" he exclaimed incredulously. "If he has, he's the best actor I've ever met."

Constantine shook his head.

"It would be the simplest solution, but it's too easy. I can't believe that, if he was planning anything of the sort, he would go out of his way to make himself so conspicuous. Anyway, if the thief is Carew, he's locked his door and got clean away, though I fail to see where he's gone to ground. He's literally bottled up here until the weather changes."

Soames appeared in the doorway.

"I'm going down to have a look at the door into the yard," he announced. "Whoever got into this house to-night must have got out of it somehow."

"Whoever got into Mrs. van Dolen's bedroom came down that rope outside Carew's room," asserted Constantine.

"I managed to convey that to old Girling, under cover of the fat lady's accusations, but I'm willing to bet you won't find Carew there, unless he's got a confederate. Girling thinks he can find another key to that door, and, as soon as he can tear himself free, he's going to fetch it. He's having a pretty thick time, I can tell you."

He departed, and his back was hardly turned before Girling came out of Mrs. van Dolen's room, closing the door carefully behind him.

"Phew!" he murmured. "This is the last time so much as a silver bracelet comes into this house! A fair caution, she is! That rope's a funny business, sir. I'll get my bunch of keys. There should be one that fits, if I remember rightly. And I'll set Joe to watch that there balcony, but I'll lay the chap's away by now."

He bustled off, and the two men made their way upstairs to their own floor. Outside Carew's room they stopped and listened. There was not a sound from inside. Soames, accompanied by Geoffrey Ford, joined them almost immediately, and, while they stood waiting for Girling, the door of the next room opened and Melnotte's head appeared cautiously round the edge. In spite of his preoccupation Stuart very nearly laughed aloud, for the dancer was wearing one of those net-work arrangements on his head that are sold to keep the hair in place during the night. At the sight of the little group in the passage he snatched it off.

"Is anything the matter?" he asked nervously.

"Lots!" was Soames's rejoinder. "Burglary, among other things."

Melnotte started nervously.

"Not really?" he protested.

"It's a fact," Soames assured him. "You'd better come and help catch the thief."

"He's not in that room, is he?" asked Melnotte, with an apprehensive glance at Carew's door.

"That's just what we're going to find out. You haven't been disturbed by any noises next door, I suppose?"

"Me? Oh, none, I assure you."

He ventured out into the passage a graceful if rather garish figure, clad in a dressing-gown that Stuart found himself envying, but which he would never have had the courage to wear.

Stuart had been explaining the situation in a low voice to Ford.

"I suppose you really did lock that door to-night?" he concluded. Ford nodded.

"I'm quite sure I did. I remember trying it afterwards. I wanted to make sure that the fellow really was bottled up for the night. I can tell you one thing: I'm quite sure that he wasn't shamming. He was as drunk as a lord when I brought him upstairs."

Stuart entirely agreed with him.

"That's what I should have said. No one in that condition could have got down that rope, broken into Mrs. van Dolen's room, taken the girdle, and got off without waking her."

Girling's voice came from the end of the passage.

"Get you back, and don't move from under that balcony till I give the word. I'll see to this."

He appeared, carrying a large bunch of keys in his hand.

"That was Joe," he informed them. "He's been round the house with a lantern, and he says there's not a sign of anything. And the yard door's shut and locked all right. I've sent him back to watch the balcony."

"The yard door was locked when I went down just now," asserted Soames. "I had an idea the chap might have got away through it."

"Did you happen to notice whether the key was on the hook in the passage?" asked Girling. "It's always hung up there last thing."

"Sorry, I didn't. If I'd known where it was generally kept, I'd have looked for it."

"Seems as if I'd better go and cast an eye on the barn," said Girling doubtfully. "The chap may have tried to get away in one of the cars."

Constantine intervened.

"Get this door open first," he said decisively. "We can't very well break into the room except in your presence, and it's high time we investigated matters here. Let one of the others go down to the barn."

"I'll go," volunteered Soames. "Stuart's got wet through once already to-night."

Ford offered to accompany him.

"You'll find the key hanging next the other in the passage, close to the yard door," called Girling after them, as they departed.

Girling tried several keys before he found the right one, and, as he fumbled with the lock, Stuart was conscious of a curious and unpleasant sensation that was not entirely due to cold. Girling's efforts were anything but noiseless, and there was something ominous about the unbroken stillness that reigned behind the closed door. Of course, he told himself, if Carew were lying in a drunken stupor.

The key turned suddenly, and Girling threw open the door.

An icy wind came out of the darkness, taking Stuart's breath away. Then he remembered the open window from which the rope was dangling.

Girling found the switch and turned on the light.

The three men crowded in after him, their eyes with one accord focused on the bed which stood against the right-hand wall. At the sight of it Stuart gave an involuntary gasp of relief.

Carew was there, after all, engaged in sleeping off his bout, and oblivious to all that was going on around him.

His clothes were heaped untidily on a chair; his shoes lay on the floor beside it. One had fallen on its side, and a swift glance assured Stuart that there was no snow or any sign of damp on the sole.

Constantine crossed to the bed and placed his hand on the sleeping man's shoulder.

He was lying, apparently, on his side, the bedclothes drawn up over his face. Only the top of his head was visible.

Constantine leaned over him.

"Major Carew," he said urgently, giving the shoulder he grasped a little shake.

Something caught his eye and he bent lower. Then, with an exclamation that brought the others to his side, he jerked the bedclothes away, and the reason for Carew's silence was revealed.

The pillow under his head was dark with blood. Stuart gave one glance at the ghastly, smeared face and turned away, sickened, for where the man's right temple should have been was now a mass of bruised and bleeding tissue.

Constantine straightened himself and stared at Girling across the body.

"He's dead," he said at last. "There's nothing we can do."

"Seems as if we ought to make sure, like," muttered Girling dazedly.

Constantine slipped his hand inside the front of Carew's pyjama jacket. They stood waiting in silence, though they knew only too well what the verdict was bound to be.

They watched him till he drew the sheet silently over the stained face. Then, suddenly, with a queer, crowing scream, Melnotte turned and made blindly for the door.

Constantine passed his handkerchief over his forehead, and Stuart became aware that the palms of his own clenched hands were slippery with sweat.

"Better leave everything as it is," advised Constantine, "and get on to the police. Is your constable on the telephone?"

Girling shook his head.

"I'll send Joe," he said. "And he'd better go for the doctor as well."

He crossed to the window and called down to the man outside. Then he rejoined the two men standing by the bed. "Best lock this room, I suppose," he said heavily.

Constantine nodded.

"We'll clear out. There's nothing further we can do here. How soon can your man get the constable?"

"Matter of ten minutes, I should think, if he dresses himself quick. The doctor's only at the end of the village, and he's not likely to be out on a night like this. He couldn't get far in that car of his, even if he was sent for."

They trooped out of the room, and Girling locked the door behind them. They reached the stairs just as Soames was coming up. He greeted them cheerily.

"Lord, I'm wet!" he exclaimed. "Nothing doing outside. Both doors were locked, and there's no indication that any one has tried to force the door of the barn. I went in, and, as far as I could see, the cars are all right. If the thief did manage to get away, he must have had wings."

He caught sight of Stuart's face and stopped dead. "I say, anything wrong?" he asked.

Stuart told him.

Soames was shocked, but he was not an imaginative man, and he had been spared the sight of the body. His attitude was one of interest rather than horror.

"The poor chap must have woke up just as the thief was going through his room," he said. "Hard luck! Have they sent for the police?"

"Joe's gone," answered Girling.

"Then it's no good going to bed, I suppose?"

"I shouldn't think so. We're sure to be wanted."

"In that case I vote for a fire and something hot inside me," announced Soames, with characteristic common sense. "You all look as though you needed it. Can you do anything about that, Girling?"

"I can, Mr. Soames, and glad I'll be to turn my hand to something and take my mind off what's happened. It's given me a proper turn, and that's the truth. If you don't mind that little office of mine, it'll warm up the quickest."

He was as good as his word, and they were thawing comfortably enough over a wood fire by the time he returned, carrying a large tray on which were cups and a huge coffee-pot.

At Constantine's invitation he poured himself out a cup and joined them.

"Where's the young gentleman?" he asked. "Doesn't he want some coffee?"

Constantine answered him. "Melnotte, you mean? I found him leaning against the wall in the passage. He was pea-green in the face, and all but fainting. I helped him back to his room, and he said he was going to bed, and that he'd be all right, so I left him."

"I don't blame him," said Stuart fervently.

Constantine nodded.

"He's a bit of a weakling, but he had every excuse> I must admit. Though, from what he said, the thing that really upset him was that it had happened in the room next to his. He was really frightened."

"I'd give something to know where that there chap got to," said Girling, staring gloomily into the fire. "Joe swears that there were no tracks anywhere near the house, and there's no sign of any one's having got away in front. I had a look when I was sending Joe off to the police station."

"What do you make of the whole business, sir?" Soames asked Constantine.

The old man was leaning back in his chair, his head supported on his hand. His face was very weary, and, for the first time since he had met him, Stuart realized his age. As he answered Soames, however, his eyes lit up with something of their old fire.

"Up to a point," he said slowly, "it seems fairly simple. Ford, here, left the key in the lock outside Carew's door, and whoever was after Mrs. van Dolen's emeralds evidently found it there. Why he chose that room, rather than mine or Melnotte's, is an open question, but I think it is significant. Carew had been drinking heavily, and no doubt everybody in the hotel knew it. He would obviously be less likely to wake than, say, myself. Old people are notoriously light sleepers. Which goes to support my theory, that the thief comes from inside, not outside, this hotel."

Girling stirred uneasily in his chair.

"That's a nasty thought, sir," he remarked. "I'd rather think otherwise."

"So would I, and, I've no doubt, so would everybody else in this room. But you have admitted yourself that it's practically out of the question for the man to have got away, and my own opinion is that he is in the hotel at this moment."

"Perhaps you'll tell me where, sir."

Constantine smiled.

"That's a job for the police. But I hope they'll make a more thorough search than we were able to do."

"Unfortunately there couldn't be a better house than this, from a burglar's point of view," said Stuart. "There isn't a passage that hasn't an exit at either end, and the two staircases would be a help, too. I'd undertake to hide here myself, until hunger drove me into the open."

"Well, no one's been after the food or the drink. That I can vouch for," asserted Girling.

"Which suggests that the person, whoever he is, is living here openly, and getting his food in the ordinary way, like the rest of us," Constantine pointed out.

"In fact, any one of us might be the murderer," commented Soames grimly. "It's a pleasant thought."

"It is one we shall have to face, once the police get here," said Constantine. "What sort of person is your village constable, Girling?"

"Tom Bates? Well, I've known him ever since he was a little shaver, and, seeing so much of any one, like, it's difficult to say. He's got his wits about him, Tom has, but he's slow, if you understand me. There's one or two have set out to make a fool of Tom Bates, but he's bested them in the end. There's one thing about him. You show Tom reason, and he'll see it. Not like some folks as jumps to a conclusion and sticks to it through thick and thin. A very fair sort of chap, he is. I shan't be sorry to feel he's in charge here."

"I'm sure I'm glad to see you making yourselves so comfortable."

The group sitting over the fire swung round as one man.

Mrs. van Dolen stood in the doorway, her eyes ablaze with wrath, and her fingers closing and unclosing on the lace handkerchief she held. She was still robed in pink silk, but both her complexion and her *coiffure* had undergone a change for the better since they had last seen her.

"As nobody's so much as thought of coming near me since my room was burgled, I thought I'd just have a look round and find out for myself if there was any one alive in this house. It hasn't occurred to any of you, I suppose, that unless you get a move on, there's very little chance of my ever setting eyes on my stones again?"

There was an embarrassed silence, then Constantine rose gallantly to the occasion.

"Girling here has sent for the police, and I'm afraid there is very little we can do till they arrive. They should be here at any moment now."

She swept forward and seated herself in the chair he had just vacated. "Well, I guess I'll see them myself when they do come. It don't look to me as if there's a single soul in this one-horse little hotel that's fit to give a clear account of what's happened."

Geoffrey Ford strolled over to the table and poured out a cup of coffee. "We can at least offer you some refreshment while you're waiting," he said placatingly, as he handed her the cup.

His manner was perfect, but the glance she shot at him was full of suspicion. The truth was that, in the stress of the moment, she had completely lost her carefully applied social veneer, and was beginning to be aware of the fact.

A bell pealed loudly, and Girling hurried to answer it. Even Mrs. van Dolen listened in silence to the sound of the front door opening, and the low murmur of voices that followed.

They heard heavy footsteps mounting the stairs, then the voices receded into the distance.

Mrs. van Dolen rose to her feet. "They're not going to my room without me there to receive them!" she exclaimed. "I wouldn't trust a dog in this place now!"

Constantine laid a hand on her arm.

"I think you would be wise to leave them alone for the present," he said quietly.

She jerked herself free.

"You do, do you? Considering I'm the person that's been robbed, I should imagine I've a right to interview the police!" she snapped.

"Unfortunately it has ceased to be a case of robbery," Constantine informed her.

She glared at him.

"What would you call it?" she sneered. "A practical joke?"

"I'm inclined to think that the police will call it murder," was his quiet rejoinder.

She gave a gasp of astonishment. Then her eyes travelled over the little group of men and read confirmation in their faces.

"For God's sake! Well, all I can say is, if your fool of a village policeman's got a case of murder on his hands, it's good-bye to my emeralds," was her only comment as she dropped back into her chair.

CHAPTER VII

AT FIRST SIGHT Tom Bates fitted the part of conventional village policeman to perfection. It was only as the night, or rather the morning, wore on that Stuart began to realize that under the heavy stolidity of the rustic was hidden all the shrewdness of the countryman. Bates went about his business in a manner which, though leisurely, was by no means so slow as it seemed.

Within twenty minutes of his entry into the inn he joined them in the office, and Stuart discovered afterwards that not only had he already thoroughly inspected Carew's room, but had made the round of the premises outside with the aid of a lantern. Whether or not Girling had prepared him for one of the chief obstacles in his path, he showed himself more than capable of dealing with the problem of Mrs. van Dolen.

He had barely entered the room before she was on her feet and delivering her ultimatum.

"See here, my good man," she began aggressively. "Let's understand one another! You're after promotion like anybody else, and I suppose you think you'll get it by catching a murderer. But I'd have you remember that I've been robbed, and that my emeralds are pretty well known at Scotland Yard. I've had their men on guard over them before now, and they won't think any the better of you if you fall down on that part of your job. If I have to get in a private detective I'll see to it that every one knows the reason why!"

Bates neither answered nor moved a muscle of his broad, fresh-coloured face, as he drew a chair up to the table, sat down, and produced his notebook from his pocket. Still in silence, he placed the book on the table before him, squared his elbows, looked critically at the point of his stub of pencil, moistened it with his tongue, and then at last spoke.

"If you'll kindly describe the jewels," he said.

Mrs. van Dolen, silent for once, had been watching his movements with a kind of fascination.

"So you've got a tongue!" she exclaimed tartly.

"Yes, madam."

Bates licked his pencil once more, and gazed at her expectantly.

Mrs. van Dolen launched forth into an elaborate and verbose description of the girdle. Stuart noticed that only the salient features of her narrative found their way into Bates's book, but he let her run on, waiting stolidly until her energy had spent itself.

"Anything else missing?" he asked.

"Two brooches and a ring; but it's the emeralds I'm worrying about."

"If you'll kindly describe them."

She did so.

"Now, if you can give me an exact account of what happened, according to your knowledge, I needn't keep you any longer," he said, when she had finished.

Mrs. van Dolen repeated her account of her movements during the night.

"But if you think I'm going back to bed until I've heard what these gentlemen have got to say, you're mistaken," she concluded defiantly.

Bates closed his notebook and tucked it away in his pocket.

"I'm goin' to ask these gentlemen to step upstairs with me to the corpse's room. It's no sight for any lady," he stated heavily. "But, first of all, I'll ask you to let me have a look at your bedroom, then I needn't disturb you again."

He rose and stood by the door, waiting for her to pass out, and, after a moment of baffled hesitation, Mrs. van Dolen went. It spoke well for his methods of dealing with her that they saw no more of her that night.

Neither were they asked to go back to Carew's room. Bates conducted his examination, such as it was, in the office, and he began with Constantine.

"I understand that it was you as first saw the rope," he said slowly; "May I ask you what caused you to look out of your window at that time of night?"

Constantine smiled.

"I know that it seems an odd thing to have done on a cold winter's morning," he admitted readily. "But the explanation is really quite simple. I had been playing chess with Mr. Soames, here, and as is the way with chess players, we got led on from one game to another, with the result that it was nearly two-thirty when Mr. Soames left me to go to his room. After he had gone I pottered about, putting away the chess-men and damping down the fire, in the way one does when one's too tired to do the sensible thing and go straight to bed. The result was that it must have been half-past three before I was undressed. I was just about to get into bed when I realized that the room was thick with smoke. We had been playing, you must remember, for a long time, and we had both been smoking heavily all the time. I put on a dressing-gown and threw up the window, meaning to leave it open for five minutes or so to air the room. Soames and I had been discussing the snowfall just before he left me, and with that in my mind, I suppose, I thrust my head out to see if it showed any signs of stopping. My attention was at once caught by the light streaming from the window of Major Carew's room."

Bates looked up sharply.

"This is the first I've heard of a light in that room. It was in darkness, I understand, when you went in later?"

"I'm pretty sure I spoke of the light to Girling afterwards, but he must have forgotten to mention it. It's been a pretty stirring evening for us all, you know."

"I can believe you, sir. You've no idea when it was turned off, I suppose?"

Constantine shook his head.

"Since I've had time to think things over," he said, "I've realized how thoroughly we played into the murderer's hands. We ought, of course, to have made a determined effort, then and there, to get into Major Carew's room; but you must remember we were all obsessed with the fact that the man was drunk, and more than likely to make a nuisance of himself. He had been locked in, and there was every reason to think that he might resent the fact, should he find it out. Indeed, we had been on the alert for something of the sort all the evening, and had been prepared, the moment we heard any noise, to go and try to quiet him, and, if possible, to persuade him to go to bed. Incredible as it seems, the one explanation that occurred to any of us when we saw the rope, was that he had used it to get out, and our one object, from then on, was to waylay him and get him back to his room before he succeeded in disturbing the whole house."

"I understand that you did try to go in. I'd like to hear exactly what you did do, in its right order, if you don't mind, sir."

"We did the stupidest thing we could have done, as it turned out," replied Constantine ruefully. "As soon as I saw the rope, which was plainly visible in the light from the window, I immediately, as I said, jumped to the conclusion that Major Carew had either used it or was just about to do so. I hurried to his room and had actually rapped on his door, when I discovered that the key was no longer in the lock. I then tried the door, and when I found that locked, called to him through it as loudly as I dared. I did not want to wake the other people on that floor, but I knew that I had made enough noise to attract his attention, supposing he were awake and in his room. I'm sorry to say that, when he didn't answer, I allowed myself to be led astray into thinking that he had escaped by way of the window to the balcony below; had somehow managed to get back into the inn, and was wandering, probably in a fuddled condition, about the house. It seemed a natural supposition that, if he were indignant at having been locked in, he would commandeer the key to prevent any other further interference with his movements."

"You didn't happen to look through the keyhole, sir?" asked Bates.

Stuart suppressed a smile. Inquisitive as the old man was, it was difficult to imagine even his pet vice leading him to such undignified depths. But Constantine took the suggestion seriously enough.

"I wish I had," he said frankly. "If the murderer had been in the room then, I might possibly have seen him. As it was, I merely went up the short flight of steps to Mr. Soames's room and roused him. He looked out of my window, saw the rope, and went for Mr Stuart. The light was still on then, but that is the last time either of us looked out, and we never realized that it had been put out until Girling opened the door and we found the room in darkness."

"While Mr. Soames was gone, what did you do, sir?"

"I tried again to rouse Major Carew. Then, when I could get no answer, I went down the passage to the stairs, where I met Mr. Stuart and Mr. Soames."

Bates thanked him and turned to Soames.

"I'll have your story now, if you don't mind, sir," he said.

Soames gave an account of all that had happened after he had roused Stuart, and Stuart corroborated it, and described his own investigations on the balcony.

When he had finished Bates rose to his feet, tucked the notebook away in his pocket and buttoned the flap. "There's one more question," he said. "Did any of you gentlemen know this Major Carew—apart from meeting him here, I mean?"

The question met with a flat denial, amplified emphatically by Soames.

"I've no wish to speak ill of the dead," he said, "but you can take it from me that he wasn't the sort of chap anybody would wish to know."

"I gather from Mr. Girling that he was not what you would call a sober sort of gentleman," suggested Bates.

"He's been drinking steadily ever since he set foot inside the place," answered Stuart.

"So that any one, coming on him suddenly, wouldn't have much difficulty in catching him unawares?"

"None, I should say. He would probably wake up thoroughly fuddled," replied Constantine.

Bates picked up his helmet.

"I'll wish you good-evening, gentlemen," he said. "There's nothing now to keep you from your beds. I've been through the pockets of the deceased, and there's some letters addressed to him at a club in London. If the wires aren't down, I'll get in touch with it to-morrow, and some one there will no doubt put me on to his relations."

He stumped out, his heavy boots clumping on the tiled passage leading to the lounge. Soames strolled to the door and listened to the sound of his footsteps mounting the stairs. Then he turned back into the room.

"He didn't ask whether it was the first time any one had attacked Carew this evening," he observed grimly.

"For which I'm thankful," said Constantine. "We don't want either Ford or that boy Trevor involved if we can help it."

"All the same, there was one moment at least when each of them would have been ready enough to choke the life out of him," Soames reminded him.

"There have been moments to-day when I could have watched him drown, cheerfully, myself," said Stuart. "But that doesn't mean that I would be capable of creeping into his room in the middle of the night and doing him in. Besides, judging by the robbery, revenge wasn't the motive."

"I'm not saying it was," answered Soames stubbornly. "What I do say is that there's only one man in this house whose movements I don't understand, and that man's young Ford. Mind you, I've nothing against him. He seems a decent enough chap in himself, but I'm not forgetting that he was up and dressed directly after Miss Adderley had started the scare about the masked man."

Constantine lifted the coffee-pot off the hob and poured himself out a cup.

"You've got Ford on the brain," he said dryly. "Have another cup of coffee and clear some of the cobwebs out of your brain. Admitting that he was up and dressed, so, for the matter of fact, were you and I, at two o'clock this morning. I'm inclined to think that Bates feels very much the same about us as you feel about Ford. His question as to why I happened to be looking out of my window at that time of night was a shrewd one, and I'm not by any means certain that he swallowed my explanation. The fact that it's a true and perfectly natural one to me doesn't make it so to him. No doubt it is the first time he's come across an old person of my age who's in the habit of sitting up till the small hours playing what he would probably stigmatize as a 'silly game.' It may be a case of the pot calling the kettle black!"

Soames laughed, but he still stuck to his guns.

"It isn't only that," he said. "I was on my way down from the billiard-room this evening when I ran into the younger Miss Ford. She was coming round the corner of that passage leading to her room, and she didn't see me till I was right on her. She'd got her head turned away and was talking to some one I couldn't see, but it was clear enough who it was. She was in a fine paddy, with her cheeks all scarlet and her eyes fairly blazing. It wasn't that though, it was what she said."

He paused.

"I suppose you want me to ask you what it was," remarked Constantine with a sigh. "Rather than spoil your effect, I'll play up. Let's have it."

"She said: 'Don't be a coward as well as a fool, Geoff. You'll have to own up sooner or later, and you may as well make a clean breast of it now.' Then she saw me and dried up, but she'd got plenty more up her sleeve by the look of her."

Stuart cast a swift glance at Constantine. In the light of his own suspicions this was interesting. To his surprise, the old man was chuckling quietly to himself.

"You are barking up the wrong tree, Soames," he said. "If Angela Ford says her brother's a fool, she's probably right, though she's hardly got the sanction of the Bible. But whatever Geoffrey may have been up to, you may take my word for it that he's neither a thief nor a murderer. If he'd any homicidal instincts, Romsey would have been in his grave long ago!" he concluded thoughtfully.

"That's all very well, doctor," was Soames's stubborn rejoinder. "They're your friends, and I should no doubt feel the same about them if they were mine. There's no other suspect in this house that I can see, so I'm keeping my eye on Mr. Geoffrey Ford until further notice. Meanwhile, I'm for bed. Anybody coming?"

Constantine rose to his feet and threw his cigarette end into the fire.

"If you're in search of a suspect," he said gently, "why not young Melnotte? His room is next to Carew's, and he never showed up this evening till everything was practically over. He may have been in his room all the time, or, again, he may not. And he nearly fainted when he saw Carew. You must admit that, considering he did not know him, and showed very plainly that he disliked him, he took his death very much to heart. And, what is more, there's a communicating door between his room and Carew's. It's locked, and he told me that the key had been missing ever since he arrived, which may or may not be true."

Stuart, who was watching Constantine's face, realized that he was unashamedly palling Soames's leg. His gravity was portentous, but his dark eyes were snapping with mischief.

For a moment Soames was taken aback, then his common sense asserted itself.

"It's an idea," he agreed solemnly. "Miss Adderley may have run into him and have mistaken that night-cap thing he wears in bed for a mask. Let's go and ask him now whether he did it. He'll probably say, 'Quate,' and commit suicide with his curling-tongs, then the whole thing will be nicely settled."

He started to leave the room, but at the door he turned and addressed them—

"I may be wrong about Ford, and, of course, the mere idea that Melnotte should have anything to do with this business is simply funny, but we've got to face the fact that every single soul in this house, barring the women, is under suspicion. Come to that, we do not know where Melnotte was this evening; he does happen to be better fitted to shin down that rope than most of us. His room is next door to Carew's; it would have been the easiest thing in the world for him to have slipped through the communicating door, and we know nothing whatever about him. He's one of these lounge lizards that crop up in every walk of life, respectable and otherwise. He may be a professional crook for all we know." He swung round and disappeared down the passage. Constantine chuckled appreciatively.

"He got his own back very nicely," he said, as he prepared to follow. "And, what's more, he's right. Personally, I'm prepared to give a clean bill both to Melnotte and Geoffrey Ford, but I'm simply working on intuition in the one case, and my knowledge of the man's character and circumstances in the other. But Soames is right in one thing. We are all under suspicion, in the sense that any one of us could have murdered Carew to-night and got away with the emeralds. There is only one bit of evidence in our favour—that of the light in Carew's room. Soames and I can corroborate each other's story that it was on just before he called you, and, from then on, we were all in each other's company and could have had no opportunity of turning it off." He pulled himself up suddenly.

"No, I'm wrong there," he exclaimed. "I'm providing myself with an alibi I haven't earned. There was a period when you and Soames were downstairs in which my movements were unchecked. I could have turned off the light then. It will be interesting to see what conclusions our friend Bates will have arrived at by to-morrow; but, given the facts as he knows them, I don't think we can blame him if he looks on all three of us with suspicion."

Stuart gave vent to a hearty yawn.

"Well, all I ask is that, if we have got a homicidal burglar in our midst, he will confine his future operations to the daytime. It's close on five now, and when I consider that I arrived here the day before yesterday and that I haven't had a decent night's rest since, I can't help feeling a little peevish!"

"It certainly does seem a wicked waste of Girling's excellent beds," agreed Constantine. "All the same, I should like to know what the doctor's verdict is before I go to mine."

As it turned out, they met the doctor and Bates on the stairs on their way up to bed.

"Fractured skull," said the doctor in answer to Constantine's inquiry. "The instrument used must have had a sharp angle to it, judging from the cleanness with which the skin is cut, but with a nasty mess like that it's difficult to tell."

"Would a jemmy have done it?" asked Constantine.

The doctor looked dubious.

"It might. But, from the damage done, I should suggest a shorter, heavier weapon, myself."

"We shall be moving the body to the station early to-morrow morning," put in Bates, with the obvious intention of cutting the conversation short. "It can go in the lock-up there till the inquest. It's a bit awkward here for Mr. Girling, what with ladies in the house and all. Good-night, gentlemen. I shall be round in the morning."

Constantine accepted his dismissal with good grace, and followed Stuart up the stairs.

All three slept the sleep of the just for the few hours of the night that remained to them, and far into the following morning. After breakfast they forgathered in Girling's office and learned from him that the constable had already put in a good day's work.

"Makin' a day of it, Tom is," he remarked, with a reminiscent smile. "Haven't seen him so busy since old Marlowe's ricks were fired. He got his man then, though, and happen he'll get him this time. He's thorough, that I will say. Had 'em all on the mat this morning, servants and gentry alike!"

"I wonder whether he arrived at anything?" said Stuart.

"If he did he didn't pass it on to me. Very close-mouthed he was, when I saw him last; but if you ask me, I'd say he didn't. Every soul, bar one, in my employ comes from the village here, and there isn't one that Tom and I haven't known all their lives like, and their fathers before them. There's only one outsider, and that's the cook. She's a Brighton woman, and her references'd satisfy anybody. As for the London lot, there's three chauffeurs and two maids. Lord Romsey, he vouched for his man at once. Been his chauffeur nine years, and was in his stables before that. Quite nasty he turned when Tom pressed him a bit over the man's habits and that. Mrs. Cloude's man was her husband's batman through the War, and she won't hear nothin' against him. As for Mrs. van Dolen—"

Girling's wizened face creased into a thousand wrinkles as he paused, his shoulders shaking with mirth.

"Let's have it, Girling, for pity's sake," urged Soames.

"Well, it seems as she took her chauffeur straight from the Home Secretary," Girling informed them, "He left because he found the work too heavy for him, him havin' been invalided out of the army. There wasn't nothin' the matter with his references, but Tom wasn't takin' no chances, so he got on to London, and the gentleman came to the phone himself. Said he was prepared to speak for the man personally if he was in any trouble. So that's that. Proper put back Tom was, over that, I fancy. I'll lay he was pinnin' somethin' on to that chap. Nice fellow, too, as I told him."

"Bates's tight lips don't seem to have availed him much so far," remarked Constantine, with a smile.

"Bless you, I didn't get all that from him," answered Girling cheerfully. "They were all in the bar after he'd got through with them, and there wasn't nothin' to prevent them talkin'. And they did talk, too! If that Mrs. van Dolen could have heard some of the things as was said about her and her jewels, I'm thinkin' it wouldn't have done her any harm."

"Has he had a thorough look round the place?" asked Soames.

"I'd say he had," replied Girling dryly. "Two of the maids gave notice before nine this morning, owin' to him pokin' about among their things, and a nice time I had of it gettin' them to stay on. He hadn't no right to do it, either, havin' no warrant. Lucky for him they didn't know that, and I wasn't goin' to tell 'em. I don't want to get old Tom into trouble, but he's goin' a bit far over this business. I think he knows that the Chief Constable will be all for applyin' to London as soon as the snow lets up, and Tom's tryin' to get on with it before the chap from the Yard turns up. I don't blame him neither, provided he don't go too far."

"Did he find anything?"

"He found a snapshot of himself, taken at the sports here last summer. It was in Bessie's room, all dolled up in a silver frame. Bessie's the head housemaid, and not so young as she was, and Tom's been a widower this four years. Proper taken aback, he was, and it was all I could do to prevent Bessie packin' her box and goin' over to her mother's, then and there! That's all he found, so far as I know, but he wasn't givin' nothin' away."

"What about Mrs. van Dolen's maid?"

"Been with her fifteen years. Mrs. van Dolen's left her three thousand pounds in her will, provided she's still in her service when she dies, and Carter—that's the maid—knows it. She told me that herself. It wouldn't be worth her while to steal. She's worried herself sick over them jewels, so she tells me, Mrs. van Dolen bein' so careless like."

"If her mistress had been bumped off now she might have had a hand in it," reflected Soames.

"Well, I wouldn't say as she hadn't got a motive for that," agreed Girling thoughtfully.

"That's the lot, then," said Stuart.

"Except for Miss Hamilton," Constantine reminded him. "Anything known about her?"

Girling shook his head.

"That I don't know. She wouldn't come gossipin' to me naturally. But she don't look that sort."

Later on in the morning he came to them to say that Bates would like a few words with Stuart and Constantine if they did not mind stepping into the office.

Soames's eyebrows shot up.

"And he doesn't want me! Pretty sinister, I call that. I have a suspicion that the net is closing round me," he called after them dramatically. He was nearer the truth than he realized.

"Sorry to trouble you, gentlemen," was Bates's brisk opening, "but it'll make my job a bit easier if you could help me as to the identity of some of the people here. There's Lord Romsey and his little lot, for instance. I understand that you've met them elsewhere."

Constantine smiled.

"If it's impersonation you suspect, you can wipe the Romseys off your slate. I've known them, on and off, for a good many years, and I can vouch for it that they are the genuine article. Mrs. van Dolen I know well by sight, though I suppose, in the circumstances, she hardly comes under suspicion. I'm afraid I can't help you with the rest. While we're about it, though, aren't you rather taking us for granted?"

Bates grinned.

"If you'll cast your eye over that copy of *The Illustrated Monthly* on the hall table there, you'll find an uncommonly good photo of yourself, sir. Girling showed it to me this morning. As for Mr. Stuart, there's been half a dozen portraits of him in the daily papers during the last few weeks. No, I ain't got no doubts about you, but there's a bare chance that some one else here may be passin' under a false name, and any help you can give me I should be obliged for. This Mr. Soames, now. You couldn't give me a line on him, I suppose?"

Constantine shook his head.

"I'm afraid not. But, if intuition and a pretty good knowledge of the world goes for anything, I think you can take it from me that he is what he claims to be. In any case, he is more likely to be able to prove his identity than any one else in the house. He must have business papers connected with his firm, and, if you ring them up, they can no doubt describe him adequately enough. And there's his luggage. If he's a commercial traveller, he's no doubt got his cases with him."

Bates nodded.

"Mrs. Orkney Cloude?" he suggested.

Constantine hesitated.

"I've got a little theory of my own concerning Mrs. Orkney Cloude," he said at last. "But, so far, it's based on such very flimsy evidence that I should prefer to keep it to myself. In any case, it has no bearing whatever on the murder or the burglary. If I am right, however, you can safely wipe her off your list of suspects."

Bates frowned and scratched his head with his pencil.

"If that's as far as you'll go, sir, I can't force you," he said slowly. "That leaves the Misses Adderley and the two young men."

"You're not going to suggest that either of the Misses Adderley hit Carew on the head and climbed down that rope afterwards!" exclaimed Stuart. "Why, the poor old things have been simply dithering ever since Miss Amy saw the man in the mask."

Bates laughed.

"I'm not worrying about them," he admitted. "But I can't seem to make much of that Mr. Melnotte, and twice this morning I've run into Mr. Trevor and Miss Hamilton with their heads together. Very hard at it, they were, and it's a fact that Miss Hamilton had as good a chance at those emeralds as any one, besides knowing where they were kept and all."

For the life of him Stuart could not resist a swift glance in Constantine's direction. But the old man looked the picture of innocence. Evidently he did not propose to inform Bates of the scene between Carew and Trevor in the passage, and, with a rather guilty feeling of relief, Stuart decided to keep what he knew to himself.

"After all, it's not an unnatural arrangement," Constantine pointed out. "People tend to fall into couples in a hotel like this, and they are the two most likely to pair. If Miss Hamilton had an eye on the emeralds she must have had many opportunities to take them, judging by the way Mrs. van Dolen seems to have left them about. Why either she, or, for the matter of that, Mrs. van Dolen's maid, should have chosen to work under such disadvantageous circumstances I fail to understand."

"I see your point, sir," agreed Bates. "Whoever did it, had this one chance and took it. That Mr. Melnotte now. He had the next room to Major Carew and above Mrs. van Dolen's. There's a door between the two rooms, though it's locked and the key's missing. Mr. Melnotte says he's never seen the key, and Girling admits that the door hasn't been opened, to his knowledge, for the last two years or more. He can't remember when he last noticed the key. Still, Mr. Melnotte may have used it. He's young and active, and, according to Mr. Girling, he was fair bowled over at the sight of the body."

"It was an unpleasant sight, you know," suggested Constantine mildly. "However, I hold no brief for young Melnotte. I can only give you the impression he has made on me. He's one of those unfortunate people whose nerve goes back on them in an emergency, and I should say he'd got an abnormal dread of physical violence."

"Meaning he's a coward," put in Bates stolidly.

Constantine smiled.

"That's what we should have called him in my young days," he admitted. "But there's a good deal to be said for the more modern theory. I don't know what his origin may be, but I've an inkling that he's had a hard fight to reach his present position. We've no idea what kind of childhood he may have had, and when or how his nerve was broken. I travelled down from London with him, you know, in a motor-coach. It was an unpleasant journey, and we had one or two very nasty skids. Melnotte was literally sweating with terror all the way. I didn't like it myself, which, I suppose, made me feel a kind of sympathy for him. He's badly frightened now, but not of the police, judging from what he said to me this morning. He wanted to know whether it was true that you were going to spend the night here, and seemed to be of the opinion that your proper place, if you did, would be on the mat outside his bedroom door!"

"He may be putting it on, sir," suggested Bates.

"He may, but I find it very difficult to believe that he would be capable of carrying through that very unpleasant business last night. However, I can only give you my own impressions."

Bates rose to his feet.

"I'm much obliged, gentlemen," he said. "If there's anything else that occurs to you, perhaps you'll let me know."

He followed them out of the room and disappeared through the swing door that led to the back regions. Stuart strolled into the lounge, and was immediately aware of the hovering figure of Miss Amy Adderley. A little smile crossed his face at the thought of her as one of Bates's possible suspects.

"Can I speak to you for a moment, Mr. Stuart?" she asked anxiously. "Somewhere where we shall not be interrupted."

Considerably mystified, he assured her that he was at her disposal, and suggested that they should make use of the deserted coffee-room.

She led him across the room and drew him into the big bow-window. He pulled a chair out from the table for her and watched her with concealed amusement as she sat down, casting an anxious glance in the direction of the big screen that concealed the service-door.

"Can you tell me if the police-officer is still in the house?" she asked, her voice hardly above a whisper.

"I think so. I was with him a minute ago. You're not nervous, are you?"

He saw her swallow suddenly, and knew that she was frightened, but she drew herself up with a pathetic assumption of dignity.

"My sister and I have talked it over," she said coldly, "and we have come to the conclusion that, as we never travel with anything of any great value, it is hardly likely that any thief would be likely to molest us. No, I wasn't thinking of myself. When that policeman asked me this morning about the man I saw the night before last, I naturally told him everything I could remember. It was only afterwards that I discovered that my sister had had a very peculiar experience during the night."

"Last night, do you mean?"

She nodded.

"What time was that?"

"I should have said early this morning," went on Miss Adderley, with maddening deliberation. "She thinks it was shortly after four, but she cannot be certain, as she had looked at her watch some time before and is not sure how much time had passed since then. It was getting on for four o'clock when she looked at the time. After that, she lay awake for some time, she thinks, trying to get to sleep. Then, finding it useless, she got up and went to her dressing-table for a sleeping-powder she sometimes takes, very much against my advice, I may say. It is a habit I detest, in spite of the fact that she is acting under her doctor's orders."

She paused, and Stuart almost groaned aloud in his impatience.

"On her way back to bed," she went on at last, her enunciation growing slower as she became more impressive, "she drew aside the curtain and glanced out of the window to see if the snow had stopped. Of course, properly speaking, I realize that she ought to see the police-officer herself about this, but, owing to her deafness, she felt she would rather that I explained matters to him first."

Stuart could contain himself no longer.

"I understand. Very wise of you," he interrupted ruthlessly. "But what did your sister see, Miss Adderley?"

Miss Adderley's voice dropped so low as to be almost inaudible.

"She saw a man, carrying an electric torch, cross the yard and enter the hotel," she whispered dramatically.

CHAPTER VIII

LEAVING MISS ADDERLEY drifting excitedly among the tables in the empty coffee-room, Stuart departed in search of Bates. Having drawn all likely places in vain, he returned to the lounge, only to meet him coming in through the front door with Girling. The clothes of both men were heavily powdered with snow.

"We've had one bit of luck, anyway," was the landlord's greeting.

Bates thrust out his hand and disclosed a large key.

"Lying in the snow underneath the balcony," he volunteered. "I'm going up to try it, but I'll wager it's the key to Major Carew's door. That settles one point for us. The chap must have chucked this away after he'd shinned down the rope, and then got back into the hotel through Mrs. van Dolen's room. She found her door unlocked, if you remember."

"Plausible enough," agreed Stuart. "But that doesn't get us anywhere."

"It helps us this far," asserted Bates. "It's an inside job, and if those jewels are hidden anywhere in this house, I'm going to find them! Meanwhile, we'll try the key."

He was already on his way towards the stairs when Stuart stopped him.

"Don't be too sure about that," he said. "Some one was seen getting in at the back door shortly after four this morning."

Bates swung round.

"What's that?" he exclaimed. "It's the first I've heard of it!"

Stuart made a gesture towards the coffee-room door, behind which a female form was to be seen hovering expectantly.

"Miss Amy Adderley is waiting to have a word with you," he said. "It seems that her sister saw a man from her window."

Leaving Bates moving ponderously in the direction of the coffee-room, he went upstairs to his room. It seemed to him high time that he made an effort to marshal his own impressions into some sort of order, a task only to be attempted in solitude. One glance into his bedroom showed him that here, at least, this was denied to him. The fire had only just been lighted, and was smoking dolorously. On the rug beside it lay a dustpan and brush, evidence that the housemaid was still in possession.

Waiting only to collect his pipe and tobacco-pouch he departed to the upper regions in search of a spot more suitable for meditation.

Peering round the door of the little room Miss Adderley had christened "the ladies' sitting-room," he perceived the crowns of two heads, barely showing above the back of a small sofa drawn close to the fire, and recognized the low, absorbed voices of Miss Hamilton and her knight-errant, Trevor. Evidently that little episode was already bearing fruit. With a silent blessing he withdrew and cautiously reconnoitred the billiard-room next door. To his surprise it was empty, and, with a sigh of relief, he drew a big armchair up to the blazing fire, filled his pipe, and set to work to sort out his impressions.

It was only natural that his thoughts should stray first in the direction of the couple next door. Miss Hamilton, as Bates had pointed out, was the one person in the house, with the exception of Mrs. van Dolen's own maid, who had easy access to the emeralds. And young Trevor was, so far, an unknown quantity. True, everything pointed to his own account of himself as being correct, and his youth and apparent ingenuousness, at any rate, were in his favour, but there was no reason why he and Miss Hamilton should not have known each other before, and nothing to show that they had not been acting in collusion. Stuart had the novelist's trick of summing up and pigeon-holing people according to their various types, and he had already endowed Miss Hamilton with the conscientiousness, method, and mediocrity of brain that so often goes to the making of an excellent secretary. Trevor he had put down as the more intelligent of the two, but both of them seemed to him singularly lacking in guile. However, in view of the circumstances, it seemed only reasonable to consider them as possible suspects, and, leaving them on the list, he turned his attention to the other inmates of the "Noah's Ark."

The Romseys, Constantine, and Mrs. van Dolen herself he passed over. Of course, any one of these people might, for some fantastic reason, have taken the emeralds, and, so far as Mrs. van Dolen was concerned, jewels carrying heavy insurances had been "mislaid" by their owners before now; but, working as a psychologist rather than a policeman, he found it difficult to entertain the idea of their guilt seriously. And yet, in view of certain knowledge that he had not seen fit to share with either Constantine or Bates, he found it difficult to dismiss Geoffrey Ford entirely from his speculations. Which, by a natural sequence, brought him to Mrs. Orkney Cloude, whom, unfortunately for the task he had set himself, he both liked and admired. An apparently rich women travelling, curiously enough, without a maid. That was all he knew of her, except for the disquieting discovery that she was on fairly intimate terms with some man in the hotel, and was at pains to conceal the fact. When he had first surprised the little scene on the stairs, he had jumped to the amazing conclusion that her companion on that occasion was Lord Romsey. Since then, however, he had realized how closely Geoffrey Ford's voice resembled that of his father. It was certainly far more likely that Ford, unknown to his family, should be having an affair with Mrs. Cloude, than that Lord Romsey, stupid and vain though he undoubtedly was, should be carrying on so undignified an intrigue. Given that this was the case, and that Angela Ford had discovered it, the conversation Soames had overheard might very well be a quite innocent one. At which point he set himself to the consideration of Soames.

Here again he was hampered by his liking for the man; but, he reminded himself, of all the people in the hotel, Soames was most fully equipped with those qualities that go to the making of a successful crook. And, looking back, he realized that it was Soames, all along, who had taken the initiative. He it was that had practically forced his acquaintanceship on the two other men, he it was who had consistently contrived to throw suspicion on Geoffrey Ford, and, later, had argued plausibly enough in favour of the possibility of Melnotte's guilt. And Soames had known of the emeralds on the night of his arrival at the inn. Constantine himself had described them to him.

Stuart, who was becoming conscious of an increasing distaste for the job he had set himself, turned his thoughts to the last person on his list—Felix Melnotte. Though he held no brief for this exotic individual, he was inclined to endorse Constantine's estimate of his character. Unless he were an uncommonly good actor, it seemed inconceivable that any one so noticeably lacking in courage and intelligence should be capable of the cold-blooded and ruthless performance of the night before.

With a sigh he knocked the ashes out of his pipe and hitched his chair nearer the fire, conscious that, as an investigator, he was cutting a pretty poor figure. If either Mrs. Cloude or Soames were involved in the murder, he would prefer, he told himself frankly, to be well on his way back to London before Bates laid his heavy hand on their shoulders. His mind drifted off on to the draft of an article entitled "Do Novelists make good Detectives?" and, with the help of a pencil and the back of an old letter, he was making a really good thing of it, when a voice behind his chair startled him.

"Are you being really busy, or just making a job for yourself?" it asked.

Angela Ford skirted the chair and propped one shoulder against the mantelpiece.

Stuart sprang to his feet.

"I was merely frowsting," he answered. "Have you anything better to suggest?"

"There is nothing better," was her decisive answer. "As a matter of fact, I've grown tired to death of my own company. May I frowst with you?"

He dragged up a second chair and she sank into it.

"I've been sitting alone in my room sleuthing," she announced gloomily. "You can take it from me it's a rotten game! As the result of an hour's hard work, I don't mind telling you, in strict confidence of course, that I haven't the remotest idea who stole Mrs. van Dolen's emeralds."

Stuart, remembering that many a true word is spoken in jest, was seized with a sudden inspiration.

"I suppose your brother didn't take them by any chance?" he asked lightly. "I've been doing a bit of deducting myself, and he's the only person who doesn't seem to have produced a perfectly good alibi!"

He grinned in a way which, he hoped, conveyed the utter absurdity of the suggestion.

"Geoffrey?"

His heart leaped with relief at the amused incredulity in her voice. It was so obviously genuine.

"If Geoffrey picked an acid-drop off the pavement, he'd spend the rest of the day looking for the child that had lost it!" she said. "He's one of those people with an over-developed bump of conscientiousness. As a matter of fact, he's probably the only person in the hotel at this moment that honestly thinks Mrs. van Dolen ought to get her ghastly girdle back again. Personally, I think she richly deserves to lose it; but then, I should make a much better burglar than Geoff!"

"That's that then," said Stuart. "Which leaves me in precisely the same predicament as yourself. I do *not* know who stole the good lady's emeralds, and I've come to the conclusion that I'm not going to bother any more about them."

"The point is rather, whether the thief is going to bother any more about us," she pointed out. "I should hate to lose my pearls, you know. Neither do I wish to be murdered in my bed. Dr. Constantine seems to have made up his mind that it's some one inside the house, and that he's still here. It's not a very cheering prospect."

"The only thing to do is to lock our doors and windows, and leave Bates to ferret him out."

"Or sleep with a poker under our pillows," she suggested sweetly. Stuart groaned.

"So that's got about, has it? In self-defence I should like to state that the poker was Miss Adderley's, and that she literally forced it on me. If I'd had my choice I should have taken something much heavier and more adequate."

"I shouldn't worry," she said consolingly. "Every one thinks you were very brave."

Stuart peered over the arm of his chair.

"I can see you grinning from here," he assured her. "My hurt feelings are not in the least assuaged. Who was the reptile that gave me away?"

"I'm afraid it's more or less in the air," she answered. "I've been discussing the whole thing with Dr. Constantine, and I admit I did ask him if it was true. He was really very nice about it, you know. He told me, by the way, that the police have been all over the house. They even got that wretched chauffeur who's laid up with lumbago out of bed and searched his mattress! Apparently half the servants have given notice, and poor Mr. Girling's frantic."

"The 'police' being one, Tom Bates, the village constable," said Stuart, with a chuckle. "Have you come up against him yet? He's a character, in his way, and no fool. According to Girling, he found more than he bargained for in the housemaid's room!"

He told her of Bates's discovery of his own photograph, after which the conversation drifted to other topics, and the atmosphere of the billiard-room became very like that of the ladies' sitting-room next door, its outward and visible symbol being two heads visible over the backs of two armchairs, the crackling of the logs in the grate, and the soft, contented drone of two voices.

The rest of the day passed uneventfully. Stuart and Soames took a brisk walk, and were unaffectedly glad when it was over and they could shed their sopping clothes and thaw themselves by the fire. Bates was seen at intervals, stolidly intent upon his business. In answer to the Misses Adderley's anxious inquiries he announced his intention of spending the night in the house, and the occupants of the "Noah's Ark" retired to bed early, anxious to secure the night's rest they felt that they deserved. In spite of the knowledge of Bates's reassuring presence, most of them locked their doors carefully before putting out the light, and Stuart was awakened in the morning by the ineffectual efforts of the chambermaid to persuade the deaf Miss Adderley to unlock her door and admit her matutinal hot water, Miss Amy being, for the moment, in possession of the bathroom and in no position to explain the situation to her sister.

Stuart, congratulating himself on having at last succeeded in sleeping the whole night through, dressed and made his way downstairs. He was met in the lounge by Girling, and one glance at the landlord's wizened countenance was enough to convey the fact that calamity had once more descended on the snowbound household.

"I'm very sorry, sir," he began in a low voice, "but there's more trouble. It's the cars this time."

Stuart's thoughts flew to his most recent possession.

"Good Lord, man!" he exclaimed. "They can't have taken those! Only a wizard could get a car away over these roads in the state they're in."

Girling permitted himself the ghost of a smile, but he was more seriously perturbed than Stuart had ever seen him.

"The cars are there all right," he said; "but some one's been in the barn during the night and slashed the cushions something cruel. At first I thought it was spite, but, seein' the way everything's turned out on the floor—tool-boxes and all—I'd say some one had been lookin' for something. Bates is in there now. You're the first I've seen, except for Dr. Constantine, and I can tell you I don't relish breakin' the news to the others. What Lord Romsey'll say, I don't like to think, and I'd give somethin' for it not to have happened here, me bein' responsible, as it were. I'm more sorry than I can say, sir."

His distress was evident, and Stuart hastened to reassure him.

"You needn't take it to heart, so far as I'm concerned," he said. "My insurance will cover any damage of that sort, and I expect you'll find that the others are in the same case. What the dickens was the fellow after?"

"Ask me another, sir," was Girling's gloomy rejoinder. "I suppose I had ought to have been more careful with the key, but nothing like the doings of the last few days has ever happened in this village before, and that key's always hung where we found it this mornin', on the nail inside the back door. The barn door's solid enough, and it hasn't been damaged. Accordin' to Bates, whoever done it must have opened the door with the key."

"How many cars are damaged?" asked Stuart.

"The six that were in there. Yours, Lord Romsey's, Mr. Soames's, Major Carew's, the one that chauffeur that's ill upstairs brought in, and the Ford we use for station work. By a bit o' luck the others are all at the coach-builder's in village, owin' to there not being room for them in the barn. I sent a man up there to inquire, and they haven't been touched. It's a queer go, and that's a fact."

Stuart hesitated for a moment, then, with a glance at the drifting snow outside: "I'll get something hot inside me first, and then have a look at the car. There's nothing to be gained by going now. You say Bates is there?"

"Him and Dr. Constantine. Dr. Constantine came down about ten minutes ago, and as soon as he heard what had happened he went over. I don't fancy Tom Bates was any too pleased."

Stuart made a hearty breakfast in spite of the bad start to his day. Except for the Misses Adderley, who were established primly at their table in the window, he had the room to himself. They both bowed and expressed the hope that he had slept well, and, from their dignified calm, he concluded that they had not yet heard of the latest outrage.

He had almost finished when Constantine joined him. He looked chilled, and, for him, distinctly ruffled.

"This business is getting too much for Bates altogether," was his comment as he sat down. "Yes, coffee please, and lots of it."

Stuart indicated the occupants of the other table.

"I gather the news hasn't spread yet," he warned him.

Constantine nodded.

"There'll be a fine commotion when it does," he said, lowering his voice carefully. "If it wasn't obvious that the perpetrator was looking for something, it would be a case of sheer malicious damage. Your car has suffered badly, I'm afraid."

"Any damage to the engines?"

"None, so far as we can find out. Lord Romsey's chauffeur has looked them over, and doesn't think they have been touched. There was an indignation meeting of chauffeurs going on in the back regions when I came through just now."

"It's no good asking if there's any indication as to who was responsible, I suppose?"

"None that I could see; but Bates is on his official dignity to-day, and intimated pretty clearly that he didn't want any elderly gentlemen poking round. The truth is, he's getting badly rattled. As soon as this snow clears he'll have New Scotland Yard on his heels, and, so far, he's got very little to show for his work."

"I don't blame him," said Stuart. "He can't arrest the lot of us wholesale, and, failing that, I don't honestly see what he's to do. Anyhow, he can't prevent me from having a look at my own car, and I propose to do so after breakfast."

"Accompanied by me," asserted Constantine firmly. "My investigations were ruthlessly interrupted just now, and I intend to get my own back."

Stuart realized, to his amusement, that the old man was genuinely annoyed at having been baffled.

"We'll let him clear out and then we'll do a little sleuthing on our own," he said soothingly.

They waited in the lounge until they had seen Bates plod off through the snow in the direction of his cottage, then, having with some difficulty run the key to earth in Girling's office, where, going on the principle of shutting the stable door after the steed had been stolen, he now kept it locked in his desk, they crossed the yard to the barn.

A glance was enough to show Stuart that the search, if search it were, had been thorough. Not only were the cushions of all six cars badly damaged, but the contents of every receptacle capable of holding anything had been turned out on to the floor of the barn.

Constantine wasted no time over the cars.

"This is what I want to see," he said, making his way to a corner of the barn, in which stood an overturned sack. "I've no doubt Bates has been before me, though."

The sack, which contained bran, was lying on its side, and at least half its contents had run out on to the ground. Constantine bent over it and plunged his arm into it up to the elbow.

"Nothing there," he said philosophically, as he straightened himself. "It was too much to hope for. But it's pretty clear what the fellow was after, and I've a strong suspicion that this is where he found it."

Stuart stared at him.

"You don't mean Mrs. van Dolen's girdle?"

"It looks like it. In which case we've now got two sets of thieves to deal with. If some one has been instituting a search in this barn, whether it is for the emeralds or not, it stands to reason that some one else must have hidden something. That's what has upset Bates! He has just realized that, while he was turning the inn upside down, the emeralds were probably here all the time!"

He brushed the bran from his clothes, and came over to where Stuart was standing by his car.

"If the emerald girdle was the objective," he went on gravely, "it is now probably back in the hotel; and if there really are two lots of people in the house, both set on getting it, some very unpleasant things are likely to happen within the next few days. One of these people we know to be ruthless in his methods, and, from the look of these cars, the other is not any too squeamish."

Stuart nodded.

"And, like a street row," he said, "the onlooker is likely to get hurt! And the thieves can't, either of them, get away. In fact, until the snow clears, we seem to be for it. I'm not sure that I care for this Corsican atmosphere! If Bates is going to do anything, I wish he'd do it."

"Bates is as much at sea as any of us. He swears the emeralds are not in the house. He searched my room at my request this morning before I came down to breakfast, and he tells me that the other members of the party have asked him to do the same to them. He is positive that he will draw blank, and I agree with him. The servants have already been through it. In fact, after their first revolt, they were anxious to be searched. And I think we may take it that there's nothing here," he finished, with a glance at the havoc that had already been wrought in the barn.

And the thief can't get away; therefore, where are they?" finished Stuart flippantly. "There's always the snow, of course."

"Which may melt in a night," Constantine reminded him. "Too unsafe. No, it looks as if they were actually in some one's pocket at this moment."

At idea struck Stuart. He turned on Constantine excitedly.

"Unless no one knows where they are!" he exclaimed. "Has it occurred to you that Carew may have taken them originally? Supposing it was he who went down the rope and robbed Mrs. van Dolen? He may have succeeded in hiding the emeralds before he was surprised by the chap who killed him. We've all taken it for granted that he was an innocent victim until now. What if he were the thief?"

"There's no real reason why he shouldn't have been," admitted Constantine. "Especially in view of this recent development. The idea did occur to me, and I dismissed it for various reasons, none of which were really very convincing. The truth is, I find it very difficult to picture him in the role of a successful burglar. Also, I cannot bring myself to believe that he was not genuinely drunk that night, in which case he was physically incapable of carrying out anything of the sort. Also remember, he was undoubtedly attacked while in bed, probably before he was properly awake. Given that his assailant knew that he had taken the emeralds earlier in the evening, it seems extraordinarily unlikely that he would have allowed him time to hide them and go quietly back to bed, or that, having done so, he would have killed him without first making some effort to find out what he had done with his booty. A more stupid, clumsy, and unnecessary murder it is difficult to imagine, and, from the neatness with which he has covered his tracks ever since, it does not look as if we had a burglar to deal with."

"He may have taken it for granted that Carew had the girdle concealed in his room," suggested Stuart.

"He may, but you have got to take into account the fact that, if he knew Carew to be a thief, he must have been on the watch when he took the girdle. If Carew did hide the thing in this barn, the other man must have known of it. It would have been the simplest thing in the world for him to have waited till Carew was asleep, and then have come here and abstracted it. Honestly, I think the theory that he used Carew's room, and only attacked him because he woke unexpectedly and threatened to raise the alarm, is the only one that holds water, but I am not rejecting the alternative theory entirely. The whole thing is so mysterious that almost any explanation may be possible. The one thing that does seem clear to my mind is the fact that some one, other than the thief, is after the emeralds. Whether he found them last night, or whether they are still in the hands of the person who originally took them, or, as you suggest, they are so securely hidden that neither party knows where they are, is at present a mystery." Stuart indicated the damaged cars.

"Supposing all this has no bearing whatever on the robbery?"

"You are at liberty to suppose what you like," was Constantine's rather tart rejoinder. "I, personally, refuse to believe that it hasn't."

As they left the barn he stooped to examine the lock of the heavy door. Then in silence he followed Stuart back to the inn; there he made a careful inspection of the lock of the door leading into the yard. This time he inserted the tip of his little finger into the keyhole.

"Smell that," he said, holding out his hand. "It's oil. The barn door has been well oiled, too. Our thief was a gentleman of fore-thought."

Some hours later Stuart, sitting on the edge of his bed, watching Bates deliberately and painstakingly going through his possessions, remembered his words, and was seized with the horrible conviction that the thief might easily have planted the girdle on any one of the unsuspecting occupants of the "Noah's Ark." His attitude from then onwards until Bates closed the last drawer of his bureau, was that of the traveller who watches the Custom-house officers at their work, acutely aware of the fact that, at any minute, they may stumble on the cigarettes he has hidden in his portmanteau. His relief when the constable thanked him and departed was whole-hearted. He discovered afterwards that Soames had been assailed by the same misgivings, and had even gone so far as to institute a hurried search of his own effects before Bates arrived on the scene.

As Constantine had predicted, Bates found nothing, but he suc-ceeded in so thoroughly upsetting the feelings of the Misses Ad-derley that Miss Connie was reduced to tears and took to her bed.

On his way to dress for dinner Stuart met her, a distraught ap-parition in a dressing-gown, clasping a sponge in one hand and a large bottle of bath salts in the other, being assisted along the passage by her sister.

"A hot bath and then a nice little dinner in bed will be just the thing for her," confided Miss Amy to him, after she had shut her sister safely into the bathroom. "Very silly of her to have taken it like this, of course, but then, as I always say, it's different when you're deaf. Everything seems to get exaggerated so. Of course, it was a *most* unpleasant experience, to have a policeman turning over all one's things! But then, as I told her, we could hardly stand out when the Misses Ford had actually asked him to search their rooms. It would have looked too odd, not to say suspicious. And, after all, if you take it in the right way, it *is* an experience, isn't it, Mr. Stuart? One, I trust, we shall never have again, but still an experience! But you can hardly expect her to see it in that light, can you?"

"I didn't like it very much myself," admitted Stuart, with his kindly smile. "So I can imagine how she felt." The door of her room had hardly closed behind her when Trevor appeared at the end of the passage. He was in his shirt-sleeves, and his round face was pink with indignation.

"I say," he shouted, at the sight of Stuart. "Has that chap been at your room again?"

Stuart stared at him.

"Bates, do you mean?" he answered. "He went through it thoroughly this afternoon."

"I know; that was when he searched mine. Well, he's been back again! I advise you to have a look at your room!"

Stuart opened his door, switched on the light, and stood aghast.

The contents of every drawer and cupboard in the room were piled on the floor. Even the attaché-case that held his papers had been emptied, and the bed was littered with manuscript, proof sheets, and correspondence.

"Pretty ghastly, isn't it?" came Trevor's voice from the doorway. "It may comfort you to know that mine's worse! If that beastly policeman's responsible for this, he ought to be sacked!"

Stuart, with the picture of the barn as he had last seen it still fresh in his mind, shook his head.

"Then that chap didn't get the girdle," was all he said.

CHAPTER IX

LEAVING TREVOR still spluttering with wrath in the doorway, Stuart ran downstairs, and, on the second floor, overtook a scared and scarlet-faced chambermaid, bound on the same errand as himself. She was on the verge of hysteria, but he managed to gather that Mrs. Orkney Cloude's room had been ransacked also, and that she had sent the girl for the landlord.

Stuart let her go on ahead, and, as he stood waiting, he heard a babel of excited voices wafted from the floor above, and guessed that others had made the same discovery as himself. The arrival of Girling, followed by a badly worried Bates, soon established the fact that, at any rate, the constable had no hand in this latest development.

A careful inspection showed that nothing had been taken from any of the rooms, and that, with the exception of the servants, the Romsey family, Mrs. van Dolen, and the Misses Adderley, no one had escaped. The search, though obviously hurried, had been very thorough, and there could be no doubt that the intruder had had some definite object in mind. Whether he had found it or not was an open question.

"If you ask me, I hope he has," announced Soames frankly, pointing to the contents of an indexed folder that lay strewn upon the floor. "It'll take me the best part of an hour to get those straight again, and there's a dozen clean collars as good as done for. Let him have the blooming emeralds, provided he leaves my things alone!"

"I wonder why the others got off scot free like that," said Trevor. "Mrs. Cloude's the only person on the floor below that suffered."

"Because the others are beyond reproach, my lad," Soames informed him. "Remember, whoever has got the emeralds must have taken them in the first instance."

The boy flushed hotly.

Constantine intervened.

"As the only person who suspects us is, on the face of it, anything but honest himself, I don't think we need concern ourselves with his opinion," he said quickly, "The interesting point to me, is that whoever is after the emeralds now, obviously hasn't the remotest idea who has got them. I fancy the Misses Adderley only escaped owing to the fact that they have been in their room all the evening."

"Your original assumption that the robbery was an inside job does seem pretty well established now," said Stuart. "It's pretty clear that the emeralds are hidden inside this house somewhere, and that the person who took them knows where they are."

"And some one else doesn't! I wish he did!" added Trevor. "The brute has forced the lock of a perfectly good suit-case that I only bought last week. I suppose I ought to be thankful that he didn't take the money that was in it."

"As he left Mrs. Cloude's jewellery alone, I take it he was after something worth a pretty penny," said Bates slowly. "I'd say you're right about the emeralds, Dr. Constantine. I thought so this morning, but I'm sure of it now."

"Well, you can cheer up, constable," remarked Soames consolingly. "If this other chap can't find them they must be pretty well hidden, so no wonder your search was in vain. I'm off to do a little tidying."

Bates watched him disappear into his room, then he turned to Constantine.

"Strikes me," he said thoughtfully, "that that there thief, or whatever he is, would be mighty careful to chuck his own things about while he was about it. It'd be a bit pointed, like, if his things weren't touched."

On that he departed, leaving Constantine and Stuart staring at one another.

"That's a nasty one!" exclaimed Stuart. "Poor old Soames!"

Constantine smiled.

"By now, I don't suppose he'd give a clean bill to any one of us," he said. "I must say, the thing is getting a little uncanny. I wish this snow would stop. I'm getting too old for these alarums and excursions."

His looks belied him. In spite of his evident discouragement, his face was as animated as that of a boy, and Stuart had a suspicion that the old man had not spent such an interesting or eventful holiday for years. He could not resist saying so.

"I believe, if the truth were known, you're enjoying it, sir," he ventured.

The wrinkles round Constantine's eyes deepened.

"You see too much, young man," he admitted. "But, to tell you the truth, I'm getting exasperated. The thing's like a chess problem one can't solve, and, till now, I've been accustomed to deal adequately with chess problems! There's a key move somewhere and I can't get hold of it. Until I do I shall be like a cat on hot bricks. Besides, you forget, there are women in the house."

"You're afraid of what may happen?"

"I'm afraid because I don't know what may happen. At the best, there's a chance that some of them may be badly frightened before we've finished. And I can't see a gleam of light anywhere!"

"I suppose, if the worst comes to the worst, one of us could sit up and keep an eye on things," suggested Stuart.

He spoke reluctantly. He was a good sleeper, and. hated to be deprived of his night's rest.

"This *is* a jolly little Christmas holiday," he complained. "When I think that I came away for a rest!"

Constantine laughed.

"You'd have got very little rest at Redsands," he retorted. "It's evident that you've never been there. Burglar hunting's a more wholesome occupation than being entertained by an energetic committee to within an inch of your life. Joking apart, though, I should keep an eye on those old ladies next door to you. Like myself, they're a little ancient for these nocturnal alarms."

As it turned out, Constantine's misgivings were shared by the ladies themselves. After dinner, Miss Amy approached Stuart and asked him whether, by any chance, he was going up early to bed that night. It appeared that Miss Connie's attack of nerves had brought on a bronchial cough to which she was subject, and her sister thought it unlikely that she would be able to leave her room for a couple of days at least.

"We don't want to feel that we are imposing on you," she finished, rather wistfully. "But it is a relief, both to my sister and myself, to feel that there is a man in the room next door. If we noticed anything in the night, for instance, we could rap on the communicating door."

"Of course! I hope you will," assented Stuart, inwardly praying that nothing unusual would obtrude itself on the Misses Adderley's attention during the small hours. Then his naturally kind heart asserted itself. He remembered the proofs he had brought from London, and, with a pang, abandoned his original plan of inveigling Angela Ford into a return match at billiards.

"As a matter of fact," he assured her, "I've got some work I ought to tackle, and I may as well do it to-night. I can start on it now, in my room, and if I sit with the door open, I can keep an eye on your sister's room till you come up to bed. How will that be?"

He was rewarded by the look of relief on her little round face.

"That will be delightful!" she exclaimed. "I'll tell my sister that you are there, and it will make all the difference to her comfort. Of course, nothing will happen; but she's apt to be nervous, you know."

The last sentence was more in the nature of a question than a statement, and he hastened to reassure her.

"You can't expect adventures every night, Miss Adderley," he said, smiling. "I'm afraid you'll find life quite dull now that things are settling down. Anyhow, I don't expect you travel with much jewellery, so you were never in any real danger of being disturbed."

Miss Adderley peered warily over her shoulder.

"My sister has got some very fine cameos that belonged to our mother," she informed him in a hushed voice; "but we've been very careful not to allude to them in public."

"Quite right," he assented, his lips twitching uncontrollably, and hurried away to find Constantine, and inform him that, if wanted, he was to be found keeping guard over the Adderley heirlooms.

The chess maniacs had retired to Constantine's room, and were already setting out the chess-men. It struck Stuart that neither of them was inclined to quarrel with the opportunity for making it an all-night sitting.

"I suppose, now you've got an excuse, you'll go on till breakfast," he gibed as he left them.

Soames grinned.

"I've got my health to consider," he said. "I propose to turn in not later than two-thirty, so don't come to me after that, carrying your little poker!"

But, as it turned out, it was Soames who came to him.

Stuart settled himself down by the fire with his proofs, leaving his door open, and thus affording himself an excellent view of the various occupants of his landing as they sped to their baths.

Punctually at ten o'clock Miss Amy Adderley flitted coyly across his vision, armed with the inevitable sponge and family bath salts. She was followed by Constantine, Rembrandtesque in his black silk dressing-gown. He had torn himself away in the middle of a fierce struggle with Soames over the chessboard, to take advantage of the bath water while it was hot. He paused at Stuart's door on his way back to his room.

Stuart, looking up, saw him standing there; his thick white hair on end, his figure instinct with vitality, his dark eyes ablaze with some emotion that the younger man could not fathom.

"Hallo!" he exclaimed.

To his surprise, Constantine did not answer, but with an inscrutable look turned and disappeared down the passage to his room, leaving Stuart gaping after him.

He returned to his work and laboured steadily over his proofs until past one in the morning; but, in spite of the concentration demanded by that hateful task, the vision of the old man, as he had last seen him, kept intruding itself on his vision. Remembering his mingled depression and exasperation earlier in the day, he could not get over the feeling that something had happened to change his mood. Stuart was no chess player, but he could not bring himself to believe that checkmating an antagonist so obviously his inferior as Soames would have induced this triumphant aspect. More than once he was on the point of following Constantine to his room and demanding an explanation, but he knew the old man well enough to realize that, if he had made up his mind to say nothing, it would be useless to question him. All the same, as the night wore on, he became more and more convinced that Constantine not only had something up his sleeve, but that in his queer, whimsical way he had intended to convey the fact to him. It was not unlike him deliberately to whet Stuart's curiosity, and then, as deliberately, to refrain from satisfying it.

When he did get to bed he was tired out with the exhaustion born of a tedious job and too little exercise, and he had been asleep for more than two hours when he was awakened by the sound of his door opening, and remembered, with a start that brought him fully to his senses, that he had forgotten to lock it on going to bed.

A hand came round the door and switched on the light. Soames was revealed to him, clad in the camel's hair dressing-gown that he was beginning to know only too well.

Stuart sat up in bed and gave vent to his exasperation.

"If I see you in my room again in the middle of the night," he exclaimed, "there'll be another murder committed in this hotel! I don't care what's happened, I'm not going to get out of my warm bed!"

He slid under the bedclothes and clutched them firmly under his chin.

Soames bore down on him.

"It's Melnotte this time," he announced cheerfully. "The poor lad's had the fright of his young life. Fortunately, the doctor was wakened by the sound of a door shutting, and sallied forth to see what was happening. He found Melnotte literally gibbering, with a story of a masked man standing by his bed, feeling under his pillow. Looks as if your friend's on the prowl again."

Stuart regarded him warily over the top of the blankets. He knew Soames to be quite capable of dragging him bodily out of bed. But he was more stirred than he chose to admit.

"Well, if he is, what do you expect me to do about it?" he demanded. "I'm not responsible for his actions."

Soames scratched his head.

"I suppose some one ought to do something," he said, rather doubtfully. "Dr. Constantine knocked me up, and I came for you."

"Thank you," said Stuart dryly. "It was a kind thought. Didn't Melnotte go after him?"

"Melnotte did precisely what one might have known he would do. He pretended to be asleep until the chap had left the room, and then lay sweating with terror, with the clothes over his head, till Constantine arrived. He's about as much use as a sick hen!"

"You don't think he's invented the whole thing?"

"Dr. Constantine says he was almost insane with funk. He thinks it's genuine enough."

"What's Constantine doing?"

Soames's grin widened.

"As far as I know, he's gone back to bed. He seems to hold the same principles about getting up in the night as you do!"

"Good luck to him!" was Stuart's hearty comment. With a fat policeman sleeping on the premises, I'm blessed if I see why we should do our own burglar hunting. Where's Bates supposed to sleep, do you know?"

"Nowhere, I should have said. I understood that he was going to sit up with a truncheon in one hand and a pair of handcuffs in the other. If you won't come, I'd better go for him alone; but if I'm knocked on the head on the way, I hope you'll have the decency to attend the funeral."

With a sigh, Stuart climbed out of bed and began putting on his dressing-gown.

"Look here," he said. "You know where Girling sleeps, and I don't. If you'll go and rouse him I'll have a look for Bates. He's probably downstairs somewhere, if he's sitting up. Then we can go back to bed and leave them to fight it out together."

He found Bates quite easily. He was sitting in Girling's office with the door open; his theory being, no doubt, that he would thus hear anybody moving on the stairs outside. Unfortunately for the success of the plan his head was sunk on his breast, and he was sleeping so heavily that even Stuart's approach did not wake him, though the latter had made no effort to move quietly. It was as well that the Misses Adderley could not see their official protector at this moment.

But he pulled himself together with astonishing celerity when Stuart placed a hand on his shoulder.

"Now then, sir," he demanded, with the truculence of one who has been found in a thoroughly undignified position, "what are you doin' here?"

Stuart mastered his natural indignation and told him what had happened. He had barely finished before the constable was out of the door and half-way up the stairs. Stuart followed more slowly.

"I'm going back to bed," he called after him when he reached his own landing. "If you want me you know where to find me."

He felt so certain of the utter futility of any kind of search that, once back in his room, he merely took the precaution of locking his door and then tumbled thankfully enough into bed. For a time he listened to the sound of muffled voices in the passage outside, but within half an hour of the alarm he was sound asleep.

Girling's report next morning was as he had expected. Indeed, from the point of view of interest, it faded into insignificance beside the chambermaid's announcement that the snow had ceased during the night and that the snow-plough at Rushton was already at work. The landlord and Bates had made a round of the house, and had drawn a complete blank. They had even been on to the roof and had searched it with the aid of pocket-torches, but had found no sign of any one's having been up there. Nothing had been taken from Melnotte's room, which had been pretty thoroughly ransacked earlier in the day, presumably by the same person. Apparently he had been acting on the assumption that Melnotte was carrying the object of his search on his person, and had been driven to the expedient of looking for it after he had gone to bed.

The unfortunate Bates came in for a good deal of adverse criticism, which he could hardly have avoided overhearing. In addition to which, according to Girling, he had been summoned to the presence of Lord Romsey, who had asked him point-blank what steps he proposed to take to ensure the safety of the occupants of the "Noah's Ark." Bates's retort that he was working single-handed and could hardly manage to be in two places at once, had, it appeared, only inspired Lord Romsey to further eloquence.

After lunch Stuart, hoping for a repetition of yesterday's peaceful interlude in front of the fire, made his way unostentatiously to the billiard-room, only to find himself involved in an informal committee meeting, presided over, to his consternation, by Lord Romsey. His attempt to withdraw, unnoticed, was ruthlessly frustrated by Constantine, who had taken possession of the hearthrug, and had evidently been goaded by Lord Romsey into a state that could only be described as one of diabolical whimsicality. A glance was sufficient to show that the old man was enjoying himself thoroughly in his own queer way. Stuart was amused to see how the general uneasiness had served to lower all class barriers. Mrs. van Dolen was engaged in an animated discussion with Soames, and Lord Romsey, who, according to Constantine, had so far spent his time in writing wordy letters to the *Times* in the fastnesses of his own room, had apparently become hail-fellow-well-met with every member of the mixed caravanserai. It also struck him as significant that the only member of the party not present should be Melnotte.

As Stuart sank meekly into a chair on the outskirts of the group, Lord Romsey, with a bleak stare that reduced even Mrs. van Dolen to silence, resumed his attack on Constantine.

"If we accept your suggestion that this—er—person is endeavouring to obtain possession of the jewels that were stolen from Mrs. van Dolen on the night of the murder—and I think I may take it that we all agree to accept that view?" he paused and cast a coldly disparaging glance at his audience, which obediently emitted those nondescript sounds which may be taken to signify assent. "If, as I say, we agree to this assumption, I think you must admit that this second attempt on the room of one particular member of this household is not without significance."

He paused once more, and Constantine cut in sharply. "If you are suggesting that Melnotte's adventure proves that the emeralds were hidden in his room, I entirely disagree with you," he retorted. "You must remember that several other people's rooms were very thoroughly searched yesterday evening."

"While those of certain members of the party were left untouched," asserted Lord Romsey, with somewhat questionable taste. "I still adhere to my contention that the thief only looks in such places as may be expected to contain the emeralds."

"So that to be the victim of this persevering gentleman is, in itself, a suspicious circumstance," submitted Constantine, his voice positively silky.

Lord Romsey, who had been led away by his own eloquence, contemplated his audience and became aware of a certain restlessness, accompanied by frank indignation on the part of at least two of the ladies present. He hastened to amend his statement.

"You must not take me too literally, Constantine," he said with elephantine playfulness. "I am merely endeavouring to emphasize my contention that the mere fact that this young man Melnotte, who, I understand, occupies the bedroom next to that of the unfortunate Major Carew, has twice been the victim of the attentions of this person is in itself suspicious. That is to say, if he really was the victim. I must point out that we have only his own word for it!"

"Your suggestion being that he deliberately manufactured this suspicious evidence against himself?" snapped Constantine.

Lord Romsey permitted himself a bland smile.

"He may not have realized his error. We cannot afford to overlook the possibility that Melnotte himself may have been the perpetrator of yesterday's search, in which case his obvious course would be to pretend that he had been one of the victims."

"Which is as good as saying that he could not have been guilty of either the original theft or the murder," pointed out Soames, who, for some time, had been holding his peace with difficulty.

Lord Romsey assented graciously.

"Exactly. I am simply pointing out that, whichever way we may elect to look at it, suspicion points to this young man of whom we know nothing, and who, if I may say so, belongs to a type that hardly inspires confidence."

Stuart, for the first time, was conscious of a distinct reaction in favour of the unfortunate Melnotte. Apparently he was not the only person thus affected. Angela Ford asserted herself suddenly.

"Come to that, father," she said, "there are hundreds of professional dancers exactly like him. If you went oftener to dance clubs you'd realize that, even if you don't like the type, there's nothing suspicious about it. I'm willing to bet he's exactly what he pretends to be."

There was a short pause, during which her sister cast an agonized glance in her direction, and a slow flush mounted to Lord Romsey's brow. He was clearly unaccustomed to such demonstrations on the part of his family.

"I admit that my experience of such places is limited," he informed the delinquent with heavy sarcasm. "But I do lay claim to some knowledge of human nature, and I repeat that the type to which this young man belongs is in itself an obnoxious one."

His daughter was not to be quelled so easily.

"You said yourself that the obvious thing for the searcher to do was to pretend that his own things had been ransacked," she pointed out ruthlessly. "Doesn't that put us in rather an awkward position? Our rooms were never touched."

Lord Romsey's colour deepened, and it seemed to the now interested audience that an explosion was inevitable. It was averted by an entirely unforeseen interruption.

The door opened slowly, and Melnotte insinuated his body gracefully round it. He looked genuinely shaken by his experience of the night before. There were dark shadows under his eyes, and his manner lacked its usual languid assurance, but his voice was as exasperatingly genteel as ever.

"Does this belong to anybody here?" he asked.

He held out his hand. The fire blazed up suddenly, and the diamonds in the brooch he held sparkled as the light caught them.

Mrs. van Dolen rose ponderously to her feet.

"That's my brooch," she announced grimly. "And it was among the things that were stolen the other night. May I ask where you got it, young man?"

CHAPTER X

THE SILENCE that fell on the room when Melnotte entered it had been ominous enough, but the dead hush which followed Mrs. van Dolen's blunt question was even more fraught with meaning. He could hardly fail to recognize its significance.

He stared in consternation at the brooch still lying in his hand, then his eyes travelled round the room. There was deprecation in them, and a quite genuine surprise.

"I found it," he stammered, "just now on the landing outside my room. It was caught in the window curtain. I—I thought some one had dropped it."

The silence remained unbroken, but Mrs. van Dolen's attitude towards this somewhat halting explanation was plainly written on her features. Melnotte's face whitened, and then grew slowly scarlet.

"Then I'd better hand it to you, Mrs. van Dolen," he said, making a painful effort to speak naturally. "It was a piece of luck, my finding it."

Constantine forestalled him.

"Properly speaking, I imagine that it ought to go to Bates in the first instance," he said, coming forward and taking the brooch from Melnotte. "You don't mind, Mrs. van Dolen?"

"Not in the least," replied that lady grimly. "The police had better deal with both the brooch and Mr. Melnotte. It's what they're here for."

Her mouth closed like a trap, and she turned away as though to indicate that she had washed her hands of the whole business. Stuart, who was watching Melnotte closely, saw the dancer's hands clench suddenly at his sides, and was seized with a horrified foreboding that, at any moment, he might burst into tears. He rose hastily to his feet and approached Melnotte with a friendliness that he hoped was not exaggerated.

"What about getting hold of Bates—if he's on the premises—and asking him to have a look at the place where you found the thing?" he suggested.

Melnotte stared blindly at him.

"If anybody thinks I've the remotest idea how it got there," he began, in a high voice that bordered on hysteria, "they're mistaken …"

Constantine slipped a hand through his arm.

"You have just told us that you found it on the landing," he said in his pleasant, even voice. "Surely that should be enough, though, you must admit, things have reached a point of absurdity sufficient to drive us all a little off our balance. As a matter of fact, we are all inwardly seething with suspicion of each other."

His smile robbed his words of all malice, and Stuart, with a view to lessening the tension, hastened to fill the silence that followed.

"The question of the moment is, how the brooch got there," he said. "And it's Bates's job to find that out. I vote we go and see that the local ratepayers get some value for their money."

Between them they drew Melnotte out of the room, and managed to get the door closed behind them before his nerve broke.

"How was I to know the beastly thing had been stolen?" he raved. "I found it, like I said. I wish to goodness I'd left it lying there. If I'd known it belonged to that cursed old woman, I should have. I've had enough of their whispering and sneering! It's bad enough to sleep next door to a drunken brute like Carew without being accused of goodness knows what! If they think I murdered him, why don't they say so? It isn't my fault that I had that room. There's such a thing as libel—"

"That's enough!" cut in Constantine sharply.

The man was literally sobbing with rage, and was fast working himself into a real fit of hysteria. Stripped of his carefully acquired veneer of gentility, he showed himself for what he was, a poor-spirited weakling. At the sound of Constantine's voice he pulled himself up with a gasp and fell silent, his face a mask of misery and humiliation.

"I'm sorry," he mumbled at last. "I suppose I ought not to have said that about Carew. But if you'd had the rotten time I've had ever since I set foot in this beastly inn, what with the ghastly things that have been going on, and everybody looking down their noses at me, you'd understand. And now to be as good as told that I'm a thief and a murderer!"

Constantine stepped squarely in front of him.

"Listen to me," he said. "I know you had nothing to do with either the robbery or the murder, if that's any satisfaction to you. As far as that goes, we're all under suspicion until the thing's cleared up. Next time an ill-advised old woman sees fit to make an unpleasant exhibition of herself, remember that and don't let your feelings get the better of you. But there's one bit of advice I should like to give you, if you'll take it."

Melnotte threw out his hands in a gesture of despair.

"I'm grateful for anything, if I can only feel that some one believes in me!" he exclaimed, with so dramatic a self-pity that Stuart's new-born sympathy died a sudden death.

"It's this," went on Constantine, ignoring his outburst. "The roads will be clear probably to-morrow or the next day. Unless you have any very pressing engagement elsewhere, do as we propose to do, stay and see the matter out. I think I can promise you that the police will lay their hands on the culprit within the next week. Take my advice, and don't be in too great a hurry to get away. Now let's find Bates."

Steadfastly avoiding Stuart's eye he led the way downstairs. The two men followed him, Stuart entirely at sea as to whether Constantine's astounding statement had been made merely with the intent to soothe Melnotte's ravaged nerves, or whether the secretive old man had really discovered something of sufficient importance to account for his change of manner the night before.

For once Bates's bucolic stolidity proved a Godsend. Whatever his opinion may have been concerning Melnotte, he gave no indication of it, but listened to his account of the finding of the brooch, and then, without farther comment, stumped off to inspect the place in which he had picked it up.

The two men, neither of whom had any desire to rejoin the company in the billiard-room, settled themselves in the lounge by the fire.

"What on earth Bates can find to do all day in this place beats me," said Stuart, as he filled his pipe. "I will say this for him, he's generally to be found when he's wanted."

Constantine chuckled.

"If one goes to look for him, yes," he answered. "The truth is, I fancy, he's afraid to go home for fear some sudden manifestation may take place in his absence! He never yet has succeeded in being on the spot when anything happened, though that's hardly his fault, I suppose."

"He certainly wasn't on the spot last night. Dozing in front of the fire in Girling's office isn't going to get him far."

"To do him justice, he had made the round of the house twice and found all quiet before he settled down. No doubt the gentleman in the mask had his eye on him."

Stuart looked the old man straight in the face.

"Do you know who the man in the mask is?" he asked bluntly.

Constantine shook his head.

"I don't," he answered frankly. "I wish I did."

"But you do know something?" persisted Stuart.

Constantine hesitated.

"I'm sorry you asked that question," he said at last. "I did make a discovery last night, a very astonishing one, and I am still trying to fit it in with the other facts in my possession. Until I've succeeded, I'd rather not say anything about it. But I can assure you that I've no idea who Melnotte's visitor was last night."

"And the original thief?" asked Stuart shrewdly.

"Was not Melnotte," said Constantine. "I refuse to say more, but of that I am quite certain."

His voice was implacable, and Stuart realized that it was of no use to press him. He made a praiseworthy effort to swallow his chagrin, and looked up to meet an appreciative twinkle in Constantine's eyes.

"I'm sorry," he said. "I admit that I'm a pestilential old person. But I must solve my chess problem in my own way, and, though I've mastered one move, I've still got the others to deal with. To go back to Melnotte. Do you realize that we've very nearly driven that young man off the rails between us?"

"I don't see that we are to blame," answered Stuart stubbornly. "Mrs. van Dolen's attack was unwarrantable, and, of course, I don't know what else may have happened during the day, but it struck me that he had let his imagination run away with him."

"Have you gone out of your way to see anything of him since we have been here?" asked Constantine. Stuart's eyes fell.

"I suppose I haven't," he admitted. "But there was nothing to bring us together."

"And that's the seat of the trouble," said Constantine. "He's nothing in common with any member of the party, and he knows it. He's suffering from an exaggerated sense of inferiority, of course, but it is a fact that we all do despise him; added to which, he has been left rather severely alone ever since he arrived. He has no doubt been brooding over it, and what happened to-night brought the whole thing to a head. We shall have trouble with him if we are not careful."

"I've only your word for it that he's got nothing to do with this business. After all, we know nothing about him," retorted Stuart.

"And you call yourself a psychologist," scoffed the old man. "However, so far as his record is concerned, I'll undertake to convince you in a day or two. The morning after the death of Carew I telephoned to a friend of mine who runs a theatrical agency in London. He knew nothing about him, but then professional dancers are not in his line. He undertook, however, to find out if he was on the lists of any of the other agencies, and to let me know what he could find out about him. I'm willing to risk giving you a short resume of what his report will be, if you like."

Stuart gave a delighted chuckle. The old man was so magnificently cocksure.

"I'll spare you the trouble," he said. "That's to say, if you're taking him at his face value, in which case I'm as good a psychologist as yourself. How's this? The son of working people, who has reached his present position by dint of sheer determination, and, as a consequence, is morbidly sensitive about his origin. In all probability is, ashamed of his family connections, and terribly afraid of giving himself away. Hence his outburst to-night. All that is plain enough for a child to read, but I still contend that you are taking a good deal for granted. You must admit that a clever adventurer, who wanted to get in touch with people like the egregious van Dolen, could hardly have chosen a better role. If things had gone according to schedule, and we had reached Redsands as we expected, he would probably be her favourite dancing-partner by now."

"My answer to that is that Melnotte is neither more nor less than what he appears to be, and, in a very short time, I shall produce convincing evidence that I am right," was Constantine's unperturbed rejoinder. "Meanwhile, I've a suggestion to make. In view of Bates's predilection for slumbering in front of the office fire, it seems about time we organized some sort of defence league for ourselves."

Stuart nodded.

"I had thought of keeping a watch myself," he said, "though I must say I heartily dislike the idea of doing Bates's work for him."

"Bates is outclassed," stated Constantine, "and we've got to face the fact. It's not his fault; nothing like this has ever come his way before, and he's working single-handed. Between us we ought to be able to keep an eye on the stairs and the two corridors. And, if we can manage to remain unobserved, we may catch the man at work. There's every reason to believe that he hasn't achieved his object yet."

"Well, if he tries again to-night, we ought to get him," rejoined Stuart cheerfully.

The prospect of sitting up all night wore a very different aspect when viewed from a cosy armchair by the fire; but, as he spoke, he had an uncomfortable feeling that he was going to regret his compliance bitterly later.

"Do we take Bates into our confidence?" he asked.

"If Bates does the job he is here for, he will find us out for himself," answered Constantine dryly. "Meanwhile, there seems no point in wounding his delicate susceptibilities."

After dinner that evening they roped in Soames, and made their plans. Constantine was anxious to enlist the help of Geoffrey Ford, on the score that, with the ground they would have to cover, the more watchers the better; but Soames, whose prejudice against him still persisted, was so insistent that he should not be let into the secret that he was eventually ruled out. They decided that Soames should take the first floor, while Stuart kept an eye on his own landing. Constantine, who, in view of his years, was obviously not in a position to tackle any intruder without help, they tried in vain to persuade to go to bed, but the indefatigable old man flatly refused to allow himself to be dismissed as negligible. He did, however, consent to keep watch from his own room, where he would be in touch with Stuart, who, with the Misses Adderley in mind, repeated his programme of the night before, and settled himself in his own room with the door open and an imposing array of proofs before him. In spite of which it seemed that Miss Amy's mind was not entirely at rest. With a disregard for her appearance, that in itself spoke volumes for her state of mind, she stopped at his door on her way back from the bath.

"Excuse me, Mr. Stuart," she began, standing primly on the threshold, her bath-sponge clasped to her bosom, "but I suppose that man, Bates, really is keeping a careful watch. He seems to have been nowhere about when Mr. Melnotte was attacked last night."

"Which will make him all the more on the alert now," Stuart assured her. "He won't allow himself to be caught napping again. There's nothing to prevent your sleeping in peace, and I shall be here in case anything disturbs you."

Miss Adderley turned to go, then hesitated.

"My sister and I have been discussing the disturbances of the last few nights," she said diffidently, "and there was one thing that struck us both. In an old house like this, with these long, rambling passages, it must be very difficult to catch a thief. That terrible masked man seemed to get away very easily, didn't he? Please don't think I am blaming you in any way, Mr. Stuart, you were wonderful, but you really had no chance from the beginning."

"Of course, once he had the place in darkness, it was easy for him to slip up the little staircase at the end of the passage. I think there's no doubt that that's what he did," agreed Stuart.

"And what I fear he will do again," said Miss Adderley portentously, "even with the police after him. Of course, the police know their business better than I do, and I should not dream of making any suggestions to the constable, polite and obliging though he is, but an idea has occurred to both of us."

She lowered her voice mysteriously.

"Has it struck you, Mr. Stuart, how much more difficult it would be for any one to get away if every door in the place were locked? As it is now, he can pop in anywhere and hide."

Stuart tried not to smile.

"We can't exactly lock people into their rooms," he protested. "And, in any case, I think that, after what has happened, most of us are inclined to sleep with our doors locked."

"Ah," said Miss Adderley; "but what about the other rooms? Take this landing, for instance. I happen to know that there is a roomy housemaid's closet on this floor, not to mention the bathroom, which can be locked on the inside. Supposing he popped into one of these. And there must be lots of cupboards and things upstairs."

It struck Stuart that her idea wasn't so unpracticable after all.

"I believe you're right, Miss Adderley," he said. "I'll put it to Bates."

Miss Adderley glowed modestly.

"You see we used to play hide-and-seek as children, and I can remember now how I used to dodge into the boot-cupboard and listen to my brother, who was a very fleet runner, flying past. Then I used to hop out and get home," she finished, with a reminiscent smile.

Stuart waited for half an hour or so after she had gone, and then ran upstairs to the floor above his. The servants had gone to bed, and he was able to reconnoitre at his leisure. He discovered that Miss Adderley had been quite right in her assumption. The old place was honeycombed with cupboards, in most of which a fugitive might very well take cover. He contented himself with turning the key in the doors of any that seemed large enough to harbour a man, reflecting that this should be enough to hamper any one who might try to use them in his flight. Once back on his own floor he locked both the bathroom and the housemaid's closet, and put the keys in his pocket. They would be easy enough to replace in the morning before anybody was about.

He looked at his watch. It was 11.30, and he could count on at least another hour's uninterrupted work before his vigil began.

Shortly after midnight Soames appeared to say that he proposed to take up his position in the bathroom on the floor below. Here, with the door ajar, he could command a fairly good view of the passage.

"Though, if I don't die of cold during the night, I shall probably go to sleep, sitting there in the dark," he said as he departed, wrapped in his thickest overcoat.

A few minutes later Constantine came along the passage. Stuart, who was standing in the doorway, noticed—to his surprise—that he was in his dressing-gown. As he passed the bathroom he tried the door and paused, in astonishment, when it refused to yield. Stuart called out softly to him.

"Do you want a bath? I've got the key here."

Constantine nodded.

"I've had nearly three hours' rest," he said, "and I'm ripe for anything. But I didn't realize I had slept so long. Are you reserving the last of the hot water for yourself? If not, why are you sitting on the key?"

Stuart handed it to him, and told him of Miss Adderley's suggestion.

"It really isn't such a bad idea," he finished.

Constantine raised his thick eyebrows.

"Bless her little heart!" he exclaimed. "I should never have credited her with such a brain-wave! Imagine it, if we win our Waterloo on the playing-fields of Miss Adderley!"

He inserted the key in the lock and disappeared into the bathroom. Stuart heard the sound of running water, then the tap was turned off, and Constantine reappeared.

"No good, I've left it too long. The water's cold," he called out, as he went back to his bedroom.

Stuart took a chair and placed it near the door, which he left ajar. Then he turned out the light and settled down to watch the passage.

It was a more eerie business than he had expected. The old house seemed alive with small, disconcerting noises. It was as though, at intervals, it stirred in its sleep, emitting strange creaks and rustlings, the sources of which it was impossible to locate. Once a board cracked so loudly that Stuart could have sworn that it had moved under a foot. He stood up and peered through the slit of the door into the darkness, and was immediately startled almost out of his wits by an equally loud report from the interior of his room. He swung round and turned on the electric torch which he had fetched from his car earlier in the evening, but the room was empty, and, as he waited, listening, another crack came from the wardrobe and he realized how his nerves had betrayed him. He sat down again, wondering how the more stolid Soames was enjoying his vigil on the floor below.

Shortly afterwards, to his shame be it said, he fell asleep, in spite of all his efforts. He woke, stiff and cold, but so on the alert that he felt convinced that some definite sound must have disturbed him. As he listened, every nerve tense with expectation, it came again.

Some one was working his way stealthily down the passage in his direction.

Stuart rose and moved softly out into the corridor, holding his torch ready in his hand. The steps came nearer.

He waited until they were quite close, then flashed his torch suddenly into the face of the intruder, hoping to dazzle him sufficiently to be able to close with him before he had time to recover from his surprise.

He caught one glimpse of a red, startled face, then the torch was knocked out of his hand and he felt himself clutched by the throat.

"Shut up, you fool!" he managed to gurgle. "It's Stuart!"

The grasp on his throat relaxed, and he heard the soft explosion of suppressed laughter in the darkness. He stooped, groped for the torch, found it and turned it on to the burly figure of Soames, who stood rocking with mirth before him. Behind him, in the thin beam of light, stood Constantine, fully dressed, his face alight with glee.

"Good Lord," gasped Soames. "Do you realize that you're practically invisible behind that beastly thing?"

A sound behind him made him turn.

"Constantine!" he whispered. "I must say, you're on the job, up here!"

"I've been on your heels ever since you reached the top of the stairs," murmured Constantine. "May I ask what you are doing up here, spoiling our best effects?"

Soames took him by the arm.

"If you come downstairs, I'll show you!" he whispered triumphantly. "I was right all along! They're both in it! The son's disappeared, but I bet I know where he is, and the old man's in the barn at this moment. If we're nippy we can get them both!"

"What on earth are you talking about?" exclaimed Stuart, utterly at sea as to his meaning.

Constantine supplied the answer.

"He means the Romseys," he said. "But the thing's impossible!"

"Impossible be blowed," was Soames' vulgar rejoinder. "They're both in it up to the hilt, I tell you!"

CHAPTER XI

STUART, CATCHING SIGHT of Constantine's face, realized that, for once, the old man was completely taken aback. He looked utterly incredulous.

"Romsey?" he exclaimed. "Preposterous!"

"I don't care how preposterous it is," retorted Soames, "I'm going to head him off before he makes off in one of those cars. We don't know how far the snow-plough may have got to-day, and I'm not taking any risks." Constantine turned and moved swiftly in the direction of the staircase.

"I'm as anxious as you are to see this cleared up," he said, as the two men followed him; "but you need have no fear of losing Lord Romsey. He'd be about as easy to mislay as the Albert Memorial."

Stuart kept his torch alight till they reached the head of the stairs. Then, warned by Soames, he slipped back the catch and the three men felt their way in darkness down to the floor below. At the bottom of the stairs they paused and listened. Stuart could hear nothing, but it would seem that some sound reached Constantine's ears, for, without a word, he left them, and they heard the soft rustle of his silk dressing-gown against the wall as he moved down the passage to their left. Soames drew Stuart in the opposite direction.

"There's a window at the end," he whispered. "You can see the barn from there."

They reached it and peered out into the moonlit night. Though the snow had stopped, dark, wind-blown clouds still scurried across the face of the moon; but the yard, with its white carpet of snow, was just visible, and, on the farther side, they could make out the grey bulk of the barn. As they looked a light flitted across what was evidently a window, vanished, and then revealed itself once more.

"A torch," murmured Stuart.

"He's in the barn all right," assented Soames. "We'd better get down there. Where's the doctor?"

"Here," whispered a voice at his elbow.

Constantine had returned from his little expedition, but whether or no it had been satisfactory he did not say.

"I'm sorry about this, sir," muttered Soames; "but it is pretty obvious, isn't it?"

A gentle chuckle floated out of the darkness.

"I'm not undergoing any apprehension concerning the reputation of my friend Lord Romsey," came a mocking whisper. "What do you propose to do?"

"Catch him in the act," answered Soames, somewhat nettled. "Are you coming, sir?"

"Not I. I've got a better use for my time. I'll take Stuart's place on the upper landing. May I use your room?"

"Of course," answered Stuart, thankful that the old man's impetuosity was not driving him out into the cold.

They parted, and he and Soames felt their way down the stairs to the lounge, and thence along the narrow passage that led to the door into the yard.

"I wish we dared use a light," murmured Stuart, as he groped his way ahead of Soames. "If there are any of those infernal little steps—"

He came full tilt up against something soft and warm that moved as he touched it. Instinctively he clutched it with both hands.

"Ow!" squeaked a voice softly in his ear. "It's Mr. Stuart, isn't it?"

"Miss Ford!" he gasped in amazement.

"I recognized your voice in the dark," she whispered. "Do, please, let go. You've no idea how it hurts."

He dropped his hand as though he'd been stung.

"I'm so sorry!" he stammered.

Soames's voice cut in out of the darkness. There was an edge to it that Stuart did not like.

"Miss Ford, will you please explain what you are doing here?"

There was a second's pause before she answered, then—

"Certainly not, Mr. Soames, unless you're prepared to answer the same question yourself."

With a pang of dismay Stuart realized that she was playing for time. But Soames was ready for her.

"Certainly," he said. "I was watching on the landing upstairs for our friend in the mask when I saw your father come out of his room and go down the passage. He went into your brother's room and called to him. Then he switched on the light. Evidently the room was empty. I watched him go down the staircase, using matches to light his way, and I followed him. When I heard him open this door I ran back to the landing and looked through the window at the end, and saw him cross the yard in the direction of the barn. But I fancy I'm only telling you what you know already." For a moment there was silence, then—

"But what on earth can either of them be doing in the barn?" she asked, her voice one of blank astonishment. Evidently, finding that they already knew as much as she did herself, she had decided on frankness.

"They?" Soames took her up sharply. "Your brother's there too, then?"

"I don't know. My room looks out on the yard. Something woke me, I think now it must have been this door opening or shutting. Ordinarily I shouldn't have bothered, but I'd gone to sleep thinking of all the things that have been happening, and I suppose I had them on my mind. Anyhow, I got up and looked out of the window. I saw a dark shadow flit across the yard to the barn, so I slipped on a coat, meaning to call Geoff. But when I opened my door I saw father going down the passage. He did not hear me, and I was just about to follow him when he opened Geoff's door and called him. And Geoff wasn't there!"

Her bewilderment was undoubtedly genuine. "I watched father go downstairs," she continued. "At first I wasn't sure what to do, then I followed I was just going to open this door when you came."

While she spoke Soames had unlatched the door and was peering into the yard.

"They're still there," he said. "Some one's moving outside the barn, I can just see him against the snow. I think it's your father. What made you think your brother was out there?"

His voice was milder, though he sounded only half convinced.

Again she hesitated, then—

"Where else should he be? He's not in his room."

"Do you know of anything that would be likely to take him to the barn?"

Soames spoke over his shoulder, keeping a careful watch the while through the half-open door.

"Nothing, unless he thought some one was tampering with the cars."

"His window looks out on the other side of the house," Soames reminded her. "He could have seen nothing suspicious from his room."

"He might have heard some one going down the stairs," she retorted quickly.

"Even then, I don't quite see why you followed him. He and your father could surely be relied upon to deal with any one they might find there."

Again there was a pause, then—

"There is such a thing as curiosity, Mr. Soames," she said. "It's one of the several failings that my sex is accused of."

Soames muttered something under his breath, but he was careful that it should not reach Miss Ford's ears.

"It's time we cleared this up, one way or the other," he said. "Are you coming, Stuart?"

He stepped out into the snow, and Stuart prepared to follow. But first he turned to the girl.

"Miss Ford—" he whispered.

He broke off with an exclamation of annoyance. Soames was with them once more.

"Did you turn out your light before leaving your room, Miss Ford?" he asked abruptly.

"I never turned it on," she answered. "I couldn't have seen anything from my window if I had. My coat was hanging on the door, and I snatched it off in the dark when I left my room."

"It's turned on now," announced Soames. "Your window's lighted up. It looks as if some one was in your room."

With an ejaculation of surprise she turned to go upstairs, but Soames stopped her.

"If it's the gentleman in the mask, you can't deal with him," he objected. "One of us had better go."

"I'll keep watch here," said Stuart quickly. "If I see the barn doors open I'll give a shout. You can do the same if you're in any trouble. The window's just overhead, we ought to hear each other."

Soames hesitated a moment, then disappeared up the stairs. He had no sooner gone than Stuart proceeded to take advantage of his absence.

"Miss Ford," he urged, as she followed him out into the yard, "won't you be frank with me? You thought your brother was going to use your car, didn't you?"

She countered his question with another.

"I don't know what Mr. Soames suspects us of doing; but do you agree with him?" she asked.

"I don't!" he assured her emphatically. "But you were keeping something back just now, and I could help you better if I knew what it was."

She hesitated, then evidently decided to trust him.

"I did think he might be going to leave. There's just a chance that the roads are clear; and when I missed him, I thought he might be going to risk it."

"Why?"

"I can't tell you that, Mr. Stuart."

Her tone was final. Stuart felt his cheeks grow hot.

"Why did you come down?" he asked at last.

"Because I wanted to be there if he and father met. Father's rather—well—difficult, sometimes."

"You mean you were afraid he'd—"

The words died on his lips. A window above their heads was jerked up, and Soames's exasperated voice floated down to them.

"I say," he cried, "come and get me out of this, will you?"

"Where are you?" called Stuart softly.

"In Miss Ford's room, of course! The blighter's locked me in!"

A soft giggle sounded at Stuart's side.

"He's dealt with him," she murmured. "Poor Mr. Soames!"

Then, as Stuart turned and vanished into the house, she ran quickly across the yard towards the barn.

Meanwhile Stuart, torch in hand, was taking the stairs two at a time. On the first landing he cannoned into Geoffrey Ford, who was moving with equal rapidity in the opposite direction. He had completely lost his rather mature air of dignity, and, once he had grasped Stuart's identity, grabbed his arm with the enthusiasm of a schoolboy.

"I've got your fellow with the mask!" he exclaimed.

"You're the very person I was after. Where does Bates hang out, do you know?"

For the moment Stuart forgot Soames and his troubles.

"How did you get him?" he demanded breathlessly.

"He's bottled in my sister's room l Went after her pearls, I suppose."

Stuart could only stare speechlessly at him. Then he swung round and tore down the passage to Angela Ford's room.

"Better leave Bates to deal with him," expostulated Ford, as he followed him. "I only caught a glimpse of him, but he seemed a pretty hefty chap."

"He is," agreed Stuart dryly, as he clutched the key which Ford had left in the lock outside the door.

He turned it and threw the door open.

Soames, his face scarlet with mingled rage and mortification, charged into them.

"Come on, you chaps," he cried. "We'll get him this time!"

Stuart caught him by the arm.

"Hold on, old man," he begged, trying to keep the tell-tale quiver out of his voice. "There's been a mistake."

Soames jerked himself free.

"What do you mean—a mistake?" he demanded. "I tell you, the fellow was here not five minutes ago. He was behind the door when I went into the room, and had whipped out and locked it before I could turn round. Now's our time to get him!"

"I'm afraid I owe you an apology, Mr. Soames," murmured Ford's voice. "The truth is …"

Stuart cast one look at his stricken countenance and made a bolt for the lower regions, where he could indulge his sense of humour with impunity.

He was half-way down the stairs when, for the second time, he encountered a flying figure. This time it was Angela Ford. Before he had time to tell her what had been happening upstairs, she had seized hold of him and was dragging him after her by the way he had come.

"Hurry, Mr. Stuart! He's in the house! I saw him come in. Where's Bates?"

Stuart came to a standstill, barring her way as she tried to push past him.

"Look here," he said firmly, "let's get this straight. In any case, Bates is sure to be downstairs, so it's no good bursting our lungs like this. Whom did you see come in?"

"The man who was in the barn," she cried impatiently. "It wasn't Geoff! I was half-way across the yard when he came out. He locked the door and ran past me into the house. I don't know who he was, but we ought to get him, if we're quick. Please let me go! I must get Geoff!"

She slipped under his outstretched arm and tore up the stairs.

Stuart hesitated for a moment, then, realizing that she was bound to run into her brother and Soames, departed in search of Bates. Contrary to his expectations, that worthy was not in Girling's office, neither was he in any of the rooms downstairs. Baffled, Stuart returned to the first landing. As he approached it he heard Angela Ford's voice. She was alternately knocking at a door and calling to her brother to come out. He hastened his steps, meaning to tell her that he was with Soames, and reached the top of the stairs, only to stand petrified with astonishment.

For the door at which she was knocking was that of Mrs. Orkney Cloude!

Before he had time to make his presence known, she had seen her brother and had run to meet him, as he appeared round the corner at the opposite end of the passage, followed by Soames, whose red face was illuminated by a rather sheepish grin. It did not take long to explain the situation to the two men, and to institute a more or less organized search.

Stuart and Soames undertook to explore the upper regions, while Ford went in search of Bates. Angela Ford, flouting their suggestion that she should retire to her room and lock herself in, went with her brother.

They found Constantine placidly keeping guard in the passage above. He was ready to vouch for it that no one had passed that way since Stuart's departure, but pointed out that he was not only out of sight but out of hearing of the back staircase, and that the chances were that the man had used that.

They hurried on to the floor above, Soames taking the flight of steps at one end of the passage, Stuart that at the other. As he turned into the long corridor that ran past the billiard-room a light was flashed in his face and Bates's deep voice boomed out of the darkness behind it.

"It's you, Mr. Stuart," he said. "What might you be doin' here?"

"Burglar hunting as usual," rejoined Stuart flippantly. "It's no good asking if you've seen anybody about, I suppose?"

"I've seen no one," said Bates heavily. "Anythin' happened?"

Soames, who had approached from the other end of the passage, came up behind him.

"Nothing out of the way," he said dryly. "Just the usual masked men and things. Where have you been, Bates?"

"Inspectin' the premises," announced Bates with dignity.

Soames's mouth twitched.

"Excuse my asking," he said, "but do you always move about behind that baby searchlight of yours?"

Bates met his gaze calmly.

"I do not, sir," he said; "but I make a point of turnin' it on anything suspicious like."

"Such as?" asked Stuart, actuated by an impish desire to see Bates make his point.

"You and Mr. Soames, sir," answered Bates stolidly.

"Joking apart," said Stuart. "Could any one have got up here from downstairs without your seeing them during the last twenty minutes or so?"

Bates meditated.

"They could. I made the round of the rooms downstairs, and then went along the passage to the back door. I found that open and stepped out into the yard, but could see nothing. I then locked the door and came up the back stairs and along this passage. When I reached the end, meanin' to go down by this staircase, I met you, Mr. Stuart."

Stuart made a quick calculation.

"Then you must have been out at the back when I looked for you in Girling's office, and Soames must have been just behind you as you came upstairs. And, of course, the man Miss Ford saw must have nipped upstairs while you were making the round of the downstairs rooms. Confound all these wretched staircases!"

"What's this about Miss Ford seein' some one?" asked Bates sharply.

They told him, and he cursed his luck in good round Anglo-Saxon. He had Stuart's full sympathy, for he realized that, according to his lights, the unfortunate constable was doing his best. The job was a hopeless one for any one working single-handed.

"Look here," he said. "After to-night we shall have to organize some kind of watch between us. Between us, we ought to be able to keep these beastly stairs covered. Until we do, the fellow's simply playing with us."

He was not exaggerating. Armed with the authority of the law they were able to make a much more thorough search than they had done hitherto; Bates even going so far as to rouse the servants and inspect their rooms, with the usual result. There was no person in the house unaccounted for, and no one had seen or heard anything suspicious.

Cold and disheartened, they gathered in the lounge in the small hours of the morning.

"What roused you, if I may ask, sir?" said Bates, addressing Geoffrey Ford.

"The sound of voices talking in the passage," answered Ford readily enough, though Stuart saw a quick glance flash between the brother and sister.

"Where were you when Lord Romsey called you, earlier in the evening?" cut in Soames, his suspicions still anything but allayed.

Ford opened his lips to answer, but a shriek from his sister cut short any reply he had been about to make.

"Good Heavens!" she cried, her eyes wide with consternation. "Father!"

"Bless my soul, yes!" ejaculated Stuart. "Where *is* Lord Romsey?"

Angela Ford's hand went to her mouth.

"In the barn!" she quavered. "I'd completely forgotten him!"

CHAPTER XII

THERE WAS a moment of appalled silence, then Geoffrey Ford spoke.

"Do you mean to say that father has been in the barn all this time?" he demanded incredulously.

His sister nodded. She was too deeply moved for speech.

"You knew he was there, and you—you left him there?"

The mingled awe and horror in his voice proved too much for her. A feeble giggle escaped from behind the hand she still held pressed against her trembling lips.

"I'm frightfully sorry, Geoff," she said, trying to control the shaking of her voice. "I really did forget. You see, I knew he was all right, because he called out to me to let him out, and I asked him if he was hurt. He said he wasn't. But he sounded frightfully annoyed. I tried to open the door, but the man had taken the key, so I told father I'd send some one. Then I ran after the man, but, of course, by then I was too late. After that father went clean out of my head!"

Bates stepped forward.

"You should have told us, Miss," he said reprovingly. "A night like this, too! Why, the gentleman will be half frozen!"

He turned to Girling.

"We'd best take tools with us, if the key's missing," le added, as he led the way to the door.

"There's plenty of straw up at the far end of the barn," remarked Girling. "He'll keep warm enough if he thinks to use it."

They trooped after him, Stuart's fancy playing fantastically with the vision of Lord Romsey couchant in the straw. He managed to catch Angela Ford's eye. She turned away, her cheeks crimson.

"I'm going to bed, if anybody wants me," she murmured in a stifled voice.

"Coward!" called Stuart softly after her, as she disappeared swiftly up the staircase.

As they approached the barn it became evident that Lord Romsey was, at any rate, alive, and, at the moment, very actively kicking. The barn doors were shaking under the impact of a heavy body which was being hurled repeatedly at them from the other side. A voice was also distinguishable, and it struck more than one of his hearers that Lord Romsey's style had undergone a marked change for the better. It was probable that never before had he expressed himself with such picturesque brevity.

Ford's attempt to mollify his father through the door met with no success. Life held but one burning question for Lord Romsey at that moment, and he continued to ask it, incessantly and in diverse forms, during the somewhat lengthy period that ensued before they managed to force the heavy doors. He wished to know why they had not come to his assistance immediately on hearing of his predicament. It spoke well for his daughter's popularity that no one gave her away, and that, to this day, he is probably unaware that this was exactly what they had done.

Girling had been right when he said that the barn door would baffle any burglar. It withstood the tools they had brought with them, and it was not till Girling had fetched a crowbar from the cellar that they were able to wrench the double doors apart.

They dragged them open, and then, with one accord, waited in silence for Lord Romsey to emerge. When he did make his appearance, it was perhaps as well that the first person his eyes fell on was the unfortunate Bates, to whom he addressed himself for the next five minutes. Bates, whose sense of humour was not unduly developed, was about the only member of the party who could have borne that impassioned monologue with impunity, coming as it apparently did from an elderly black-face minstrel who had been rolling in a haystack.

For Lord Romsey's face, from the tip of the nose upwards, was stained a rich, oily black, in contrast to which his double chin seemed positively livid. This, combined with the enormous quantity of straw with which he had managed to embellish himself in the course of his efforts to keep himself warm, produced an effect that made it difficult for any ordinarily constituted person to regard him with equanimity.

Soames, after a moment of fascinated and awestruck contemplation, turned to Stuart.

"After all, we've only his word for it that he *is* Lord Romsey. He's the very spit of a chap I used to see on the beach at Margate," he whispered, thereby demolishing the last vestige of Stuart's self-control.

Geoffrey Ford's attitude towards the whole affair was characteristic. His face bore an expression of frozen disgust, though he contented himself with reiterating patiently at intervals, "If you'll come upstairs with me, father. I'll explain matters."

Stuart realized that, for the moment, he was obsessed with but one thought, the desire to get his father's face washed at the earliest opportunity.

But Lord Romsey, who had not yet seen himself in the glass, recked little of his appearance.

"When I think," he boomed, with an assumption of dignity that, in the circumstances, was incredibly funny, "that, owing to sheer callousness and inefficiency, I might not only have died of exposure in this abominable place, but that the thief, whom I actually surprised in the act of tampering with my car, has had ample time in which to get away, it makes my blood boil! If you think you've heard the last of this, sir, you are mistaken!" he finished, turning savagely on Bates.

"That's as may be," returned the constable. His round face had reddened slowly during the outburst; but, apart from this, his stolidity was unshaken. "You surprised this man at his work, you say. I take it, then, that you can furnish me with a description of what he looked like."

His hand crept towards the pocket in which reposed the inevitable notebook.

Lord Romsey exploded into the ejaculation that had so fascinated Stuart on a former occasion.

"Pshaw!" he exclaimed. "If I had had time to see the man, do you suppose I should have allowed myself to be—er—overpowered? He was bending over the engine, with his back to me, when I entered. At the sound of the door opening he turned and leapt on me. There is no other word for it."

Lord Romsey gave a reminiscent shudder.

"He must have had some filthy rag in his hand," he went on, "for he rammed it over my face, nearly choking me; then, as I staggered back, he put his foot behind mine and bore me down. Bore me down," he repeated impressively. "Then, by the time I had managed to get my mouth and eyes free, he was gone, locking the door behind him. Almost directly after that I heard my daughter's voice on the other side of the door, and I still entirely fail to understand why her efforts to summon assistance should have been in vain!"

He glared at his distinctly sheepish-looking audience. Bates alone returned him look for look, though, when he spoke, his tone was perfectly respectful.

"It seems a pity, if I may say so," he said slowly, "that your Lordship couldn't lay hands on the man while you had the chance. We've been searching for him ever since he was seen to slip into the house, but we've none of us so much as caught a glimpse of him. That's how it was we didn't come along sooner."

Lord Romsey's blackened features relaxed into a sarcastic smile.

"One would imagine," he retorted, "that there were more than enough of you to deal with one burglar. Surely somebody could have been spared to open the door of this barn?"

Ford, goaded beyond endurance by his father's undignified exhibition, seized him firmly by the arm.

"We can settle all that later," he said decisively. "What you want at the moment is a fire and a hot drink, otherwise we shall have you laid up."

"And some warm water," murmured the irrepressible Soames.

Lord Romsey turned to his son with a pomposity that ill became him.

"I imagine, Geoffrey, that I am the best person to decide what my immediate needs may be."

The altercation was becoming more than Stuart could bear with equanimity. As he turned towards the house, his shoulders heaving uncontrollably, he realized that Geoffrey Ford's patience had given way at last.

"My God, sir," he whispered fiercely, "do you realize that you look like a negro minstrel?"

Lord Romsey's ebony countenance became a mask of outraged dignity.

"A what?" fell on Stuart's ears as he fled, whimpering, towards the house.

But he was not fated to reach it.

As he neared the door a little figure emerged, picking its way delicately over the snow. Even seen from a distance, the neat black coat and the woollen fascinator would have betrayed the younger Miss Adderley.

"Oh dear, what has happened now, Mr. Stuart?" she exclaimed apprehensively. "Not that dreadful man again?"

Before he could answer she recoiled with a shrill scream of terror.

"Oh! Oh, they've caught him! Why don't the; make him take off that frightful mask? And Bates hasn't even put the handcuffs on!"

Stuart turned, to discover that the group he had left at the door of the barn had joined them. Lord Romsey was regarding Miss Adderley with marked severity.

"They have not caught him, madam," he said, totally unaware that his own appearance was the sole cause of her distress. "Nor, as matters are at present, are they likely to do so."

He passed majestically on into the house.

Miss Adderley peered after him.

"Surely that wasn't Lord Romsey?" she piped in amazement.

"It was," Stuart assured her.

"Then why has he disguised himself? Was he trying to trap that man?"

"I'm afraid the truth is that the man trapped him," said Stuart, trying to attune his countenance to her shocked gaze.

In as few words as possible, for the yard was growing colder each moment, he told her what had happened. He had just succeeded in making the situation clear to her when they were joined by Soames.

"I'd like a few words with you, Stuart," he said in a low voice.

Miss Adderley, in her excitement, ignored him.

"Did Bates find any clues?" she asked.

Stuart smiled.

"I don't think there were any," he replied. "In any case, we were all rather absorbed in the rescue of Lord Romsey, and I'm afraid we didn't look for any."

"I wish I had a light," she said wistfully. "Then I could have a look round while you are talking to Mr. Soames. One never knows, I might stumble on something."

Stuart produced his torch from his pocket.

"Take this," he suggested. "But I'm afraid you'll find it a cold, fruitless job. Do you want me to come with you?"

She drew her short figure up to its full height.

"I'm not afraid, thank you," she assured him. At least, not so long as you and Mr. Soames are within hail."

Stuart regretfully abandoned his plan of making a speedy retreat to a warmer sphere.

"Don't be long, will you?" he begged, as she departed.

Soames waited until she was out of hearing.

"Well, what do you think of the Romsey crowd now?" he asked.

Stuart stared at him.

"You don't mean to say that you're still harping on that old string?" he exclaimed.

Soames reddened.

"Take the facts," he retorted. "Ford's room was empty to-night, not for the first time, remember. It doesn't look out on the yard, so that, even if his father's story that he left his room because he saw a light in the barn is true, the son was not burglar hunting. Where was he? Then, when we go down, whom do we find in the barn? Lord Romsey; and to make it all the more mysterious, we run into his daughter, obviously keeping watch behind the yard door. If she wasn't there to warn him of any possible interruption, I should like to know what she was doing!"

Stuart laughed, though he was beginning to feel more angry than amused.

"You're not seriously going to suggest that Lord Romsey blacked his own face and locked himself into the barn on purpose?" he exclaimed.

"So far as his blacking his face is concerned, little Miss Adderley gave me a hint as to that just now," returned Soames triumphantly. "She as good as recognized him as the man in the mask, before she realized that he was Lord Romsey. No one's set eyes on this blessed mask except her, and there's no reason why the man she saw shouldn't have been the old boy with his face blacked, just as it was to-night!"

This time Stuart's laugh was one of sheer mirth. It nettled Soames, but he stuck to his guns.

"It's all very well to laugh," he continued stubbornly. "But the truth is that you're all such infernal snobs that you won't look facts in the face. Just because the chap's got a title——"

"Nonsense!" interrupted Stuart sharply. His own temper was beginning to suffer. "The fact that the man's Lord Romsey has nothing to do with it. But what you refuse to take into account is his position. He's a rich man, against whose name there's never been a breath of scandal. Why in the name of goodness should he start pinching other people's jewels at his time of life? According to Constantine, he's got plenty of his own."

"If he was the public prosecutor himself, it wouldn't alter the evidence against him! And he wouldn't be the first rich man that's been found to be penniless when he turned up his toes! Who saw this man to-night? The Romseys. If you ask me, we've been nicely had, and the whole lot of us have been wasting our time on a wild-goose chase. Who was the only person near the barn after the assault Lord Romsey declares was made on him? His daughter. What was to prevent her from turning the key on him, once she realized that the whole house was roused, and that a get-away was out of the question? He couldn't get back to his room, and the only thing for them to do was to concoct some sort of story to account for his presence in the barn. Then she conveniently forgot he was there, while we were footling round the house."

"As you've worked the whole thing out so nicely, perhaps you'll tell me the reason for that," said Stuart.

"The reason's obvious. She wanted us, and more particularly Bates, kept away from the barn until her father and brother had finished their work."

"Their work being … ?" pursued Stuart in his most annoying drawl.

"I don't know," admitted Soames. "But I shall soon, if you people will only concentrate on Romsey, and stop treating him like a little tin god."

Stuart gathered his forces together to demolish Soames's arguments, and, as he did so, he realized, with some misgiving, the formidable array of facts he was called upon to meet. The mere idea of any complicity on the part of Lord Romsey or any member of his family still seemed to him absurd; but, on the whole, Soames had succeeded in making out a pretty good case against them. And the one piece of knowledge he now held concerning Geoffrey Ford, he did not care to use without his sister's permission. He was not sorry to see Miss Adderley speeding towards them from the barn.

"We can't discuss it now," he contented himself with saying; "but you can take my word for it that you're on the wrong track altogether."

Soames's indignant snort was drowned by Miss Amy's voice, high and shrill with excitement.

"I have found something!" she exclaimed. "You see what a good thing it was that I decided to have a good look round. How did this get there?"

She held up a small red leather case.

"A jewel-case," she went on breathlessly. "And look what's on it!"

She turned the light from Stuart's torch on to the lid and revealed, stamped in gold letters, the initials: "B. O. C."

"O. C. Orkney Cloude!" she carolled. "They must be her jewels!"

"Where did you find them?" asked Soames.

Miss Adderley turned on him a face beaming with innocent joy.

"Underneath the seat in that big motor-car of Lord Romsey's," she answered.

CHAPTER XIII

THEY TROOPED BACK into the house, Miss Amy triumphantly leading the way, Mrs. Orkney Cloude's jewel-case clasped to her bosom. It was to Soames's credit that, after a futile attempt to catch Stuart's eye, he refrained from any comment on Miss Adderley's singularly opportune discovery.

Bates having taken charge of the jewel-case, Stuart and Soames adjourned to their own landing, where they found Constantine still keeping guard in Stuart's bedroom. He had nothing to report save the abrupt arrival of Miss Amy at the bedroom door, bursting with the news that "something was going on in the barn," and that she had watched the lights and moving figures until she could bear it no longer.

"She invited me to accompany her," he informed them; "but running about in the snow with a lantern in the early hours does not appeal to me, so I cunningly suggested that it was the duty of old gentlemen like myself to hold the fort in the absence of the more active members of the community. I assured her that her sister would be quite safe in my care, upon which she dashed off in search of adventure. I hope she found it?"

"She found something worth having, at any rate," said Stuart. "It's probable that Mrs. Cloude would never have seen her jewels again if Miss Adderley hadn't happened on them."

He told Constantine of the evening's work.

"Finishing up," he concluded, "with the usual fruitless paper-chase. The chap, whoever he is, had vanished into thin air as he always does."

Constantine frowned.

"That's the most puzzling element in the whole case," he said. "Try as I will, I can't place him."

Stuart took him up sharply.

"Which means, that you *have* placed the original thief?"

But Constantine still declined definitely to commit himself.

"I'm not sufficiently sure of my facts yet to say for certain," he answered; "but I think so."

Soames, who had been restraining himself with difficulty, burst into speech.

"Look here, doctor," he exclaimed. "After what happened to-night, you can't rule Lord Romsey out any longer. Stuart's talk of the man vanishing into thin air is all bunkum. If you ask me, he's washing the black off his face at this minute, and cursing Miss Adderley for having stumbled on the jewel-case he'd tucked away so neatly in his car. The whole bunch of them's in it, and you must admit that they'd got it worked out pretty cleverly. If I hadn't been on the watch, the thing would have gone like clockwork, and none of us would have dreamed of suspecting them."

"Speaking for myself, I should have been mildly surprised if the entire Romsey family had disappeared during the night," suggested Constantine slyly.

Soames snorted.

"They're not such fools as that! Young Ford would have slipped away with the loot, and his family would have been suitably anxious till they got a wire from him saying he was safe in London. And it might have been all of twenty-four hours before Mrs. Cloude missed her jewels!"

Stuart lost the rest of the argument. His mind had gone off at a tangent, which had been suggested by Soames's last words. Angela Ford, in her search for her brother, had gone straight to Mrs. Orkney Cloude's room. Supposing that, for purposes of his own, Geoffrey Ford had been conducting an intrigue with that lady and had, earlier in the evening, passed the jewel-case out to his sister! It was a relief to Stuart to feel that Soames was mercifully unaware of this further complication. He came to the surface again in time to hear Constantine's closing remark.

"You've got a good enough case against them. I'm quite ready to admit it. But I still stick to my original contention that, knowing the Romseys as I do, I find it impossible to connect them in any way with a theft of that kind. I repeat once more, there is no earthly reason why they should do it!"

"Which means that you'll simply leave them a free hand till they have done it, and, what's more, got away with it!" retorted the disgusted Soames. "I'm fed up with this, and I'm going now to put a few plain facts to Bates, and see how he takes them.'"

"You'll probably find that he's come to much the same conclusion as yourself," returned Constantine, "which will be a pity. Bates has only room for one theory in his head, and, once it's firmly established there, he'll work blindly on it till he suddenly discovers how his time has been wasted. He's not been much good so far, I admit, but he's more useful with an open mind than he will ever be trying to make a burglar out of poor old Romsey."

Soames was frustrated in his retort by the sound of footsteps in the passage, followed by the appearance of Miss Amy Adderley in the doorway.

"It *was* Mrs. Orkney Cloude's jewel-case!" she exclaimed impressively. "Would you believe it, she had never even looked to see if it was safe! And she'd probably never have missed it if I hadn't seen it! She actually said that she'd forgotten all about it!"

"Where did she keep it, do you know?" asked Constantine.

"In her dressing-case. It's got a special lock, not the kind of one that the cheap cases have. Of course any one can open those. This one would be much more difficult."

From her tone it would seem that her knowledge of locks was profound, and Constantine's lips twitched as he realized that she was merely quoting Bates.

"Was the lock forced?" he asked.

Miss Amy's manner became even more portentous.

"No. Picked! And very cleverly too. It wasn't till Bates tried to open the case that we found it out. He says it is the work of a professional!"

She paused to give her words full effect, then continued breathlessly—

"You realize what that implies, Dr. Constantine? We are harbouring a *professional* burglar in this house!"

Constantine nodded.

"I find it even more disquieting to remember that we are harbouring the murderer of Major Carew," he said mildly.

Miss Amy blenched. Her little triumph collapsed like a pricked bubble, and she became a very frightened elderly lady.

"Oh!" she whispered. "I'd forgotten poor Major Carew. And if he thinks we suspect him, the man must be desperate by now. I wish we could get away!"

Stuart came impetuously to the rescue.

"Don't you worry, Miss Adderley," he said reassuringly. "We're on the watch now, and we'll take good care of you and your sister between us. He won't find much further scope for his activities."

"He got Mrs. Cloude's jewels quite easily," pointed out Miss Adderley with unerring logic. "The moment the roads are clear I shall take my sister away."

"You suggested that the thief might know we suspect him," said Constantine. "Had you any one special in mind, Miss Adderley?"

The panic in her eyes gave place to bewilderment.

"Whom could I have?" she asked helplessly. "There *is* no one, unless it's that Mr. Melnotte. He never seems to be there when anything happens, does he? But that's not really a reason for suspecting him, and he certainly doesn't look like a professional burglar."

"What is everybody doing downstairs?" asked Stuart, more in the hope of turning her mind to more harmless topics than from any real desire for information.

"When I came away, Girling was just about to lock up the barn, and Bates was going with him to take a last look round."

"How was the barn first entered this evening, by the way?" asked Constantine. "As you had to break open the door to release Lord Romsey, I gather that the lock hadn't been forced in the first instance. I thought Girling had put the key in a safe place."

It was Miss Adderley who answered. Since her interview with Bates she had become a fount of information.

"He had. It was locked up in his desk, and Bates says that the lock of the desk was picked too. Just as skilfully as Mrs. Orkney Cloude's dressing-case. It must, of course, have been the same man."

"What's he done about it now?" asked Soames. "The lock's smashed, and, in any case, he hadn't got the key."

Miss Adderley was vague on this point.

"I think he's doing something with a padlock. He'd got his tools with him. Shall you be sitting up, Mr. Stuart?"

Her voice was pathetically anxious, and Stuart hastened to set her mind at rest. He assured her that he and Soames would be on guard till the servants were up and about.

"So you see you needn't be anxious," he concluded. "You're lucky in one thing. You haven't got a balcony to your room."

Miss Amy cast a stricken glance at him as she backed out of the doorway.

"For all we know, he may be a cat-burglar," she said.

Stuart waited till he heard her door close, then he turned reproachfully to Constantine.

"You frightened the poor old thing half out of her wits," he said. "She's been jumpy enough over the whole business, as it is."

Constantine's thoughts were evidently elsewhere.

"I'm sorry," he murmured vaguely. "It was stupid of me to say what I did, but my mind was so full of the vanishing gentleman that I forgot to allow for Miss Adderley's nerves. What is bothering me is this. The roads will be clear very soon now, and, as soon as they are, we shall have the man from New Scotland Yard upon us. A professional burglar won't take the risk of being recognized. If we're not careful he'll slip through our fingers before the London man gets here."

"As he was trying to do to-night," insisted Soames stubbornly.

Constantine smiled.

"As the Romseys will have no chance of doing so long as you're about, my dear Soames," he amended. "I'm trusting you to look after them."

The muscles round Soames's mouth stiffened.

"I shall," he rejoined shortly, as he left the room, presumably to take up his old post on the landing occupied by his special quarry.

In less than a quarter of an hour he was back again.

"Things are getting beyond a joke," he announced acridly.

Stuart was feeling both jaded and sleepy, and he cordially agreed with him. Constantine, who, a book in one hand, the other fondling the bowl of his pipe, seemed to be the only member of the party completely unaffected by the long vigil, surveyed him quizzically.

"You are not going to tell me that the Romseys have taken French leave while your back was turned?" he protested.

Soames ignored the gibe.

"Did you look at any of the tyres in the barn when you were there?" he demanded of Stuart.

"No. I never went into the barn. Bates said they were all right. Why do you ask?"

"Because they're anything but all right now. Somebody's had a go at the tyres with a knife, and done the job pretty thoroughly, too. The only car that's escaped is yours. Every one of the others has been put out of action."

Stuart gazed at him in consternation.

"When could they have done it?"

"That's what Bates is asking," answered Soames grimly. "He and Girling found them like that when they went to lock up the barn just now. Lord Romsey swears his tyres were all right when he last saw the car, and, as Bates corroborates him, it looks as if he was speaking the truth."

"Of course he was speaking the truth," said Stuart impatiently. "Do you mean to say that, during the short time that elapsed between our rescue of Lord Romsey and Girling's return to the barn, some one got in and slashed the tyres?"

"I mean to say that the chap we've been chasing half the night not only got away, but had the nerve to go back again and finish his job," exclaimed Soames savagely. "Whoever he is, he's got the laugh of us all along the line. Much good we've done by sitting up and watching!"

"He could have got down the back stairs, I suppose, while we were all gathered on the landing," said Stuart. "But it was pretty quick work. Anyway, you can't attribute this to the Romseys!"

"I don't. I saw them into Lord Romsey's bedroom, and they didn't come out while I was there. They're out of this, unless—"

He paused as a thought struck him.

"Did anybody see Miss Ford after we started to fetch Lord Romsey?"

"She went to bed," Stuart informed him shortly.

Soames's smile was sufficient to aggravate a less hot-tempered person than Stuart.

"She did, did she? And her bedroom, if you remember, is at the top of the small flight of stairs leading to the back passage. Except for Melnotte, Mrs. Cloude, and Mrs. van Dolen, she's the only person that was not with us in the passage. We can wipe out the other two ladies, and I'm not putting my money on Melnotte at the moment."

"But what earthly object could she have in disabling her father's car?" asked Stuart.

"Why do you suppose your car was left unmolested?" demanded Soames.

"I can't imagine."

"Tut! Use your brain, my dear fellow," put in Constantine unexpectedly. "The lighter the car the easier it will be to manipulate with the roads in their present condition, and yours is the smallest car in the barn. The others were disabled with a view to preventing pursuit. The vandal who slashed the tyres has a quicker brain than the thief who made off with Mrs. Cloude's jewel-case."

Soames stared at him, his mind diverted for the moment from the Romseys.

"Then you don't believe that they are one and the same person?" he asked.

"I doubt it. The jewel-case was found in Lord Romsey's car, and, according to him, he surprised the thief in the act of starting the engine, so that he evidently intended to use it. He may, of course, have changed his mind before his second visit to the barn; but, considering the little time at his disposal, it doesn't look as if he could have given much of it to reflection. He would be much more likely to carry on with his original plan."

Soames hesitated, then returned to his old line of argument.

"It doesn't follow that Miss Ford hasn't a quicker brain than her father," he said.

"It's an undisputed fact that she has," returned Constantine. "But, all the same, without in any way supporting your theory, I would point out that if, as you suggest, the robbery of Mrs. Cloude's jewels was the result of a carefully laid plot on the part of the Romsey family, it's obvious that they must have discussed it in all its aspects first. Angela Ford, if I know anything of her, would have had her say then. In spite of which, there seems little doubt that the person who purloined Mrs. Cloude's jewels intended to use the big car."

"What is your theory about the whole thing, sir?" asked Stuart. "I can see you've got one."

"It's pure guess-work, of course," answered Constantine slowly. "But it looks as though the person who has been searching for Mrs. van Dolen's emeralds had given it up as a bad job, and decided to get away with whatever he could lay his hands on. Hence the theft of Mrs. Cloude's jewels. If he's known to the police, it's probably essential that he should clear out before the arrival of the Scotland Yard man, which is imminent now. No doubt the other thief who, so far as we know, still holds the emeralds, has an equally strong reason for wishing to get away at the earliest opportunity. It speaks well for his intelligence that he should have decided to use the smaller and lighter car."

"Which, being of a cheaper and more popular make, would be less easy to trace," assented Stuart, shamelessly decrying his new toy.

"It's all very well as a theory," broke in Soames impatiently. "But what I want to know is, where the devil are these people? It's absurd that this sort of thing should go on under our very noses, and that we shouldn't be able to spot one of them! You've turned down my Romsey theory, but have you any other to put in its place?"

"If I have, I'm keeping it to myself for the present," said Constantine calmly. "And I admit frankly that I find myself very much at sea on certain points. To go back to the chess problem analogy, some of my pieces seem to have been making some curiously unnatural moves. From a psychological point of view they are impossible, and I refuse to accept a problem in which the castles move obliquely and the bishops in a straight line, which is what they seem to be doing at present!"

"Are you sure that it isn't the knights who have been misbehaving themselves?" suggested Soames maliciously.

"Lord Romsey is one of the few barons of the United Kingdom who would bitterly resent being taken for a knight, and his moves, though ponderous, are invariably correct," retorted Constantine calmly. "Also, I can honestly assure you that neither he nor his family have anything to do with my perplexity. The person I have in mind is far more astute than Lord Romsey."

"Then it certainly isn't Melnotte, unless he's a very dark horse indeed!" exclaimed Stuart.

Constantine smiled.

"I'm giving nothing away at present," he said. "If I'm on the wrong tack altogether, which is still possible, I shall at least have the advantage of being able to blush unseen. Meanwhile, I don't wish to hasten Soames's departure, but I doubt if it is wise to leave Lord Romsey's door unguarded for so long."

Soames took the thrust in good part.

"There'll come a time when you'll, both of you, eat your words," he threatened, as he left the room.

"He's wrong about the Romseys, of course," said Stuart. "But I must say he's managed to make out a pretty good case against them. Especially over this business, of the tyres. Miss Ford could easily have reached the barn without being seen."

"So could I, for the matter of that, or Mrs. Cloude, or Melnotte, or Mrs. van Dolen. I have an idea that by to-morrow evening we shall have elucidated the Romsey problem, and a very shrewd suspicion as to what the explanation will be."

Stuart stared at him.

"I've got an inkling myself as to how matters stand," he said; "but how you've managed to tumble to it, I don't know. One thing I do feel certain about, is that Geoffrey Ford had nothing to do with either of the thefts."

"Am I to gather from that that you do suspect his sister?" asked Constantine, with a mischievous twinkle in his eye.

Stuart met his gaze squarely, though he felt his cheeks grow warm.

"I don't suspect any member of the family, least of all Lord Romsey," he answered stoutly.

Constantine sighed.

"I shall never cease to regret that I did not see him to-night," he said sadly. "If I had known of the spectacle that awaited Miss Adderley downstairs, a blizzard would not have kept me away."

The rest of the night passed uneventfully enough. Stuart tried in vain to persuade Constantine to go to bed and leave him to keep watch; but the old man flatly refused to be dismissed, and, when the first house-maid clattered sleepily down the stairs, he was undoubtedly the fresher of the two, Stuart climbed thankfully into bed, leaving instructions that he was not to be disturbed until he rang.

It was past midday when he opened his eyes, and he reached the lounge just as the house-party was trooping in to lunch. Soames reported that his suspects had made no move during the night, and were now engaged in lunching decorously in their private sitting-room. He confessed to being half asleep, and even Constantine announced his intention of spending the greater part of the afternoon on his bed.

Stuart hung about the lounge for a while in the hope of capturing Angela Ford; then, concluding that she too was sleeping off the effect of the events of the night before, he spent a boring half-hour chatting with Melnotte, whose company he had tried his best to put up with since he had discussed the dancer with Constantine. But he was not an enlivening conversationalist, and Stuart was glad to escape to his room and the work that awaited him there.

It was close on tea-time, and he had reached the last long, un-wieldy page of galley-proof, when he became aware of voices just outside his door. Certain isolated words penetrated his absorption, and, with an exclamation, he sprang to his feet and made for the passage.

"Did I hear you say that Dr. Constantine had been hurt?" he demanded.

The housemaid, who was standing waiting at Miss Adderley's door, reassured him.

"I don't think it's much, sir," she said. "Mr. Melnotte had an accident with a spirit-lamp, and Dr. Constantine got his hand a bit burnt putting it out."

At that moment Miss Amy appeared, a bottle in her hand.

"Here it is, Maggie," she said. "I meant to give it back to you yesterday. My sister does not need it any more."

Stuart was already on his way down the passage.

He found Constantine endeavouring to stem the confused apologies of Melnotte. His left hand was wrapped in a handkerchief; otherwise, to Stuart's relief, he seemed more amused than hurt. On the arrival of the housemaid Melnotte took his departure, and Stu-art watched her while she administered first aid to an angry-look-ing burn on the back of Constantine's hand.

"I'm sorry to have been so long, sir," she explained, "but I couldn't find the oil at first. I'd forgotten that Miss Adderley asked for it some days ago to rub her sister's chest with when she was bad."

"Well, it's an old saying that there's some good in all things evil," remarked Constantine thoughtfully.

The girl looked puzzled.

"I beg your pardon, sir?"

Constantine, who was seated on the edge of his bed, looked up at her with a very charming smile.

"What I should have said is that it is only when we old people get into trouble that we are looked after so delightfully. You've got a very gentle way with you, my dear."

She flushed with pleasure.

"There was a First Aid Course at the Village Institute, and we all of us took a course, not knowing when it might come in useful. I think you'll find that's quite comfortable now, sir. I'll come and do it up again last thing to-night."

When she had gone Stuart turned to Constantine.

"What on earth have you been up to?" he asked reprovingly.

Constantine chuckled.

"Melnotte has been having a little private conflagration. He appears to have started by upsetting a spirit-lamp on to the window curtain. Then, characteristically, he lost his head and threw open the window, thereby creating a thorough draught. Fortunately his next move was to batter madly on my door, and I arrived on the scene in time to pull the thing down and smother the flames. If it hadn't been a flimsy muslin affair we should have had the whole place alight. I don't think I've ever met any one with so little presence of mind in an emergency. Of course he's full of apologies now."

"I don't see anything funny in that," was Stuart's rather grim comment. "It might have been a good deal worse, and, as it is, you've got a nasty burn."

"You will in a minute, though," said Constantine, his eyes dancing with mirth. "It's a shame to give him away, but he deserves it for being such an incredible fool. I very nearly laughed in his face when I caught him picking up the tongs. He so evidently hoped I hadn't seen them!"

For a moment Stuart was baffled, then his face lit up with joyful recognition.

"You don't mean to say that he was curling his hair?" he exclaimed.

"I do," answered Constantine. "It was that kind of spirit-lamp, and, what's more, if you'd observed him more closely just now you'd have seen that it was only half finished."

He waited till Stuart's appreciation had subsided, then, with his uninjured hand, extracted a letter from his pocket.

"It's curious it should have happened just now," he said. "I was reading this when he knocked at my door. It came by the afternoon post. You remember I told you I had written about him to a theatrical agent I know. Well, he's just sent his complete dossier."

He handed the letter to Stuart, who glanced through it. He could not resist a smile at the discovery that Melnotte's real name was Spadger, though, in view of his profession, he could hardly blame him for having abandoned it. The son of a small Manchester shopkeeper, he had gone on the films, but had had to leave them owing to his lack of nerve. The legitimate drama being closed to him on account of his accent, which he had obviously been at great pains to improve since, he had taken up ballroom dancing, and had managed to achieve something of a reputation in that line. Owing to his reliability, he was seldom out of an engagement, and had the reputation among his fellow artists of being a hard worker and generous to his people, though he was known to be morbidly sensitive as to his origin.

"That wipes out Melnotte, as far as I am concerned," said Stuart as he handed the letter back to Constantine.

"I never really suspected him," answered the old man. "And, if I had, his performance just now would have cleared him. He hasn't got the nerve to kill a fly, and is quite incapable of planning and carrying through a robbery, much less a murder. By the way, Soames and I had an interview with another of our suspects this morning while you were sleeping off your night's work."

Stuart looked up sharply.

"Geoffrey Ford?" he exclaimed.

Constantine nodded.

"He said he thought he owed us an explanation. As you know, his father could not find him when he went to his room."

Stuart smiled. For once he felt that he had beaten Constantine at the post.

"I fancy I can guess where he was, though," he observed.

Constantine's eyebrows rose.

"So you have been keeping something up your sleeve," he said. "I felt it in my bones. That's the worst of you Scotsmen. Then you won't be as surprised as Soames was at his explanation."

"If you mean that he and Mrs. Orkney Cloude knew each other before they came here, I'd tumbled to that already."

"Then there is something you don't know," said Constantine complacently. "My dear fellow, he married Mrs. Orkney Cloude over a month ago. And Lord Romsey is still ignorant of the fact!"

CHAPTER XIV

STUART'S MIND ran swiftly back over the data he had collected concerning Geoffrey Ford and Mrs. Orkney Cloude.

"So that's it," he said slowly. "I'm afraid I credited him with a baser motive. This accounts for a good many things. Mrs. Goude's collapse when she first caught sight of Lord Romsey, for instance, and the conversation Soames overheard between Miss Ford and her brother on the stairs. I can imagine Mrs. Cloude's feelings when she found herself marooned in the same hotel with her father-in-law!"

Constantine nodded.

"It spelt ruination to all their plans," he said. "They had arranged to spend Christmas at Redsands, but not, of course, in the same hotel. The idea was to introduce Mrs. Cloude to Lord Romsey and break the news of their marriage to him after he had been suitably impressed with her charm and beauty. I don't think it would have worked, though he's more susceptible than you would think, and Mrs. Cloude's a clever woman. As it turned out, their hand was forced and Ford had to confide in his sister, who tried in vain to persuade him to go to his father. As you've no doubt grasped, she's the one member of the family who doesn't stand in awe of Lord Romsey."

"But why on earth should he take exception to Mrs. Cloude?" demanded Stuart.

"Because Mrs. Cloude comes of an old Roman Catholic family, and, to make matters worse, Geoffrey Ford joined the Catholic Church when he married her. And Lord Romsey is one of the few people who still allude to the Church of Rome as 'The Scarlet Woman.' This marriage will be the tragedy of his life. My own opinion is that, if they had carried this plan through before their marriage, he might have given his consent, provided it remained a mixed marriage. Mrs. Cloude would probably have given way there, and this deadlock might have been avoided. As it is, I feel sorry for them all."

And that's why Miss Ford was on the watch last night."

"Yes. She got it into her head that her brother was going to try to get Mrs. Cloude, or rather Mrs. Ford as she is now, away at the earliest opportunity. She honestly thought that he was in the barn, and that her father had surprised him in the act of taking the car. She ran down in the hope of preventing a rupture between them. As soon as she realized that the intruder was not Geoffrey Ford, she guessed where her brother was probably to be found."

"Then her father's plight really did go out of her head?"

"Completely. I'm sure she's genuine there, and she's thoroughly ashamed of herself. She saw the man and gave chase. In her excitement she entirely forgot her father."

"That wipes the Fords off, then. Is Soames convinced at last?"

Constantine laughed.

"Soames is busy looking for another victim. As he sapiently remarks, 'If they didn't do it, some one else did.' He's now divided in his mind between young Trevor and Melnotte, in spite of my agent friend's letter."

"I can't bring myself to suspect Melnotte. As for Trevor—"

"I've been keeping a quiet eye on that young man, and, going by appearances, his mind seems to be entirely taken up with Miss Hamilton. He's the only person, by the way, that seems to have remembered that it's Christmas Day."

Stuart's jaw dropped.

"Good Heavens, so it is!" he exclaimed. "I suppose the post, if there is one, would have reminded us when it came in."

"There's a post all right, or I shouldn't have got my letter this morning, and, what's more, the roads are almost clear and the trains are beginning to run fairly regularly. Our cruise in the 'Noah's Ark' is nearly over!"

An idea struck Stuart.

"Do you suppose the Scotland Yard man will keep us hanging about here long?" he asked.

"It's difficult to say. I don't see how he can detain us as matters stand at present. He's either got to find the emeralds or produce some evidence that they have been disposed of. As for the murder, he won't find it easy to involve any one member of the party in that."

Stuart chuckled.

"I should like to see Mrs. van Dolen's face as she speeds the parting guests," he said. "I've no doubt she'd like to see the whole lot of us arrested."

"I don't fancy the Yard will submit to any dictation from her. Those emeralds have been a bugbear to them far too long, and she's had more than one warning from them. By the way, Soames suggested that you should remove the magneto from your car. It's not a bad idea. If the thief does try to get away, as I'm convinced he will, yours is the only one that is available now. I've persuaded Bates to veto any repairs on the other cars for to-day, at least."

"I'll do it now, if Girling can let me have a lantern. This means, I suppose, that we shall have to be on the watch for the next twenty-four hours."

"Till the man from the Yard gets here, at any rate. And if you do put your car out of action, I should do it as unobtrusively as possible. If the thief thinks he can still use it, it's all to the good."

"Right. I'll use the torch; it's less likely to attract attention than a lantern. Some one's keeping a lookout, I suppose?"

"Since my suggestion this morning that the man had very little time left at his disposal and that he might try to make a get-away, the whole household has been on the job. Even Melnotte's glued to his window, which, as he pointed out to me, 'commands the front door.' What he omitted to explain was how he proposes to transport himself from the second storey to the ground, supposing he does see some one departing!"

"Especially as I'm willing to bet that he's locked himself in, for fear of an attack from the rear. It's not going to be as easy as I thought to get to the barn unobserved."

"Miss Ford's keeping an eye on the barn from her window, I believe. You may be able to enlist her sympathy," suggested Constantine demurely.

Stuart fetched his torch and slipped it into his pocket. He was amused to see Bates, looking ineffably bored, hanging about on the first landing. Trevor, with the help of Miss Hamilton, was busy decorating the lounge with holly. Stuart did not offer to help them, though it struck him that they were not getting on very quickly with their job. Two bunches of mistletoe, cunningly suspended in dusky corners, showed, however, that Trevor's time had not been entirely wasted. Turning down the passage he found Girling smoking a pipe in his office, his chair so placed that he could keep an eye on the window that gave on to the yard. Any one going from the house to the barn would be bound to pass it on his way.

Going on the principle that, in the case of a secret, the fewer people that share it the better, he gave the excuse that he wanted to fetch a map from the pocket of his car. Girling handed over the key of the padlock with which he had secured the door.

"It's not much of a protection," he confessed, "but I can't get no one to see to it to-day, bein' Christmas, and it was the best I could do at the moment. Any one could get that hasp off, provided they'd got the tools."

Stuart, as he unlocked the padlock, was inclined to agree with him. However, if they were counting on catching their man in the act of taking the car, it was all to the good that he should be given fairly easy access to the barn. He unshipped the magneto and slipped it into his pocket, then, carrying a road map ostentatiously in his hand, went back to the house.

He found Angela Ford and Miss Amy standing in the doorway of Girling's office.

"I've just been settin' the ladies' minds at rest," vouchsafed Girling, with a broad grin. "They saw you goin' into the barn from their windows, and they came down to know if it was all right. I was tellin' them they're sharper off the mark than Tom Bates!"

"No one will get into the barn without my seeing them," announced Miss Amy firmly. "My sister is sitting up to-day, so you can be sure that one of us will be on the watch."

Stuart suddenly realized that, in their absorption, they had all completely forgotten to inquire after the elder Miss Adderley's indisposition, and he hastened to repair the omission.

"She's much better, thank you," Miss Amy assured him. "Sitting up in a shawl to-day, and, I hope, well enough to come down to-morrow, though, what with the exciting life we've been leading, I feel it's just as well that she hasn't been up and about. She's so much more easily upset than I am."

"About to-night, sir," said Girling, as they turned to leave. "I've done the best I can for you. There'll be turkey for dinner and plum-puddin'; but I'd been countin' on gettin' the mince-pies from London, and, from all appearance, they're not goin' to turn up. As regards wine, I think I can satisfy you."

"You won't find me much of a critic, I'm afraid," answered Stuart. "I'm a good enough judge of beer, but I don't fly any higher."

He accompanied Miss Ford to the door of her room.

"I suppose it's no good trying to persuade you to play truant," he said wistfully. "With the Misses Adderley so enthusiastically on the job, you're not really needed, you know."

She hesitated.

"I'll play you fifty-up at billiards," she decided. "Then we'll have to go and get ready for Girling's feast. Do you realize how late it is? Our Christmas Day seems to have been badly wasted."

Stuart flushed, swallowed once or twice, and then spoke with almost unintelligible rapidity.

"I shall always look upon it as one of the happiest Christmases of my life," he stated surprisingly.

Miss Ford stared at him.

"Do you really enjoy this sort of thing?" she asked. "Up to a point it's quite pleasantly exciting, barring the death of poor Major Carew; but, I must say, my idea of a good night is to go to bed and stay there. How much sleep have you had since you arrived at the 'Noah's Ark' Mr. Stuart?"

"I neither know nor care," he retorted recklessly. "All I do know is that in a few days now we shall all go our several ways, and, to you, all this will be a queer, nightmare sort of memory. While, for me …"

Then confusion overcame him. He turned away abruptly.

"I'm sorry," he said. "Let's go up, shall we?"

Angela Ford followed him in silence, but as they entered the billiard-room she spoke.

"Mr. Stuart, you are going on to Redsands from here, aren't you?"

His voice was strained as he answered. He was miserably conscious of having made a fool of himself.

"If I get away in time, I thought of seeing the New Year in there."

"Then, what have I done?"

He swung round on her.

"You?"

"Is there any reason why you should cut me at Redsands? We shall be there together, you know, and unless you've got some reason for not wishing to pursue the acquaintance …"

Stuart strode over to the door and closed it carefully.

"I haven't," he said.

The dinner-gong had already pealed loudly when they emerged from the billiard-room, and, if they succeeded in playing their fifty-up, it would seem to have been a singularly silent game.

"Old Girling's done us proud, all things considered," was Soames's comment as he surveyed the table.

Indeed, for the first time that day, the landlord had managed to bring his guests to the realization that it was Christmas Day. Perhaps the advent of the post, a few minutes before, with its load of greetings forwarded from London, had helped matters; but it is certain that, for a space at least, the cloud of foreboding and suspicion lifted from the "Noah's Ark," and it harked back, if somewhat decorously, to the good old days of punch, pink coats, and jollity. Even Miss Amy became slightly arch over her dessert, and Lord Romsey, who with his family had condescended to dine downstairs, wore an air of benevolent affability that somehow suggested a tactful chairman at a committee meeting. Even the figure of Bates, as seen at intervals through the door, morose and watchful in the lounge, did not serve to cast a blight over the festivities.

Constantine's suggestion that they should forgather in the lounge after dinner met with instant approval; but the same thought was in all their minds, and it was a noticeably quieter party that trooped out of the dining-room. For, from the lounge, they could command a view of the stairs and at least one of the exits, and it would be easy for those members of the party who had undertaken to keep guard in the upper regions to slip away in turn. Constantine was the first to leave them, indignantly refusing Stuart's offer to take his place.

"I won't be treated as a back number," he objected. "Stay here and enjoy yourself, my boy. If you've been cheated out of your fun at Redsands, at least you shan't spend your Christmas skulking behind a bathroom door. Girling's undertaken to watch the first floor, and Bates and two of the outside men are in charge of the barn and the top storey, so neither you nor Soames is needed yet awhile. Make the most of your time!" he added, with a sly glance in the direction of Angela Ford, who was dancing with Trevor to the strains of a decrepit gramophone that he and Miss Hamilton had unearthed in the village.

Stuart protested that he was no dancer, and a far less valuable asset to the party than Constantine; but the old man was adamant.

"If you're determined to treat me as your aged grandfather," he retorted, "I hasten to assure you that this sort of thing no longer amuses me, and, what's more, I find myself a clog on the wheel. That is one of the penalties of growing old, as you will find out for yourself one day. Get into your head that I wish to go and sit behind my door!"

He said good-night, and the storm of protest that arose from the entire party gave the lie to his words. In spite of which he departed, thus missing the great excitement of the evening.

It had struck midnight; the voice of the B.B.C. had proclaimed its last Christmas greeting from the loud-speaker in the bar, and Lord Romsey was, with some difficulty, shepherding the least tractable member of his family up to bed, when Girling hurried into the lounge.

"Perhaps you'd take my place upstairs, Mr. Soames," he said. "They've sent up for me. There's a car just driven up to the door."

With a nod of understanding Soames ran upstairs, while Girling hurried to the door and threw it open.

At first glance it seemed to Stuart that the man who stood on the threshold was the largest he had ever seen. Later he realized that some of his bulk, at least, was due to the thickness of the rough frieze coat he was wearing; but even when he had slipped it off and stood thawing himself by the fire, both his height and breadth of shoulder was arresting. His clean-shaven face and the huge hands he held gratefully to the warmth were red and raw with the cold.

"I'm sorry to disturb you so late in the day," he said pleasantly, "but I've had a time of it getting through at all. I'd be grateful for a bite of something and a bed for a couple of nights."

"I can give you a room, though I'm afraid it will be a small one," answered Girling. "We're a bit full up, as you see. And I'll have supper served in the coffee-room in a minute or two."

"Don't mind how small the room is, provided the bed's large enough," returned the stranger, with a jolly laugh. "What about the car?"

Girling hesitated. He had no mind to tell the new-comer what had been happening to the cars in his barn during the last few nights.

"We're full up in the barn here, sir," he said at last. "Your car would be safer at the wheelwright's, if you're minded to let my man run it down there."

The other looked dubious.

"No need to go routing people out of their beds," he objected. "The car's only a small two-seater. Haven't you a shed you can put her in for to-night?"

"There's a shed," confessed Girling reluctantly; "but it's got no lock, and it's not over weather-tight."

The other laughed.

"Well, no one's going car-stealing on a night like this," he said. "The shed's good enough for me."

He followed Girling upstairs. Trevor looked after him with a grin.

"I wonder what sort of house he'll think he's got into," he said to Stuart, "if he looks out of his bedroom door during the night and finds a prowler on each landing. Anyway, he's hefty enough to tackle a dozen masked burglars."

Stuart nodded.

"He'll be a useful ally, if we do get our man," he agreed. "I wonder who he is?"

Girling answered that question when he rejoined them. He looked badly worried.

"That's just what I hoped wouldn't happen," he said. "The fewer strangers we get the better, till this business is cleared up. The inn's in a fair way towards gettin' a bad name already. As it was, I had to tell him the trouble we've had with the cars, seein' as he was set on leavin' his in the shed. I've left him to find out the rest of the story for himself. I daresay he'll hear it soon enough," he finished despondently.

"What's his name?" asked Soames.

"Captain Macklin. He's from Redsands."

"Redsands!" exclaimed Stuart. "Then the road's clear?"

Girling's gloomy features relaxed into a smile.

"You wouldn't say so if you'd heard his account of how he got here. He's not recommending any one to try it for the next day or two. Seems to think it will be Monday, at least, before the roads are really clear."

"Christmas Day seems a curious day to leave a place like Redsands," remarked Soames thoughtfully.

Stuart's eyes lit up with mirth.

"Another suspect?" he inquired gently. "You're getting insatiable, Soames."

"All the same, it is a funny day to choose," insisted Soames doggedly.

"According to his account there wasn't much to cheer any one up at Redsands," said Girling. "Half empty, he said the place was. This snowfall's done the hotels in properly. Half the people were afraid to start, and the other half didn't get there."

"Did he give any reason for leaving when he did?" asked the pertinacious Soames.

"Said he had to be back in London the day after to-morrow, and wasn't goin' to risk bein' hung up on the way. As it was, he'd meant to make London tonight. Said he was thankful he'd allowed himself the extra day."

"Where have you put him?" asked Soames. "If we're going to watch to-night, we'd better know where he hangs out."

"He's in the room next to Miss Hamilton," said Girling. "At the head of the little staircase near the Misses Adderley. But you needn't worry your head about him, sir. I've seen too many come and go in this place not to size 'em up pretty well, once I've had a word with them. He's what he makes out to be, a retired navy man in business in London."

He took himself off, and shortly afterwards a general move was made in the direction of bed. Those fortunate members of the household who had not undertaken to sit up presumably retired to rest; the others joined Constantine on the second floor before settling down to their job. They learned from him that, with the exception of Miss Connie Adderley, who, draped in a multiplicity of shawls, had padded to and from her bath, and the new-comer, with Girling, on his way to his room, no one had passed that way.

"I forgot to mention Trevor escorting Miss Hamilton to her room," added Constantine. "But there was nothing suspicious about *their* attitude!"

At that moment Melnotte appeared at the top of the stairs. Soames called a cheery good-night to him, but he took no notice. Without a glance in the direction of the little party standing at the door of Stuart's room, he strode down the passage, and, the next moment, his door shut with a resounding bang.

Soames's eyes widened.

"What do you think of that?" he asked. "Sounds like naughty temper to me."

Before any one could answer, Girling came down the short flight of stairs that led to the back premises. He looked even more perturbed than when they had last seen him.

"More trouble," he announced. "Has Mr. Melnotte come up yet?"

"Blew up just now," answered Soames. "What's the trouble with him?"

"I'm thinkin' 'blew up's' the word for it," said Girling. "A fine time I've had with him and Tom Bates downstairs. Now that he knows the road's clear he wants to go off by the first train to-morrow. Tried to get me to send him to the station in the Ford. I told him the trains weren't runnin' regular yet, and he'd have a time in gettin' anywhere, but there was no gettin' him to listen to reason. And me knowin all the time that Bates would stop him, sure as fat#. I didn't want to tell him so to his face, him bein' so touchy like. Then Tom Bates must needs come along, and, what with him bein' none too gentle like, and the young gentleman flying into a rage, I've had my hands full."

"Where did he want to go? Redsands?" asked Stuart.

"Didn't seem to care where he went, so long is he got away from here," answered Girling grimly. "Frantic, he was."

Constantine smiled.

"Another suspect for you, Soames," he said slyly.

Soames grinned good-naturedly.

"Oh, I haven't whitewashed him yet, by a long way. Which reminds me, I've got a little job of my own to see to before I go to my observation-post."

He beckoned Girling on one side, and said something to him in a low voice. Then the two disappeared together in the direction of the back staircase.

"I wonder what he's up to now," said Stuart, gazing after him with an appreciative smile.

"The tiger foiled of his prey," murmured Constantine. "Now that the Romseys are no longer fair game, he's on the prowl for another victim. Melnotte was bound to make a fool of himself, of course, but I'm sorry he's chosen this moment to do it."

"Why do you suppose he's in such a tearing hurry?"

"Sheer fright, part of it." answered Constantine decisively. "He's been aching to get away from this place ever since his adventure the other night. And he's got the dislike of his kind for being mixed up in a police case of any sort. He wants to get clear of it all before it comes to a head. Though, as a matter of fact, he's only anticipating the attitude of the rest of the party. By this time to-morrow they'll all be talking of getting away, and, once they've got the idea into their heads, they'll resent Bates's interference just as much as he does."

Stuart changed into a thick sweater, chatting desultorily with Constantine the while. He was stoking up the fire preparatory to his night's watch when Soames put in an appearance once more. He held a newspaper in his hand.

Stuart stared at him, poker in hand.

"He's struck oil," he announced solemnly, before Soames could speak.

Soames's retort was swift.

"You stick to your little poker," he gibed, "you may need it yet! Joking apart, there is something fishy about this chap Macklin! You thought I was an ass just now when I pointed out that no self-respecting person would travel up from Redsands on Christmas night. Well, he hasn't come from Redsands!"

He held out the paper to Constantine.

"Look at that," he said triumphantly.

Constantine took it.

"It's the late edition of the *Evening Standard*," he said slowly, "for December 24th. I see what you mean."

"Of course. It's obvious. According to Girling he claims to have started from Redsands at ten o'clock this morning. Letters forwarded the night before from London didn't reach us here till seven o'clock to-night, and we're half-way between London and Redsands. This paper couldn't have reached Redsands before he started this morning."

He leaned forward impressively and lowered his voice.

"If the chap that took the emeralds has got them hidden here he's bound to get them away somehow. The phone's been in working order ever since we arrived. What's to have prevented him from ringing up a confederate in London from the post office here? If this fellow, Macklin, stays the night here and goes up to town to-morrow, who's going to stop him? I'm willing to bet that Bates won't. And ten to one he'll have the emeralds in his pocket. Am I talking sense or not?"

Constantine, who was engaged in lighting his pipe, did not answer.

"It sounds sensible enough," commented Stuart, with true Scottish caution. "You're sure the paper's his?"

"It was in the pocket of his car. I had my doubts when Girling reported on him, so, just on the chance, I got Girling to show me where he put his car. First I spotted that it was a London car, which, of course, might not have meant anything. Then I had a look in the pockets, and the first thing I found was this. He's no more come from Redsands than I have! And he bought that paper in London last night!"

CHAPTER XV

WHATEVER his business, it would seem as though that dark horse, Captain Macklin, had brought peace to the "Noah's Ark." The night passed uneventfully, and Stuart went through agonies in his attempts to keep off the overpowering waves of sleep that kept on threatening to overwhelm him. He succeeded in so far that he was able truthfully to assure Soames, when he came up for the third time to inquire whether Macklin had made any move, that that individual had remained closely immured in his room.

He certainly showed no signs next morning of having had anything but a peaceful night, and the sight of his fresh, clean-shaven face filled Stuart, who was feeling jaded and out of sorts, with unfair resentment. Girling reported that all was well with the cars, and that neither he nor Bates had observed anything unusual during the night.

After breakfast, Stuart was amused to see Constantine and Macklin conversing affably by the fire in the lounge. Macklin appeared to be doing most of the talking, and Constantine's face wore that expression of ingenuous sympathy that Stuart was beginning to know only too well. He had little doubt that the other man would respond to it.

It would seem that he had, for when the old man joined Stuart later he was able, at any rate, to verify Soames's suspicions.

"He certainly has not come from Redsands," he said.

"Nor, I should say, has he ever been there. I got him on the subject of music, in which he is genuinely interested. We discussed modern composers, and then I asked him if he had had the luck to hear the Castaldi Quartet, which was booked to play at Redsands during Christmas week. Having confessed to his love for music, I suppose he couldn't very well admit to having missed the most interesting musical event of the Redsands season! Anyway, he committed himself hopelessly by telling me that the quartet had got to Redsands, in spite of the weather, and that he had heard it play twice at the Moot Hall. It was that extra little bit of detail that was his undoing! Owing to the fact that the chess tournament was originally to have taken place at the Moot Hall, I happen to be better informed than he is. As a matter of fact, extensive alterations, which will not be complete for some months, are being made to the hall, and all the fixtures which have been booked there have been transferred to the Excelsior Hotel, so that it is quite impossible that the Castaldi concert could have taken place there. Also, it is difficult to reach the sea without passing the hall, which was a mass of scaffolding when I saw it a month ago, so that it is difficult to believe that any one could stay in Redsands long without discovering that it was not available. I must say that that was the only point on which he gave himself away. His description of the concert was masterly!"

"Then it's one up to Soames this time," observed Stuart. "It's difficult to see what object the fellow can have in lying if he's honest."

Constantine agreed.

"I shall stick closely to my landing while he's here," he said. "And, if I may make a suggestion, this afternoon would be as good a time as any to overhaul your car. I suppose, like everybody else, you will be making tracks directly, and that, I gather, is one of the indispensable ceremonies."

Stuart nodded.

"It's not a bit of work I hanker after," he admitted ruefully. "Apart from the fact that it's a cold and beastly job, it's one I'm not used to, and shall no doubt do very badly. You see, I'm not one of those fortunate people who have always had a car to play about with, and, until now, there's always been an accommodating garage round the corner. However, if I'm to be used to further one of your little schemes, I suppose I must stop putting off the evil day. Am I allowed to rope in Soames as adviser?"

Constantine laughed.

"There's nothing so very Machiavellian in the suggestion," he said. "It merely struck me that, the thief having left himself your car to get away in, it might be as well to stick closely to it for the present. If you don't see that it is in running order, no doubt he will!"

"I wish he would! However, after lunch, I'll go and mess about with it, and I only hope none of the chauffeurs will be there to watch me! Afterwards, Soames can tackle his tyres! That ought to keep him busy for some time. You're not going to ask me to sleep in the barn, are you?"

But Constantine was merciful.

"I'll spare you that," he said. "If I use all my wiles I may be able to persuade Bates to take on the job. If not, I can easily work Soames up to it! He's more of a sticker than you are!"

Stuart, when he reached the barn, was obliged to admit that Constantine was right. Soames was already on the job, working over his tyres with the thoroughness and efficiency that one would expect of him. It was fortunate that the barn was a large one, for two of the chauffeurs were also at work. One of them Stuart recognized as belonging to the Romseys, the other was a stranger to him.

"Who is the other fellow?" he asked Soames in a low voice. "I don't remember to have seen him before."

"A chap called Grimes. He belongs to the Citroen over there," answered Soames. "I've been giving him a hand. He's not fit to work, but he says his master's expecting him at Redsands to-morrow, if he's able to drive. He's the chap that came in the day you arrived, and went down that night with lumbago. I should say he'd been pretty bad by the look of it."

Stuart told him of Constantine's suggestion.

"There's something to be said for the idea," was Soames's comment. "There's no harm in keeping an eye on the place, especially as by to-night most of the cars will be in working order. I'd best lend you a hand now, and keep my own job till after you've gone. I'm dashed if I'll watch here to-night, though! I'm beginning to wonder what my bed looks like!"

He took Stuart in hand, and proved an admirable instructor. By the time he had finished Stuart knew more about his own car than he could have believed possible in so short a time, and had quite forgotten his reluctance to begin the job. He was also to see a manifestation of that inherent kindliness that was one of Soames's most engaging characteristics.

He had just satisfied himself that Stuart's engine was running sweetly, and was wiping his hands on a bit of cotton waste, when he gave vent to a muttered exclamation.

"That chap'll have to go back to bed," he said. "He'll knock himself up for good at this rate."

Stuart followed the direction of his eyes. One of the chauffeurs was standing over the other, who was sitting on an upturned box, his head in his hands. Soames strode over to them.

"What's up?" he asked in his bluff, friendly way. "Is the job too much for you?"

The man looked up. His face was drawn with pain.

"It's my back, sir," he gasped. "I thought I was through the worst of it when I came down, but it's the stoopin's done it. All tied up again, I am."

"And there'll be no untying you if you stay in this ice-house any longer. Bed's the place for you, if you really think of driving to-morrow."

He cast a practised eye over the man's work.

"I'd finish it myself, sir," put in Lord Romsey's chauffeur. "But his lordship's set on getting off as soon as possible, and I've got my work cut out to get through with it"

Soames nodded.

"I seem to be the only one of the lot that isn't in a tearing hurry," he observed with a grin. "I don't mind making the weather an excuse for staying away from my job for another day or two! My car can wait." He turned to the sick man.

"You hop along back to bed," he said. "There's nothing here that I can't tackle within the next hour. Don't you worry about it. Leave it to me, and then, if you're fit to move to-morrow, you can join your master. But, if you take my advice, you'll do as I do—take a few days off and blame it on the weather!" Cutting short the man's thanks, Soames helped him to his feet, and hustled him out of the barn. It was all he could do to straighten himself, and the other chauffeur had to give him an arm or he would not have managed the short distance between the barn and the house.

"That's a good bit of work," said Soames as he rejoined Stuart. "I've got my excuse now to stay on here indefinitely. You might ask old Girling for a lantern when you go in, and send it out to me."

"You got your excuse to do a damned kind action," returned Stuart warmly. "Not many people would have bothered about the poor chap."

Soames reddened.

"You'd have done the same yourself, if it wasn't that you're such a mug at this kind of thing," he retorted. "It's a comfort to think that, at least, you know a little more now than you did when I took you in hand! No, you can't help me! You'd only be in the way. But, for Heaven's sake, don't forget that lantern. It'll be dark in another half-hour."

"I'll bring it out myself," Stuart assured him, "if you're sure I'm too much of an ass to be of any help."

"Quite," was Soames's unflattering rejoinder.

As Stuart was leaving the barn he called after him.

"By the way, you might give Girling a hint about that chap. Tell him to see that he's got hot bottles, or whatever he ought to have."

"I had thought of that," returned Stuart meekly. "I'm rather good at those more effeminate jobs."

He interviewed Girling, and then visited the sick man, and saw to it that he had all that he needed. He found him in bed, in comparative comfort, and very grateful for the kindness that had been shown him.

"It's not the way I'd reckoned to spend Christmas," he said, with an attempt at humour. "But, from all accounts, it's been a queer time for everybody. Do you reckon they're on the track of the murderer, sir?"

"If Bates knows anything, he's keeping it to himself," answered Stuart. "You didn't hear or see anything suspicious, I suppose?"

Grimes shook his head.

"Lying here, with the door shut, I shouldn't be likely to. Lucky for me I didn't! If the house had been on fire I couldn't have moved, even to turn round in bed. Makes you feel a bit helpless when there's anything going on," he finished with a rueful smile.

Stuart left him, promising to bring him some books and magazines later, and went to his room. To his surprise he found Constantine there, a travelling chessboard on his knees, busy composing a chess problem.

"I seem to have taken possession of your quarters," he apologized with a smile. "Turn me out if I'm in the way."

Stuart hastened to reassure him.

"I've got a letter or two to write," he said, "that's all. Yesterday's post made me thoroughly ashamed of myself. I'd completely forgotten Christmas."

"Which you'd never have been allowed to do at Redsands! It was a shame to trespass on your good nature, but I stupidly let my fire out, and didn't want to bother the maids to re-light it. You might leave that open, if you don't mind," he went on quickly, as Stuart prepared to shut the door. "There will be no harm in keeping track of the people who use this passage."

Stuart grinned.

"At bottom, you're as bad as Soames," he exclaimed. "Between the two of you, you ought to catch somebody!"

"Only, unlike that butterfly Soames, I have a pretty shrewd idea where my goal lies," returned Constantine quietly. "Soames flits from flower to flower, and only settles for a moment on each. It's a fruitless method."

The idea of Soames in the role of butterfly was too much for Stuart.

"Have you any more poetic comparisons to make?" he asked.

"One might compare the Misses Adderley to a daisy and a rather full-blown peony," he said thoughtfully.

"Not bad," Stuart agreed. "Miss Amy's ingenuous little round face isn't unlike a daisy. She tells me that her sister is thinking of coming down to-morrow."

"I don't fancy she'll get far beyond thinking. Miss Connie is much too comfortable where she is. She's the kind that takes to her bed years before she dies, and little Miss Amy was intended by Providence to nurse other people. They're marvellously true to type, those two," was Constantine's appreciative comment.

As it turned out, they might have spared themselves the draught from the open door. No one came down the passage save Captain Macklin, on his way to his room. But just before the gong sounded for dinner Constantine raised his head and listened.

"That was either Macklin's door or Miss Hamilton's," he said.

"You can hardly take exception to their going in and out of their rooms," remarked Stuart mildly.

"I don't," retorted Constantine. "But I like to know where they're going. Neither of them has come past this door."

A few minutes later Miss Hamilton came down the passage. Instead of coming from her room she was on her way to it.

"That settles it," said Constantine. "It was Macklin. He must have been using the back staircase."

But when they reached the dining-room, Captain Macklin was not there. Neither did he turn up later, and Soames was a prey to the direst forebodings, all through the meal, in consequence. The moment it was over he sought out Girling.

"He says he's dining with the vicar!" he announced incredulously, on his return. "Did he give you the impression when he arrived that he knew any one in this neighbourhood?"

Stuart gave vent to his mirth.

"If you'll tell me how one gives an impression of that sort on first entering the portals of a country inn, I might be able to tell you," he said. "There's no earthly reason why he shouldn't dine with the vicar, unless you've added *him* to your black list since I saw you last?"

"Macklin's car is still in the shed," went on Soames doggedly. "I went out to see. All the same, if he's walked off with the emeralds, don't blame me!"

"I should be the first to admit that you had done everything in your power to avert such a catastrophe," asserted Stuart solemnly. "Did you manage to convince Girling of the danger?"

"Girling's altogether too slack about the whole thing," said Soames disgustedly. "The only thing that worries him is the reputation of his blessed inn. If I can get hold of Bates I'm going to talk to him, but he seems to have taken himself off too."

"Perhaps he, too, is dining with the vicar," suggested Constantine meekly.

Soames treated his remark with the silence it deserved, and took himself off on business of his own.

"He's gone to keep an eye on the barn," said Stuart. "And he'll sit in some icy nook all the evening, for all the world like a dog watching a rat-hole. I'm beginning to feel a real affection for Soames."

Constantine agreed.

"There's something engaging, even about his foibles," he said. "And he's a very sound chess player. I hope to enjoy many games with him in the future."

Stuart looked up sharply.

"Then he's not one of your suspects!" he exclaimed.

Constantine's eyes twinkled.

"I congratulate you on your powers of deduction," he said. "But you won't get anything more out of me."

But Stuart had yet another shot in his locker.

"By the way," he observed casually, "I looked into your room on my way down to dinner, and was glad to see that your fire was burning beautifully."

Constantine's voice was very bland as he answered—

"Was it? Then that nice little maid must have been attending to it. I needn't have obtruded myself on you after all."

At about ten o'clock Stuart went to his room and busied himself with his belated Christmas letters. He left the door ajar, with the result that, at about a quarter to ten, he saw Macklin returning from his dinner engagement. Though he had flouted Soames's suspicions he took the trouble to rise from his chair and stand listening in the doorway after Macklin had turned up the short flight of steps to his room. Thus it was that he caught the sound of murmured conversation, and was sufficiently curious to step lightly along the passage.

He arrived at the foot of the steps just in time to see him parting from Miss Hamilton. Neither of them was aware of Stuart, standing watching at the foot of the steps, and when Macklin handed the girl a good-sized key, he did so quite openly. His voice was so carefully lowered, however, that Stuart could not hear what he said as he gave it to her. Then they both disappeared into their respective rooms.

Stuart hesitated for a moment, then he hastened down the passage, and called softly to Soames.

"Is there a communicating door between your room and Trevor's?" he asked, as Soames appeared at the foot of the stairs.

"Yes. Why do you want to know?"

"Only that your room corresponds with the one Captain Macklin is using at this end of the passage."

Soames's eyes widened.

"But he's got Miss Hamilton next door to him," he said.

"I know," was Stuart's cryptic rejoinder. "That's all I wanted to know."

He withdrew so swiftly that he missed Soames's next question, and returned to his room, gleefully conscious of the fact that he had, at least, left him something to ponder over.

About fifteen minutes later Miss Hamilton passed his door on her way downstairs, presumably to Mrs. van Dolen's room. Ten minutes afterwards she returned, evidently on her way to bed. Of Macklin there was no sign, and Stuart was certain that his door had not opened. At 11.30 Constantine joined him, and he told him what had occurred.

"The key was a good sized one," he said. "The kind that might fit any of these old-fashioned doors. I'll wager it was either the key of his door or of the communicating door between their two rooms."

Constantine, who was standing with his back to the fire, frowned.

"It really looks as if Soames was going to have the satisfaction of saying 'I told you so,'" he said. "Macklin is a darker horse than I thought."

He looked up sharply at the sound of an opening door, then relaxed as Miss Amy Adderley's blameless figure trotted past on the way to the bath.

He turned again to Stuart.

"If Captain Macklin—" he began, then, with a swiftness astonishing in one of his years, made a dive for the door.

But he was too late. As he reached it, the key turned on the other side.

Stuart, who had reached his side, tried the handle, but the door was securely locked.

Constantine eyed it malevolently.

"Caught!" he said bitterly. "Did you see who did it?"

Stuart shook his head.

"I'd got my back to it," he answered. "And I never heard a sound. Whoever it was must have slipped down behind Miss Adderley."

He shook the door violently, but there was not a sound from outside. Then he tried shouting, but the door was too solid for his voice to travel far, and, in any case, Miss Connie Adderley, his only neighbour, was too deaf to hear him.

He turned to find Constantine standing by the fire, his finger on the bell.

"Unless they've cut the wire this ought to bring some one," he said.

It did, but not until another five minutes had passed, and they had to wait, helpless and exasperated, until they heard the footsteps of the chambermaid and the sound of the key turning once more in the lock.

While Constantine was explaining to her what had happened, Stuart went down the passage and up the flight of steps leading to Macklin's room. As he reached it Macklin came out.

"Anything wrong?" he asked. "I thought I heard some one shouting."

"You did," answered Stuart. "Some bright spirit locked me into my room. You didn't hear any one down this end, did you?"

"Not a soul. What did they do it for?"

"That's what I want to know," returned Stuart, as he went back to his room.

He found Miss Amy in the doorway, much perturbed by this new menace to their security.

"It's a dreadful thought," she wailed, "that one might be locked in at any moment. Supposing there was a fire!"

"You could always come out through the communicating door into my room," said Stuart soothingly.

"But supposing you were locked in too!" she objected, and he found that argument impossible to meet.

She was eventually sufficiently reassured to return to her room. Not, however, until she had seen Stuart take his doorkey out of the lock and slip it into his pocket.

He did not share with her his conviction that, in all probability, most of the locks on the bedroom doors were alike, and the keys interchangeable.

He accompanied her to her room and saw her safely inside, then made his way along the passage, only to meet Constantine coming out of the bathroom.

"He couldn't have been in there," said Stuart. "Miss Amy was in possession when it happened."

"I know," answered the old man calmly. "All the same, I propose to keep the bathroom door locked till the time arrives for my own nightly ablutions."

Stuart stared at him.

"I call that pretty arbitrary," he said. "Supposing some one else wants a bath?"

Constantine stowed the key away in his pocket.

"You know where to come for this if you want one," he answered. "And I happen to know that every one else on this landing baths in the morning, with the exception of Captain Macklin, who will simply have to go without."

But at midnight when, persuaded by the untiring Constantine, Stuart lay down on his bed for a couple of hours' sleep, Captain Macklin had shown no desire to wash, and Constantine, still in triumphant possession of the key, was comfortably established with a book in his old place by the door. He had promised to wake the younger man so that he might relieve him in two hours' time, and Stuart, after five minutes of intense wakefulness, drifted off into complete oblivion.

He was awakened by the low murmur of voices, and opened his eyes to see Mrs. Orkney Cloude in conversation with Constantine in the doorway. He looked at his watch. It was close on two o'clock.

Hastily getting to his feet he joined them.

His first thought was that Mrs. Cloude was looking extraordinarily pretty. Her hair was in disorder, and she had evidently flung a wrap hastily over her nightclothes. She had obviously only just arrived, and was still panting from her race up the stairs.

"Geoffrey's trying to get in," she was saying; "but the door's locked, and there's a most frightful shindy going on inside! I've been trying to find that policeman, but he's nowhere to be seen!"

Constantine seized her arm and hurried her out of the room.

"Put your finger on the bell and keep it there," he called over his shoulder to Stuart. "Girling's bound to hear it in time. But on no account stir from this landing till I come back!"

With that he departed, sweeping Mrs. Cloude with him. But Stuart was not to be disposed of so easily. He followed them on to the landing.

"Here, I say! What's it all about?" he demanded.

Constantine took no notice, but Mrs. Cloude turned a startled face in his direction.

"Something awful is going on in Mrs. van Dolen's room," said she, "and we can't get in!"

CHAPTER XVI

IT SEEMED HOURS to Stuart before Constantine returned, though, as he afterwards discovered, the old man could not have been gone for more than five minutes. He arrived breathless with the haste with which he had mounted the stairs.

"You must admit that I've been merciful," he gasped. "I left at the most exciting moment in the game! If you're quick, you'll get there just in time. Off with you!"

"Then there really was some one in Mrs. van Dolen's room?"

"From the noise I should say there were at least half a dozen of them!"

Stuart hesitated.

"I don't like to use you like this, sir," he said. "If you really do feel that this landing ought to be guarded, I'm ready to stay."

Constantine picked up his book.

"Wild horses wouldn't drag me from this landing," he announced contentedly. "And, before you go, I'll tell you this, my friend. Bates may be arresting the murderer of Carew at this moment, for all I know, but he hasn't laid hands on the emeralds. Put that in your pipe and smoke it!"

But Stuart had little time to ponder over these cryptic words. Things happened so swiftly and unexpectedly during the next half-hour that Constantine and his conundrums went completely out of his head.

Every occupant of the "Noah's Ark" seemed to be gathered outside Mrs. van Dolen's door when he arrived there. It was still closed, and presented an ominously blank surface. Mrs. Orkney Cloude, as they continued to call her, joined him.

"Girling and the policeman have gone round by the balcony," she informed him. "They thought they could get in more easily there."

"Is Mrs. van Dolen all right?"

"Goodness knows! She hasn't made a sound, but there's been a struggle of some kind, and we could hear a man's voice."

There was a cry from one of the maids in the foreground.

"Get back! They're coming out!"

The crowd surged back on to Stuart and Mrs. Cloude. Then the door opened and Girling came out. On his face was a broad grin of triumph.

"We've got one of them, at any rate," he announced.

Mrs. Cloude pushed her way through the crowd, and the servants fell back to let her pass. Stuart followed her through the door and into the bedroom.

The first person his eyes fell on was Captain Macklin. His collar had been torn from its stud and was under one ear, and there was a bruise on his cheek-bone that was colouring rapidly, but he seemed as cheerful and self-possessed as ever. His hand was grasping the cuff of an individual even more battered than himself, who was dabbing his bleeding knuckles with a handkerchief, considerably hampered in his work by the handcuffs that encircled his wrists.

Stuart gave a gasp as he recognized the sick chauffeur he had tucked up in bed so tenderly only that afternoon.

Mrs. van Dolen was nowhere to be seen.

"Better get out of this!" said Macklin briskly. "Can we use your office, landlord?"

"Right, Inspector," agreed Girling, who was engaged in shooing the maids down the passage as though they were a pack of hens.

Trundling his silent prisoner in front of him, Macklin led' the way, Stuart treading dose on his heels. As they entered Girling's little office Macklin turned and caught sight of him.

"I'm afraid I played a dirty trick on you to-night, Mr. Stuart," he said, with a friendly smile. "I had to change places with Mrs. van Dolen unperceived. There was too much risk of running into the servants on the back stairs, so there was nothing for it but to lock you into your peep-hole for a minute or two. You see, coming fresh to the job as I did, I couldn't take any of you for granted, and could only let Bates and Mr. Girling into the secret."

Stuart could not help laughing.

"It's only fair to tell you that we've been cherishing the basest suspicions of you," he answered. "We knew you hadn't come from Redsands."

Macklin's eyes widened.

"That's one up to you," he exclaimed. "I must have made a bad slip somewhere! Perhaps, some time, you'll put me wise to how you caught me. By the way, Macklin's not my name. Detective-Inspector Arkwright, at your service. As you guessed, I came straight down from the Yard."

He swung round and faced his prisoner.

"Now we'll have a word with this chap. I won't bother you with all the names we've known him under, Mr. Stuart, but his friends call him Puggy Walker, because he began his career in the ring. And I will say this for you, you haven't forgotten everything you learned there, Puggy!" he finished, fingering his cheek tenderly.

"You've no call to bring that up against me, Mr. Arkwright," muttered Walker sullenly. "If I'd known it was you I'd have come quiet; but I can't see in the dark."

"Thought you'd only got a woman to deal with, eh? "

Walker snorted.

"I knew it wasn't no woman as soon as our little party began! No. I thought it was the village flatty."

He cast a vicious glance at Bates, who stood, stolid as ever, by his side. But if he hoped to draw him he was doomed to disappointment.

"It may be a comfort to you to know that, if it hadn't been for this officer here, we shouldn't have got you to-night," was Arkwright's brisk retort. "Let's have that parcel I left with you, will you, Mr. Girling?"

Girling unlocked the front of his heavy bureau and handed Arkwright a parcel wrapped in newspaper.

"Bates found this up the chimney in a box-room upstairs," went on Arkwright, as he undid the string. "He brought it to me, and, when I heard of the sick chauffeur, my thoughts naturally turned to you, Puggy. You've played that game once too often, son. Why don't you fellows vary your methods?"

Stuart's eyes were on the man's face. The colour was ebbing slowly from it, leaving even the thin lips white. He moistened them with his tongue before he answered.

"Whatever you've got in there's got nothing to do with me," he asserted hoarsely.

"Then why did you try to fetch it to-night?" snapped Arkwright. "You'd got your hand on the box-room door when you saw Bates at the end of the passage. As a matter of fact, you'd been under observation ever since I arrived."

He undid his parcel and took out the object it contained.

"I suggest that you were going to wash this, and put it back in the car," he said. "Though why you left it so late I can't imagine."

Stuart broke into the conversation.

"I believe I can explain that," he exclaimed. "He probably did try on the night I locked the box-room door. It was the only door that I forgot to unlock next morning, and I only remembered it to-day."

Arkwright nodded.

"What about it, Walker?" he asked. "You're not bound to talk, you know, but you may as well tell us now as later."

He held out the object in his hand to Stuart.

"You see?"

Stuart saw and shuddered. It was a heavy sparer and, even to his unpractised eye, it was obvious that the stains on it were not those of rust.

Walker found his voice.

"Whoever used that has got the emeralds," he retorted defiantly. "Wait till you find them before you try to put it on me!"

"I wonder what makes you so sure of that, now?" said Arkwright gently. "We've no evidence that the man who killed Major Carew was after the emeralds. That may have been another job altogether."

He was watching his man closely, but, conscious of how nearly he had blundered, Walker was moving very warily now.

"You won't find no emeralds on me," he repeated stubbornly. "I'd have been out of this, snow or no snow, long ago, if—"

He broke off and relapsed into stubborn silence.

Stuart's excitement got the better of him.

"If some one hadn't pinched them from you," he cut in, completing the man's sentence for him.

Walker looked up quickly. Only for a second was he taken unawares; but that second was his undoing, and Stuart knew that his shot had found its mark.

"You hid them in a sack of bran in the barn, and some one took them from there," he went on, almost involuntarily.

Arkwright placed a restraining hand on his arm.

"Just a minute," he said. "Keep anything that you know to yourself till I come back."

He hurried out of the room, and Stuart heard his footsteps on the stairs outside.

In a few minutes he was back again, carrying a coat and a dirty shirt over his arm.

He threw them on the table and examined them rapidly, concentrating his attention on the sleeves and buttonholes. It was not till he had turned down the cuffs of the shirt that his search was rewarded.

"Another score for you, Mr. Stuart," he observed, as he shook the open cuff over the table, and watched a little drift of bran trickle out of the fold. He picked up the spanner and turned to the hand-cuffed man.

"I think it was you who said that the man who used this got the emeralds," he said, all the lightness gone from his voice now. "I'll talk to you again when I've heard what Mr. Stuart here has got to say. You can take him, Bates. Got another man who will go with you?"

Bates nodded.

"There's Mr. Girling's Joe as'll oblige, if he'll spare him," he said.

He opened the door to find Joe's face on the other side of it. He and the entire staff of the "Noah's Ark" were congregated in the passage.

When the door had closed behind him and his prisoner, Arkwright turned to Stuart.

"Who *has* got the emeralds, Mr. Stuart?" he asked, with a twinkle in his eye.

Stuart laughed.

"I wish I knew," he answered ruefully. "I admit that that's baffled us."

"'Us' being yourself and the big gentleman with the gimlet eyes?" suggested Arkwright.

"It's as good a name for him as any," admitted Stuart. "What little I do know is certainly due to him."

"Has he got anything else up his sleeve?" asked the other.

Stuart hesitated. He did not propose to put a spoke in Constantine's wheel if he could help it.

But Arkwright's eyes were on him.

"He has, eh? Where is he now?"

"Keeping an eye on the landing outside my room," answered Stuart, and immediately regretted it.

"Then we may take it that he's got a good reason for being there," reflected Arkwright. "Who is on that landing? I've got a plan of the rooms upstairs, but I can't place them off-hand."

"Miss Hamilton, the Misses Adderley, Constantine, Melnotte, Soames, Trevor, and myself," answered Stuart.

"And the emeralds, if your Dr. Constantine., is all I take him to be," added Arkwright. "I don't see him watching a mouse-hole unless there's a very substantial mouse in it. Do you know, I think we'll pay your friend a visit."

Stuart agreed with alacrity. He anticipated a considerable amount of entertainment from the interview.

A chuckle from Girling, who had been once more dispersing his staff in the doorway, made them pause.

"There's the doctor himself," he announced, as Constantine's face appeared over his shoulder.

"Dr. Livingstone, I presume? In other words, Detective-Inspector Arkwright," he remarked, the wrinkles round his eyes deepening.

This was more than Stuart could bear.

"Dr. Constantine, how do you do it?" he murmured.

"By the simplest of all methods, letting the other person talk," answered Constantine. "I met Mrs. van Dolen in the passage upstairs. There was nothing, literally nothing, she did not tell me," he finished meditatively, "except one thing."

"What was that?" asked Arkwright appreciatively.

"When you were coming up to ask why I was playing Cinderella," concluded the old man slyly.

Arkwright chuckled.

"I'm more interested to know why you have abandoned your post," he said.

Constantine turned up the collar of his greatcoat and buttoned it deliberately.

"Because I have found another place more worthy of my attention," he answered. "With your approval, we will now adjourn to the barn."

CHAPTER XVII

WITH A whimsical glance at Stuart, Arkwright prepared to follow Constantine.

"Do you know anything about this?" he asked in a low voice.

Stuart shook his head, but his heart warmed towards the Scotland Yard man. There was nothing of derision in his attitude towards the old man, rather he seemed to appreciate his foibles and realize that they were but the natural manifestation of an unusual and interesting personality. It was evident that the fact that he chose to wrap his discoveries in an almost childish veil of mystery did not rob them of their value in Arkwright's eyes.

"So you've decided to abandon your post upstairs?" he observed, as they went down the passage. Constantine cast a glance over his shoulder.

"I've left Soames in charge of a very interesting situation," was all he would vouchsafe, and Arkwright did not press him further.

Constantine opened the door into the yard, being careful to make as little noise as possible. He cast an eye on the yard, then beckoned to Arkwright.

"Look," he said.

Stuart, peering over the other's shoulder, could see light move inside the barn. Whoever was at work there was evidently carrying a torch in his hand.

Constantine led the way across the yard. The crackle of their footsteps on the frozen snow made so light a sound that it was unlikely to carry through the heavy door of the barn. Half-way across the yard he paused and faced Arkwright.

"May I give you a word of advice?" he asked.

"Of course, sir," was the answer.

"Then I would recommend you to detain the person you find in there, no matter whom it may be. That is, if you want a full bag to-night."

"I do," came back Arkwright's emphatic whisper.

He took an electric torch from his pocket, stepped swiftly across the intervening space to the barn door, and threw it open.

As he did so, the light within went out.

There was a moment of absolute silence while the inspector and Miss Amy Adderley faced each other. She stood, plainly revealed in the circle of light cast by the torch, her little round face utterly expressionless, her hands still clutching the oil-can from which she had been filling the tank of Stuart's car. She wore the felt hat and heavy coat in which Stuart had first met her.

Then Arkwright spoke.

"May I ask what you are doing here, Miss Adderley?" he demanded.

She came forward, blinking a little, as though blinded by the light.

"It's Captain Macklin, isn't it?" she murmured vaguely.

Then the heavy oil-can swept upwards, and Arkwright's torch fell with a clatter to the ground, leaving the barn in darkness. It was a bold move, and might very well have succeeded if she had not been too dazzled by the light to observe the two men standing behind him. As it was, she ran full tilt into them.

There was a short struggle, during which Stuart's shins suffered surprisingly, before she stood passive, Arkwright's hand gripping her cuff.

"You've done it," she said. "I'll come with you."

On the way to the house she spoke again.

"I never set foot in Major Carew's room that night," she said.

"I'm inclined to believe you," answered Arkwright. "Who put him out?"

"I don't know."

"That I don't believe," said Arkwright cheerfully; "but you can keep your information to yourself for the present. I'm bound to warn you that anything you say may be used in evidence against you."

"I know all about that," she answered, with a placidity that astonished Stuart. From their manner she and Arkwright might have been discussing the weather. "I'm British by birth, you know, though it's a long time since I operated in this country. That's why I wasn't wise to you. I ought to have guessed that a split was about due by now. I'll talk. May as well do it now as later."

Once inside Girling's office, Arkwright planted her on the hearthrug, and, placing himself between her and the door, observed her closely. She bore the scrutiny with complete equanimity, though there was a hint of derision in her eyes. When he pulled out an official-looking envelope from his pocket and examined the photographs it contained, she smiled openly.

"Well?" she asked.

He grinned.

"Got it, I think. Must have been a bit blind myself, but it's a good make-up, and I'd never seen either of you. Belle Gearie, isn't it? And the lady upstairs is Flo."

"All I'll say to that is that it's up to you to prove it."

"Flo must be feeling a bit neglected, by the way," he continued. "It strikes me it's about time I paid her a visit."

He dived into his pocket and produced a pair of handcuffs.

"I'm sorry to inconvenience you," he said; "but, as you see, we're short-handed, and I shall have to leave you in charge of Girling. You wouldn't like to tell me where the emeralds are before I go, I suppose?"

She shook her head.

"I should not," she answered emphatically. "Even if I knew, which I don't."

"I shall have to ask your mother, then. Here, Girling!"

He snapped the cuffs round her wrists. Then he took the key out of the door and handed it to Girling.

"Lock yourself in when we've gone," he said, "and keep a close eye on the lady. This little job oughtn't to take us long."

On the way upstairs he spoke over his shoulder to the two men.

"They're the Gearies, all right," he explained. "The New York police notified us of their arrival, and we've been on the look-out for them; but I admit that I never expected to find them here. Must have been on their way to Redsands. Mother and daughter they are, and two of the cleverest operators in the United States, but they're not known to us here. It's possible we shall have trouble with the mother. She's down in the report as 'likely to carry fire-arms.'"

"I don't think so," said Constantine mildly.

Arkwright halted and swung round on him.

"What *have* you been doing up there?" he demanded.

Constantine looked the picture of innocence.

"Nothing, I assure you. But Miss Connie Adderley was in the bath when I came down, and I can answer for it that she was carrying nothing but a sponge when she went into the bathroom."

"She's probably out of it by now, and dealing with your friend Mr. Soames," remarked Arkwright grimly.

Constantine shook his head.

"When I left them he was on one side of the door and she was on the other," he said. "And I didn't anticipate any trouble, as the key was in my pocket."

He held out his hand with the key lying in the palm.

Arkwright stared at him, then he threw back his head and laughed.

"You haven't got the emeralds up your sleeve, by any chance, as well, sir?" he inquired.

"Not exactly," answered Constantine composedly; "but, if they're still where I last saw them, I think I can hand them to you."

It was a comedy after his own heart, and he was playing it with a gusto that delighted Arkwright.

"Lead the way, sir," he exclaimed, stepping aside to let the old man pass. "You've stage-managed the affair so well up to now, that it's only fair you should be in at the finish."

But Constantine drew back.

"The fun is over, so far as I'm concerned," he said, the glint of humour dying in his eyes. "We've arrived at a part of the business which I heartily dislike. I've got a genuine admiration for those women, you know, and when I compare them with the real owner of the emeralds, I could almost wish they had got away tonight. They've been up against a very dangerous antagonist, and their pluck and skill was amazing."

"I have your word for it that you won't connive at their escape?" demanded Arkwright swiftly.

Constantine smiled.

"You're crediting me with more ingenuity than I possess," he said. "And, if it's any comfort to you, though I may be a misguided old person, my instincts are generally on the side of the law. But I prefer the police to do their own dirty work, if I may say so without offence."

"It's what we're paid for," answered Arkwright dryly, as he led the way to the second landing.

They found Soames leaning stolidly against the bathroom door. His stolid face bore a look of perturbation, however, and he was unfeignedly glad to see them. There was not a sound from the other side of the door.

"I say, you know," he exclaimed doubtfully. "It was a bit strong, locking the old lady in like that. She all but had hysterics when she found she couldn't get out, and she hasn't made a sound for the past five minutes. I hope to goodness she hasn't fainted."

"It's all right, Soames," answered Constantine. "Inspector Ark-wright's in charge now."

Soames's face was a study as he stepped aside to let the inspector get to the door.

Arkwright unlocked it.

"You can come out, Miss Adderley," he called out.

The door opened slowly, and Miss Connie Adderley stood in the opening. She wore a dressing-gown and carried a sponge in one hand, a big jar of bath salts in the other.

"What happened?" she asked in the husky whisper that was habitual to her. "Did the door jam?"

Constantine stepped forward. He had meant to keep out of this final scene, but his sense of drama was too strong for him.

"The door was locked, Miss Adderley," he said. "Let me carry those for you."

He placed a hand on the bath salts, but she shrank from him, clutching them to her.

"I can't hear what he says," she murmured, with an appealing glance at Stuart. "I've left my trumpet in the bedroom."

Arkwright, with a firmness that made resistance useless, took the sponge and the bath salts from her.

"You won't need your trumpet any longer, Mrs. Gearie," he said briskly. "The game's up. We've got your daughter, and now we'll take you, if you don't mind. Get a coat on over those things, and we'll see what sort of accommodation Bates can rig up for you."

Constantine held out his hand, and, automatically, Arkwright handed him Miss Connie's impedimenta, keeping a firm hold on her shoulder the while. She twisted under his grasp, realized his immense strength, searched his countenance to see if he were bluffing, and then suddenly capitulated. There was a business-like element about the Gearies that appealed to Stuart's sense of humour.

"All right," she assented, in a voice totally unlike the one she habitually used. "I can put a few things in a bag, I suppose?"

"Provided you do it in my presence," said Arkwright, leading her down the passage and into her bedroom.

It presented an unusually neat aspect, tidy though the Misses Adderley had always been. Their modest luggage was packed and strapped as for a journey, and Miss Connie's coat and hat were placed ready on the bed.

"Going away?" queried Arkwright, with a gleam of humour in his eye.

"There was nothing to prevent our leaving, that I know of," she snapped. "What you're holding us for now, I don't know."

"For being in unlawful possession of a car would about meet it, I think," Arkwright informed her suavely. "There may be other charges of a more serious nature."

For a moment she looked nonplussed.

"Mr. Stuart would have lent us his car if we'd asked for it," she muttered.

"The point being that you didn't ask for it," Arkwright reminded her. "Your daughter was taken in the act of removing it from the barn. Which of these do you wish to take?"

He pointed to the two neat suit-cases standing by the bed, and waited with interest to see which she would choose. He was convinced that she would not leave without the emeralds if she could help it.

Her only answer was to open one of the cases and remove her toilet articles from it. These she packed in the other, Arkwright watching her closely the while.

"That's got enough for the two of us," she said, as she closed it.

Arkwright picked it up and stood holding it while she removed her dressing-gown. As he had surmised, she was fully dressed, all but her shoes and stockings, underneath. He waited while she put them on.

"Anything else you wish to take?" he asked.

He was frankly puzzled. The fact that she had shown no perturbation when he took possession of the suit-case argued that the emeralds were not in it. It was beginning to look as though they had found a hiding-place for them so safe that they could afford to leave them in it until they were in a position to fetch them.

She glanced at him with a look of real malice, very different from her daughter's debonair humour, in her eyes.

"Meaning those emeralds, I suppose," she retorted. "If I'd got them, I'd take them all right."

They were leaving the room when her eyes fell on Constantine, still patiently holding the paraphernalia of her bath.

"I'll take those," she exclaimed. "I suppose one can wash at your police station."

Arkwright nodded and put down the suit-case. Constantine obediently handed her the sponge.

She knelt down, opened the case and tucked the sponge into a pocket, then she held out her hand for the bath salts.

"Those cost five dollars a jar, I'd have you know," she said.

But Constantine shook his head gently, and, with the jar still under his arm, drifted out of the room and down the passage.

It was then that the scene for which Arkwright had prepared them earlier in the evening took place. The almost painfully correct little spinster from Tunbridge Wells became a spitting termagant, and Stuart marvelled at Arkwright's forbearance as she writhed and twisted in his huge hands, employing language as forcible as that used by her sisters on this side of the Atlantic, but infinitely more picturesque. It ended by Arkwright's picking her up bodily, carrying her downstairs, and depositing her beside her daughter in Girling's office.

He stayed long enough to arrange for their accommodation, pending their removal next day to London, and then made his way hot-foot to Constantine's room.

The old man was sitting by his bedroom fire, peacefully smoking his pipe, and delightedly parrying the questions of those of the house-party who had managed to crowd into the room. Mrs. van Dolen was the only one of them who might be said to have entirely lost her temper, but the baffled curiosity on the faces of most of his audience bore testimony to the amount of enjoyment the old man had been getting out of the situation.

Mrs. van Dolen turned on Arkwright as he entered.

"I suppose you consider yourself in authority here," she exclaimed, her voice shaking with fury. "Perhaps you'll kindly tell me whether my emeralds have been found or not, and whether it's true that it's this Dr. Constantine here that has found them?"

Arkwright, who had already had his fill of Mrs. van Dolen that evening, set her gently aside.

"You must ask Dr. Constantine that," he said, his eyes on the old man's face. What he read there told him that his suspicions were correct.

"What about it, sir?" he asked; and Stuart realized gratefully that he was not going to clear the room and cheat Constantine of his dramatic moment.

The old chess player rose, opened a cupboard; and took out the jar of bath salts. Untying the pink ribbon that held the glass stopper in place, he turned the jar upside down over the table.

The big crystals ran like a stream of sugar candy over the dark cloth, and with them, slim, glittering and serpentine, slithered, coil after coil, the emerald girdle, until it lay in a scintillating heap in the middle of the pile of bath salts.

There was a little gasp of sheer admiration from Angela Ford and Mrs. Orkney Cloude, and what amounted to a shout of triumph from Mrs. van Dolen.

Arkwright interposed a massive arm between her and the table.

"One moment, madam," he said.

Constantine was contemplating the girdle.

"And they left that, day after day, unprotected in the bathroom," he said, with a note of real admiration in his voice. "The one place in which they guessed the thief would never look for it. The sheer nerve of it!"

"How did you tumble to it, sir?" asked Arkwright.

Constantine separated the bath crystals with his finger.

"Look," he said.

Arkwright bent over the table. In the clear space where the crystals had been piled was a little mound of bran.

CHAPTER XVIII

IF STUART and Soames had hoped that by lingering in Constantine's room after the rest of the party had dispersed they would get the old man to talk, they were disappointed.

As the last excited voice died away along the passage, and the closing of doors showed that the "Noah's Ark" had at last retired to rest, he rose and knocked out his pipe.

"Bed," he announced. "And, for the first time since I entered this place, I can feel certain of staying there."

"But, I say, aren't you going to tell us how you did it?" objected Soames childishly.

"Do you know what time it is?" demanded Constantine.

"So near breakfast-time that we may as well make a night of it," was Soames's answer. "Have mercy, doctor."

But Constantine shook his head.

"I'm going to try and sleep to forget it," he said, his voice weary and dispirited. "And I advise you to do the same."

"You're tired out, sir," exclaimed Stuart. "It's a shame to bother you."

Constantine's face softened.

"I believe you'll understand when I say that it's not my body that's tired," he said slowly. "The hunt was good fun while it lasted, but it's fallen a little flat at the end. I liked those two women, and, of all the qualities, I think pluck is the one I admire most."

"They seemed very small, somehow," agreed Stuart thoughtfully, "when one saw them with their backs to the wall. Their helplessness in their role of Adderley had been so absurdly convincing, that it was difficult to rid one's mind of it."

Constantine sighed.

"Good material wasted," he said, "and I hate waste. They're clever enough, too, to know that they've chosen not only the worst but the silliest and least profitable profession in the world. They'll work harder all their lives than many a more honest woman, and probably die penniless. The world's a queer place, and, for to-night, I would prefer to forget it."

Stuart understood him even better when, as he was undressing, he found his mind straying to the empty room next door. He, too, had liked Miss Amy, and, from the beginning, had been conscious of an absurdly protective feeling towards her—a feeling that he now knew to be entirely unwarranted. If ever there was any one perfectly able to look after herself it was the woman they had surprised in the barn that night. As he got thankfully into bed, he told himself, and it was no doubt the truth, that it had flattered his masculine vanity and soothed that inherent sense of inferiority that had always been his stumbling-block, to play knight-errant to a pathetic little old lady. But, as he fell asleep, he knew that he would miss Amy Adderley, and that, had she existed outside Belle Gearie's imagination, he would probably have looked her up, sooner or later, in her neat little retreat at Tunbridge Wells.

He and Soames were present at the interview between Constantine and Arkwright next morning.

The inspector was quite frank about his own attitude towards the crime.

"Walker killed Major Carew," he said decisively. "You agree with me there, sir?"

Constantine nodded.

"I should say there was no doubt about it," he answered. "I'm sure the two women had nothing to do with it. But how you propose to prove it I can't imagine."

"Neither can I," admitted Arkwright ruefully. "I am morally certain that he committed the murder; but, barring the fact that he undoubtedly was trying to get into the box-room when Bates scared him away, and that his only reason for wishing to go there could have been to remove the spanner, I've nothing against him whatever. I can charge him with 'breaking and entering' all right, but beyond that I am helpless. He came into Mrs. van Dolen's room, as I guessed he would, through the window, but he spotted me earlier than I had intended, and his pockets were empty when I took him."

"What made you hide in Mrs. van Dolen's room last night?" asked Soames. "I mean, why take it for granted that he would choose that particular night to make the attempt?"

Arkwright smiled.

"I had the advantage over all of you there," he said. "I knew my man. Walker has most of the qualities that go with brutality. He's stupid, very pertinacious, and, up to a point, singularly courageous, though I think lack of imagination rather than bravery is at the root of this. Twice he has been arrested as the result of his own foolhardiness. I laid a trap for him last night, and risked his falling into it. I argued that, seeing he had lost the emeralds and failed in his attempt to get Mrs. Orkney Cloude's jewels, he would have a shot at something before he made his get-away. He'd already wasted his time trying to locate the emeralds, and he knew that his tether was getting shorter every day. Mrs. van Dolen still possessed a tempting enough haul, and I hoped he would try her. I told Bates to let drop among the servants that a Scotland Yard detective was due this morning, and the news was of course passed on to Walker, who was in the habit of questioning the maid who took up his food as to how things were going. He must have realized that it was imperative that he should get away that night, and, as it turned out, I was right in thinking he would not go empty-handed."

"It was extraordinarily foolhardy of him to have attempted such a thing with the whole house on the alert," said Constantine.

Arkwright agreed.

"It was insane, but absolutely characteristic of the man; and remember, if it hadn't been for my presence, he would probably have brought it off. No one in this house suspected him of being anything but bed-ridden, and the back passages here made it comparatively easy for him to dodge any one who was watching. Also, lie was able to find out from the servants exactly what every one was doing. He probably knew, for instance, that Mr. Soames here was in the habit of using the bathroom as an observation-post. All Walker had to do was to watch his chance and get to the window on the stairs. Coming back would have been his main difficulty. The balcony was his only means of egress, owing to the excellence of both the locks and the doors in this house."

"Why didn't he have a try earlier?" asked Soames.

"For two reasons. One was that, as I have said, his mind was centred on the recovery of the emeralds, and, unfortunately for him, he had already succeeded in putting every one on the alert by his efforts to find them. The probability is that he did try, later, and was frustrated by one or other of the watchers. Also, you must take into account the fact that, so long as the snow persisted, he could not get away, and he had had one lesson already as to the risk of hiding anything on the premises here. No, the obvious moment for him to make his attempt would be the actual night on which he intended to leave."

"Have you got the movements of the two separate parties at all clear in your mind?" asked Constantine. "I've been going over the events of the past week or so, and it's a ticklish business trying to decide which was responsible for the various things that have happened."

"I've got the advantage of you there too," Arkwright admitted. "The two Gearies have been quite frank as to the part they played.

The truth is that they are scared to death of being implicated in the murder and are only too anxious to come clean, so far as they themselves are concerned. They stick to it, by the way, that they only saw Walker twice, and each time too indistinctly to identify him. This is the only part of their statement I do not believe, but it is impossible to get more out of them."

"Did the masked man exist? Or was he a fiction of our friend Miss Amy?" asked Constantine. "My own impression is that Melnotte was speaking the truth when he said that he was visited by him that night."

Arkwright looked up quickly.

"You've raised rather an interesting point," he answered. "Belle Gearie admits to having invented him. As a matter of fact, she was after Mrs. van Dolen's emeralds that night herself. She did not believe for one moment that they would be snowed up for any length of time together, and was anxious to take advantage of the opportunity the Fates had sent her. She had actually opened the window on the stairs when she was disturbed by some one bound, as she realized almost at once, on the same errand. This person was undoubtedly Walker, though she sticks to it that she never saw his face. She heard him, however, and beat a hasty retreat, but had not time to shut the window. It appears that he did not see her. She watched him from the flight of stairs at the end of the passage, but only saw his back. When she saw him make for the window and prepare to get out, she realized that there was some one else on the job, and, with a quick-wittedness that did her credit, spiked his guns by knocking up Mr. Stuart with her story of a masked man. Girling's man, Joe sleeps downstairs, and Walker, afraid he might have been roused by the ringing of one of the bedroom bells, did not dare attempt to escape in the direction of the lower regions, and was driven to turn out the light so as to get across the passage unperceived. But Belle Gearie, who has not been quite well enough primed by her mother, gave away the fact that he was not wearing a mask. On the face of that, I don't quite know what to make of Melnotte's story."

"All this talk about a masked man may have put the idea into Walker's head, and he may have taken advantage of it on the occasion of his visit to Melnotte," suggested Stuart.

"It's possible," agreed Arkwright. "But Walker has always worked in a way singularly true to type, and this isn't like him."

"Then Miss Connie's story of the man she saw crossing the yard on the night of the murder was a fake?"

Arkwright shook his head.

"She says not, and I'm inclined to believe that she is speaking the truth there The Gearie women not only saw him, but waited till they had watched him back into the house and then slipped over to the barn, pretty well wrecked the cars in their efforts to find the girdle, and eventually discovered it in the sack of bran. From that moment it never left their possession. The mother took to her bed, and, from then on, their room was never unprotected. But they got scared, and fell back on the bath salts. It was a brilliant stroke, as they knew that Mr. Stuart was keeping an eye on that part of the passage from his bedroom opposite the bathroom door. It was the one place in which Walker literally could not look, even if the idea had occurred to him."

"And Walker never spotted them?"

"He never saw them at any period of the whole affair. If he had, it is doubtful if he would have jumped to them. They have not worked in England for years, and would not be known to a thief of his calibre. I refuse to believe, however, that they did not see him sufficiently clearly to identify him."

Constantine gave a reminiscent chuckle.

"Do you remember Miss Amy's innocent suggestion that you should lock the doors before you settled down to watch?" he asked Stuart. "You fell for it like a child, and she knew that, for the time at least, the emeralds would remain undisturbed. I nearly gave the show away when you told me what you had done."

"You knew then where they were?" demanded Stuart. "I had my suspicions of you that night." Constantine nodded.

"I knew," he said. "And, incredible as it seemed, I knew that one of the Misses Adderley must have put them there. When you told me of her suggestion I felt quite certain of it."

"What first put you on their track, sir?" asked Arkwright.

"I started by eliminating certain people, such as the Romseys and Stuart. They simply seemed to be outside the pale of suspicion. I don't defend my method, but it did, at least, prevent my wasting my time on the most unlikely people. Later I ruled out Soames, for the simple reason that we were together practically all the time on the night in question. It was nearly half, past two when he left my room. About fifteen minutes later I saw the rope outside Carew's window, and ten minutes or so after that I woke him. I admit that he could conceivably have committed the murder or the robbery during that period, but it seemed to me so unlikely that I dismissed him from my mind. I tumbled to the connection between Geoffrey Ford and Mrs. Orkney Cloude almost immediately, and, though I did not know exactly what it implied, it was enough to clear her, from my point of view. Young Trevor seemed to me to be genuinely interested in Miss Hamilton, though I took the precaution of having a look round his room one day when he was out. When I discovered that he had been trying to solve the mystery himself, and had even got so far as to work out his theories on paper, I decided to give him the benefit of the doubt, at any rate for the moment. Miss Hamilton I never suspected. She had had far too many opportunities to steal Mrs. van Dolen's jewels to be likely to choose such an unpropitious moment. Unless she were working under the influence of Trevor, there seemed no reason to suspect her. So far as the sick chauffeur was concerned, I knew nothing about him, though I do remember hearing that Bates had had him out of bed and had searched his mattress. This left me Melnotte and the Misses Adderley. Of the two, Melnotte seemed the darker horse, but from the little I knew of him, I could not believe him capable of carrying through such an enterprise. I kept an open mind about him, however. The Gearie impersonation was so perfect that I should have dismissed all idea of their guilt as incredible if it hadn't been for one thing, a slight incident that occurred on the second day of our stay here. I thought little of it at the time, but, later, it recurred to me. We were in the lounge discussing Miss Amy's story of the masked man she had seen the night before. Soames turned to me and suggested, in a voice so low that I should have said that no one but myself could have heard it, that the corridor window over the stable-yard was the most likely place for an intruder to use. Miss Connie heard him, however, and gave a little cry of horror. She started to say something about their bedroom looking on to the yard, and then was cleverly silenced by her sister. At the time I was inclined to put this down to one of those strange freaks of hearing peculiar to deaf people, and certainly did not take it seriously. Later, as I say, it came back to me with an added meaning. So far as I know, that was the only serious oversight either of them made during the whole of their visit, and I can see now that it was entirely due to the almost exaggerated thoroughness with which Miss Connie was playing her part. On the night the tyres were slashed in the barn, I noticed that the locks, both of the barn and the door into the yard, had been carefully oiled, and, once more, a flash of memory came to my aid. I remembered that Miss Amy had addressed some remark to me, and I had started to get up from my chair. She had expostulated and placed a hand on my shoulder. Now, I've got a very keen sense of smell, and that hand had smelt strongly of oil—a small thing once more, but one that fitted in with the discovery which had put me on their track. I refer, of course, to the bath salts. Those bath salts had always both amused and perplexed me, they were so out of keeping with the Misses Adderley and their ways. Orange water or lavender I could have understood, but I could not see either of the Misses Adderley spending, at the least, thirty shillings on a Bond Street production of that sort. On the other hand, many elderly ladies have extravagant nephews who pay them these little attentions, and the incongruity had no real significance, though I must confess that I used to lie in the bath and stare at that jar, and invent quite innocent little stories to account for it. That, I suppose, was how I came to notice what the others missed, a little scattering of bran wedged between the salts and the side of the glass jar. The girdle was beautifully packed. The job must have taken a long time, and been a very difficult one, and I had the deuce of a time in locating it without disturbing the salts unduly. I did, however, manage to verify the fact that it was there; after which, as I say, several small incidents came back into my mind and served to confirm my suspicions. One was the fact that on Christmas night I had seen Miss Connie's head and shoulders leaning out of her sister's window, and had noticed that she was, apparently, fully dressed. Ordinarily it would have struck me as a foolish thing for an old lady with bronchitis to do, but, in the light of the discovery I had made, it all fitted in nicely. Once I had located the girdle it simply remained for me to keep watch on the jar of salts and wait till some one materialized from Scotland Yard. I was afraid to put the affair into the hands of Bates. I had a conviction that they would prove too clever for him. Meanwhile, they couldn't get away, and I could afford to bide my time, though I admit that I grew a little jumpy when the snow stopped."

"And the oil was borrowed from the chambermaid by Miss Amy, to rub her sister's chest with," remarked Stuart. "I must say, they were an ingenious couple."

"And then, by sheer chance, I managed to burn my hand at the crucial moment. I was amused when I discovered where the oil had come from," said Constantine. "By the way, it was my little friend, Miss Amy, who punctured the tyres that night, I suppose?"

"And I lent her my torch and waited for her outside while she did it!" groaned Stuart. "I suppose she really did find Mrs. Cloude's jewel-case? Or had she planted it there herself?"

"According to her own account, she really did find it," answered Arkwright. "Of course, she had the advantage of knowing that the original thief would try to make a get-away, and the sense to guess that he wouldn't go empty-handed. When she heard that he had been in the act of taking Lord Romsey's car, she knew where to look. I think she is speaking the truth there."

"Now that one has heard the Gearie version of what happened on the night of the murder, it is easier to reconstruct Walker's part in it," said Constantine thoughtfully. "It looks as though he must have chosen Carew's room, knowing the man to be bemused with drink and less likely to wake than any other occupant of any of the rooms overlooking the balcony. Carew must have awakened at an unfortunate moment for himself, and Walker killed him. He then had the nerve to go on with his original plan, slide down the rope, get into Mrs. van Dolen's room and take the emeralds, depart by the door, leaving it unlocked, and make his way back to his own room. Then, while we were occupied with our search for Carew, he must have slipped down the back staircase and over to the barn. Either he had amazing luck, or he chose his time with great skill, for if the Gearies really saw him at the time they say they did, he must have got there and back while we were gathered on the landing outside Mrs. van Dolen's room, just before we sent for Girling. Once Girling and the household were roused, he would have had little chance of getting out of the yard door."

"I went down myself directly afterwards to see that it was locked," Soames reminded him.

"If this is more or less what happened, there's one thing that I for one can't account for," said Constantine slowly.

Arkwright shot him an appreciative glance.

"I believe I know what's worrying you," he said. "I've been trying to work it out myself. My reconstruction of events is pretty nearly the same as your own. At any rate, nothing will make me believe that Walker went back up that rope to Carew's room. It would be an almost impossible task in that weather, and there were no traces of snow on the window-ledge inside the room. It was, roughly speaking, about two-thirty when you saw the rope from your window, wasn't it, Dr. Constantine?"

"Yes. And the light was on in Carew's room then."

Arkwright smiled.

"That's the snag, isn't it? The light was out when you went into the room at five-fifteen. And Mr. Stuart didn't notice it when he went out on the balcony at about three o'clock. I'm willing to bet that he would have seen it, and remembered seeing it, if it had been on. After all, his interest was centred on that room and its occupants. My own impression is that that light was put out some time between two-thirty and three o'clock, though, I admit, it may have been much later."

"And if Walker made his exit through Mrs. van Dolen's room, how and when did he go back to Carew's room to put out the light? And why? And if it wasn't Walker, who did put out the light? You can't get that out of him, I suppose; it's an interesting point."

Arkwright shook his head.

"Walker's an old hand. He won't open his lips until he's seen his 'mouth-piece,' and, after that, we can whistle for any help he'll give us. It's an infernally awkward position. I've got my man; but, so far as the capital charge is concerned, I see every prospect of his slipping through my fingers."

CHAPTER XIX

ON LEAVING Constantine's room, Stuart made his way downstairs, and, strolling into the coffee-room, stood in the bay window, looking thoughtfully out on to the village street.

The thaw was well on its way, and the snow was rapidly degenerating into slush. Provided they did not freeze within the next few days, the roads should offer no obstacle to motorists. His car was in good running order, and there was nothing to keep him at the "Noah's Ark," but he felt a singular reluctance to leave. He had grown genuinely fond of the place, and he liked Girling and the solid, unostentatious comfort of the old inn. Now that all the alarums and excursions were over, he felt a desire to stay on and sample its hospitality under more normal conditions. But the Romseys were bound for Redsands, and so, in consequence, was he, though he told himself that he would be wiser to cut them out of his life altogether. In any case, he had every intention of returning to the "Noah's Ark" during the summer months. It would be an ideal place in which to write, not too far from London, and sufficiently off the beaten track for peace and quiet.

He was joined by Melnotte. In pursuance of his determination to be friendly with that young man, he pulled out his cigarette-case and offered it to him.

"I was just thinking that we shall all be making tracks now," he said.

"I wanted to talk to you about that," volunteered Melnotte, in his rather mincing way. "I ought to get away as soon as possible. There's my work, for one thing, though I'm not sure if my engagement at Redsands still holds good. Anyway, I want to get away. I hate this place!"

He brought out the last sentence with a passionate intensity that would have surprised Stuart if he had not been accustomed to Melnotte's almost hysterical outbursts.

"Why don't you go, then?" he answered soothingly. "There's nothing to prevent you now."

Melnotte's eyes shifted uneasily.

"That fellow Bates was so offensive when I spoke of leaving that I don't care to broach the subject again," he said undecidedly. "But I don't see how they can keep me, do you?"

"Of course not. The whole thing's cleared up and they've got quite a good bag. They won't interfere with any of us now. Why don't you see Arkwright about it?"

Still Melnotte hesitated. Stuart had the impression that there was something at the back of his mind, and that he was trying to brace himself to reveal it.

"Bates was a bit fussed when you spoke to him about it," he added. "I don't honestly think you need be afraid of any further trouble."

"What have they found out, Mr. Stuart?" asked Melnotte, abruptly changing the subject. "I seem to have been a bit out of things. I know that those two women had the emeralds, of course, and that the man the inspector took was after the rest of the old woman's jewellery, but I'm a bit at sea about Major Carew's death. Do they know who murdered him?"

"They know, all right," answered Stuart frankly. "It all points to its having been the man Walker. But whether they'll be able to charge him with it is another question."

"You mean there's no evidence against him?"

"None that's fit to take before a jury. The Gearies are just as much implicated."

"Will they try to pin it on to them, do you think?" Melnotte's voice sounded husky, as though his throat had become dry. Stuart, watching him, had a sudden intuition. There *was* something the dancer wanted to say, but it would require more than a little tact to overcome his hesitancy.

When he spoke it was with this object in mind.

"The Gearies are in a very nasty position," he said gravely, "and they know it. They've been absolutely frank about their share in the business, but that won't help them much if they're up against a clever counsel." Melnotte swallowed convulsively. Stuart thought that he had never seen a man give himself away so badly.

"Do you mean that they'll be hung?" asked Melnotte shakily.

"I suppose so," answered Stuart with intentional callousness. "I don't see how they can escape, if they do manage to bring the murder home to them."

He held out his case. For the last few minutes Melnotte had been drawing at an extinguished cigarette.

The dancer shook his head.

"No, thanks. I've got packing and things to do. Are you going to-day, Mr. Stuart?"

"I shan't make a move till to-morrow, at the earliest. I want to see what the weather's going to do. By the way, if you want a lift to Redsands, I can give you one."

Ten minutes before he would not have made the offer. He was prepared to treat Melnotte with ordinary friendliness, but the last thing he desired was his company on the road. Now, however, he would have done more than this rather than let him out of his sight. He was convinced that he had been concealing something.

The move was a success. Melnotte's face flushed with gratification.

"That's really exceedingly kind of you, Mr. Stuart," he said in his most refined tones. "But I can't say yet whether they expect me now at Redsands. I'm going to get them on the phone to-day."

He took himself off, and Stuart, after a moment's thought, decided to forgo the walk he had intended to take, and establish himself in the lounge. If Melnotte had anything to say, he should find him available.

He was doomed to disappointment. Melnotte did not materialize again, and, after lunch, Stuart was driven to make the first advances himself.

"What about a cup of coffee in my room?" he asked as they left the table. "These two maniacs are spending the afternoon scowling over the chessboard, and everybody but myself seems to be packing furiously."

"Rather!" assented Melnotte, a look, half of relief, half reluctance, on his face. Constantine's eyebrows rose a fraction of an inch, but all he said was—

"I'll drop in on you for a pipe before dinner."

"Trust you for that," reflected Stuart, with an internal chuckle, as he led the way upstairs.

He called over the banisters to the aged waiter and told him to bring up coffee, and ask Girling for a bottle of the brandy Dr. Constantine liked.

"I'm such a poor judge of brandy that I don't even know what to ask for," he confessed to Melnotte with a grin. "But the others said this was something quite exceptional, and even I was able to enjoy it. I hope you're more of a connoisseur than I am."

"Champagne's the only wine I know anything about," answered the dancer. "Not that I ever buy it myself. But it comes my way at night-clubs and so forth."

He had already begun to shed many of his little affectations when alone with Stuart.

"If it wasn't for all the beastly things that have happened in this place," he said as he sank gracefully into the chair Stuart had drawn up to the fire, "I should have been grateful for the peace and quiet of it. I'm a domestic sort of chap, really, and I wasn't brought up to the sort of life I have to lead nowadays. My people were the religious sort. I used to sing in the choir, and all that sort of thing."

He spoke bashfully, with an anxious glance at Stuart's face, as though he dreaded to surprise a derisive smile on it. But Stuart showed no disposition to laugh at this rather unexpected self-revelation.

"I can imagine one's getting pretty sick of nightclubs," he answered. "I've had to work too hard for that sort of thing myself, until quite lately, and, even now, I find it rather hard to play. That's probably my Scottish blood coming out."

Melnotte sipped his brandy thoughtfully. Stuart waited in silence till he had finished it, then filled up his glass again.

"Oh, I say!" expostulated Melnotte, but continued to sip with appreciation.

Stuart watched the colour deepen on his cheekbones, noted the added lustre in his eyes, and felt ashamed of himself. A little Dutch courage was so obviously all that the man needed to bring him to the point.

"It's curious how much I miss those two funny little spinsters next door," he remarked conversationally. "I know that, whatever happens, I shall never be able to think of them as anything else. Mother and daughter seems preposterous."

Melnotte's face grew suddenly haggard. Under the influence of the brandy he had cast off his troubles for the moment; now they came back to him with added intensity.

He sat hunched in his chair, staring into the fire. The grip of his hands, which hung clasped between his knees, tightened until the knuckles whitened with the strain. Then suddenly he spoke.

"I—I've been wanting a word with you alone," he said. "The truth is, I'm in a hell of a mess."

His voice died away. Now that he had committed himself he looked aghast. Stuart hastened to reassure him.

"Whatever it is, it's probably not nearly so bad as you think," he told him. "Things are apt to look better once they are put into words."

"This is going to look worse," was Melnotte's gloomy rejoinder. "I don't know what you'll think of me when you hear what I've got to tell you, and I know what I think of myself. I've been a fool and worse. My only excuse is that part of it, at least, wouldn't have happened if I hadn't felt that every one's hand was against me."

He fell silent again, and Stuart did not dare to speak.

"I can clear those women," came Melnotte's voice at last.

Stuart forgot all caution and sprang to his feet. This was more than he had expected.

"You mean you know who committed the murder?" he exclaimed.

"I've known all along," said Melnotte miserably. "I saw the chap as clearly as I can see you."

Stuart hesitated for a moment, then laid a hand on Melnotte's shoulder.

"Look here," he said. "This is too serious a business for me. Won't you let me fetch Arkwright? He's an understanding sort of chap, and it'll save your having to go through the whole thing twice. Let me fetch him."

But, at the mere idea, Melnotte's nerve deserted him entirely. He wrung his hands together.

"I can't see him. I'll tell you. I've got to get it off my chest somehow. After that, I'll sign anything you like, if it'll get those two women off; but I won't see Arkwright until I have to. When you've heard what I've got to say, you'll understand why."

Stuart sat down again and drew his chair closer.

"Do you want me to write it down?" he asked. "You'll have to answer Arkwright's questions sooner or later, you know."

Melnotte flinched.

"I know," he said. "I've brought it on myself, and I suppose I shall have to go through with it. But it'll be easier once you've told him the facts."

Stuart reached out a long arm and took a block and pencil from the table.

"All right," he said, "I'll jot down the facts as you give them to me, so as to pass them on correctly. Go ahead."

There was a moment of tense silence, during which it seemed as if Melnotte would never bring himself to the point of speech; then, with his eyes fixed rigidly on the fire, his face drawn with misery and humiliation, he plunged.

"I wasn't asleep on the night of the murder," he began. "When I came out of my room I'd been awake for hours. I ought to have said so then, of course, but I couldn't. I suppose, even when I've told you the whole story, you won't be able to understand why, but, I give you my word, I couldn't. It's the way I'm made, I suppose," he finished bitterly.

Stuart said nothing, but waited in silence for him to continue. He did so almost immediately. Now that the first agonizing effort was over, he seemed inclined to luxuriate in self-revelation. "Something woke me," he went on. "You know how you can wake and have a more or less clear idea what has awakened you, without having actually heard it. I'm pretty sure now that I was roused by the opening of the window in Carew's room. Then I distinctly heard Carew shout. I looked at my watch and saw that it was ten minutes to two. It never occurred to me that there was anything wrong, and my only feeling was one of annoyance. I thought Carew had woke up and was on the rampage again, and that we should have the same trouble with him that we had had earlier in the evening. I wondered whether Mr. Soames and Dr. Constantine were still playing chess, and decided that, if Carew showed any signs of being on the move, I would fetch them. I lay and listened, but I give you my word that I never suspected there was anything really wrong with him. Then I heard a bump, as if some one had knocked into a bit furniture, and the very faint scrape of a chair or table. I made up my mind that I must tell some one, and got out of bed. It was then that I thought of the communicating door between the two rooms, and remembered that the key was on my side of the lock."

Stuart looked up quickly.

"That's the key they couldn't find," he interpolated.

"Yes. It was in my dressing-gown pocket when I came out of my room after the murder. Later, when everything was quiet, I threw it out of my window. I didn't know what else to do with it."

"And Bates found it in the snow next day," exclaimed Stuart. "But that key fitted the lock of Carew's door."

Melnotte nodded.

"I found out afterwards that the locks of the two bedroom doors and the communicating door were all alike," he said. "If you try your communicating door-key you'll probably find that it's on the same plan. I don't think any of the other keys on this landing suit my door. I tried Dr. Constantine's, and it doesn't. I was sweating with fear that Bates would discover that it fitted the communicating door. You see, I'd got something else he never spotted when he searched my things."

"I can quite believe it," remarked Stuart. "I've been thinking all along how futile a search of that sort really is. Bates asked us to turn out our pockets, but he never searched them for himself. We could have kept back anything, even the girdle if we'd had it, though I believe he was much more drastic with the servants."

Melnotte nodded.

"He never actually searched me," he said. "If he had, he'd have been bound to find it. As a matter of fact, I suppose I'm the only person in the house that possesses a revolver."

Stuart could only stare at him. He made up his mind never again to judge by appearances. Melnotte was the very last person he would have suspected of even handling, far less carrying, such a thing.

The dancer must have guessed his thoughts, for a dull flush crept over his face.

"I know it seems a bit unnatural," he went an. "But the place where I lodge in London has been burgled twice, and a fellow lodger, a man who'd been through the War, decided to rout out his old army revolver and get out a licence. Then he remembered that he'd been rather a good shot, and took to going to one of those shooting-galleries. He persuaded me to go with him, and I got quite keen. I'm fairly decent at it, too, though you wouldn't think it," he finished ingenuously.

"What made you bring it here?" asked Stuart.

"Well, this chap left after a time and, well, I'm a nervous sort of person, and I didn't like to think of the place left unprotected. There was another burglary, in the house next door this time, and I suppose that decided me. Anyway, I got myself a revolver, and used to sleep with it under my pillow. I suppose I got accustomed to the feeling that it was there; anyway, I always have taken it away with me when I've had a job in the provinces. That's how it came to be under my pillow that night, and I was thankful for it, I can tell you."

"How did you manage to keep it out of Bates's hands?"

"I had it tucked inside my shirt, under one arm, when he searched my things. If he'd touched me he'd have found it."

"Let's get back to the door," said Stuart. "Did you open it?"

"Yes. And I wish now that I hadn't, though I suppose the Gearies would be in the soup if I'd done what I first thought of and gone to fetch the others. The truth was, you'd all made me feel a bit small, and I wanted to be able to say that I had looked into the room. Anyway, I turned the key as softly as I could. As you can imagine, I didn't want to tackle Carew single-handed. I must have got the door open without making a sound, because the man inside never heard me."

"Could you see him?"

"Plainly. He was standing by the open window, leaning out. Of course I thought he was Carew. I wasn't expecting to see any one else. Then he straightened himself and I saw his profile."

He paused. Stuart could see the perspiration shining on his forehead, and began dimly to realize the sheer torture such a temperament as Melnotte's could be to a man.

"Was it Walker?" he asked, when he could contain himself no longer.

Melnotte nodded.

"I know now that it was Walker. I didn't then, of course. I don't think I even knew of the existence of the sick chauffeur, certainly

I'd never seen him. All I did know was that he ought not to be there. How I got that door shut without making a noise I don't know. But I must have, or I don't suppose I should be here now, because I didn't dare lock my bedroom door for ages, for fear he should hear it."

"What did you do after that?"

Melnotte looked acutely uncomfortable.

"I got out the revolver from under my pillow and waited. You see, when he stood up I saw the rope. He was holding the end in his hand. I knew then for certain that he was up to no good, though I'd no idea what had really happened. You must remember I couldn't see the bed from where I stood, and, for all *I* knew, the man might have been an accomplice of Carew's. I know I ought to have given the alarm, but I wasn't absolutely sure then whether he had seen me, and I simply couldn't bring myself to move. After what seemed hours, I heard Dr. Constantine's voice saying good-night to Mr. Soames. That seemed to be my chance. I made for the door of my room and tore it open. I didn't care then how much noise I made, and I wonder Mr. Soames didn't hear me. He must have stopped to say something to Dr. Constantine, because he wasn't in the passage when I put my head out. Some one else was, though! The man I had seen in Carew's room was standing at the foot of the flight of steps at the end of the passage, and he was looking straight at me."

"What did you do?" asked Stuart, conscious that his own breath was coming a bit faster.

"I did the only thing I could do," answered Melnotte naively. "I bolted back into my room and locked the door. He was carrying something that looked like a spanner in his hand, and if you'd seen his face, you'd have done what I did."

"When you looked through the communicating door into Carew's room did you see the spanner?" cut in Stuart.

"Distinctly. It was lying beside him across the window-ledge. I noticed that first, and wondered what it was and what on earth Carew was doing with such a thing."

"What happened after that?"

"I simply waited. I'd have given anything to get along the passage to Dr. Constantine's room, but I didn't dare open my door again. I know I looked at the time every now and then; it seemed so endless. It was about half-past, two when I heard some one unlock Carew's door softly and go in. What I suppose happened was that Walker was on his way to Carew's room when he saw me. He must have bolted then, and made his way back later. Judging from what happened afterwards, it must have been Walker I heard going in the second time. Anyway, I made sure it was him at the time, partly because he was so quiet over it. If I hadn't been listening I shouldn't have heard him. Almost directly afterwards I heard Dr. Constantine's window open. Then I heard him come along the passage and knock at Carew's door."

"Then Walker was actually inside the room when Constantine first tried to rouse Carew?" exclaimed Stuart.

"He must have been. Anyhow, I took it for granted he was. If I hadn't I should have come out then. I wish now that I had. I heard Dr. Constantine go along the passage, and, a few minutes later, I heard Mr. Soames's voice. I was a fool not to have gone out then, but I simply couldn't as long as I knew that that man was in the next room. Then, about three o'clock, I heard the snap of the light-switch in Carew's room and stood listening by my door, thinking I should hear the man come out. But he didn't. I heard a window open somewhere down below, but there wasn't a sound from the room next door."

"Any idea what time it was when you heard the window?"

"About three, I should think. Five minutes or so after I heard the light-switch go in Carew's room."

"That must have been when I went out on to the balcony the first time. Then all that time Walker must have been inside that room, with the door locked."

"From what I could hear, I feel certain of it. It must have been at least twenty minutes after that that I heard the key turn gently in the lock, and knew he had come out at last. It must be a stiff lock, or I shouldn't have heard it."

"Why didn't you come out then?" demanded Stuart.

Melnotte cast him a look of horrified protest.

"How was I to tell he wasn't lurking in the passage? I'd run into him once already, and I wasn't going to risk doing it again, now that he knew I'd seen him. I just sat tight and waited for one of you to come back."

"I suppose it didn't occur to you that Walker might do one of us in, if we came on him unawares in the passage?" Stuart could not resist asking.

Melnotte coloured painfully.

"I know it all sounds pretty beastly," he moaned. "But you don't realize the position I was in. I didn't know then that the man had killed Carew. I simply thought he was a thief. But there was murder in his face when he saw me in the passage, and I'm certain, now, that he would have done me in if he'd been able to get at me."

It seemed more merciful to change the subject.

"Did anything else happen? Before we arrived on the scene, I mean?"

"Some one came along the passage and knocked again at Carew's door. I'd looked at my watch a minute before. That was just on three-fifteen. I nearly opened my door then, but I thought it might be a trap of Walker's to get me out. After that, no one came near me, and I sat there waiting, expecting every minute that that brute would somehow manage to get into my room, for two solid hours. It was past five when I heard your voices in the corridor and came out."

"But why on earth didn't you say anything when you did come out? You were safe enough then," exclaimed Stuart.

"Was I? Try to put yourself in my place. All the time I'd been sitting there waiting, I'd been putting two and two together. Before that it had begun to strike me as odd that nobody seemed able to rouse Carew. Either his room was empty or something was the matter with him. The thing I couldn't determine was whether he was hand in glove with this other man and was lying low on purpose, or whether he'd been drugged, or hurt, or possibly killed. Whichever it was, it was a beastly position for me. If I gave the show away, and Carew was listening in that room, I should be for it, sooner or later. You must remember that the other man was still at large, and I didn't know who he was. He'd seen me, and whether he was a confederate of Carew's or not, he was free to get his own back whenever he chose. As it was, I knew he'd got his knife into me, and what I didn't know was whether he was lurking round the corner of the passage, waiting to see what I'd do. Of course I meant to tell Bates or some one later, when I could be sure of not being overheard; but I simply didn't dare do it then."

"Then that's why you've been so anxious to get away all this time!" exclaimed Stuart.

Melnotte nodded.

"I haven't had a decent night's rest since Carew was murdered," he said simply. And it was obvious he spoke the truth. "It was bad enough in the daytime. I tried to tack myself on to one or other of you, because I was terrified that he'd catch me unawares. But you weren't any too friendly, you know, and I couldn't make out to what extent I was suspected of being mixed up in the murder. You see, that key was on my conscience, and I was terrified Bates would try it on the communicating door. And the nights were awful. I didn't dare let myself sleep."

"I should have thought you'd have felt much safer if you'd made a clean breast of it and put yourself in Bates's hands," said Stuart bluntly.

"What earthly protection would Bates have been? He never even succeeded in hampering Walker's movements. Besides, once I knew that Carew had been murdered, I'd got my own safety to consider. I'd no idea whether Bates suspected me or not, but Mrs. van Dolen's attitude was pretty clear, and, in any case, I couldn't produce any kind of proof that the man I had seen existed. Even if Bates had believed my story, he wouldn't have let me go, and as long as that man was in the same house with me I didn't dare give him away. I suppose I behaved like a cowardly fool, but you must see that my hands were tied."

Stuart did not argue the point. One thing he could not resist saying.

"And yet, as it turned out, you were safe enough. Nothing did happen to you."

Melnotte positively glared at him.

"Didn't it? What about the night Walker got into my room?"

Stuart sat up.

"That clears up one point," he cried. "That masked man story was true, then?"

"It was true that he came. He wasn't masked. Miss Adderley's story put that into my head."

"What did he want? Was he just searching for the emeralds?"

"He came to kill me," stated Melnotte, simply and with the utmost conviction.

CHAPTER XX

MELNOTTE, in spite of his little affectations, struck Stuart as an essentially truthful person. That he could lie convincingly, to save himself from physical hurt, he had proved conclusively enough, but he showed none of the gusto and fluency of a born liar. When he set out to tell the truth he told it, and Stuart felt convinced that his account of what had happened was substantially correct. This being the case, he could not be said to be exaggerating when he declared that Walker visited him with the intention of killing him.

Not only did he hold Walker's life literally in his hands, should he choose to speak, but, in Walker's eyes, was of all the people in the house the one most likely to have robbed him of the emeralds. There could be no doubt that Walker had all along been quite unaware of the identity of the Misses Adderley. But he knew that Melnotte had seen him, and, very shortly afterwards, had heard of the theft of Mrs. van Dolen's jewels. What could seem more likely than that he had watched Walker, and, later, gone himself to the barn and taken the girdle. Melnotte had been right in his assumption that only extreme vigilance on his part had saved him from Walker's vengeance.

All through the following day and night he had been baffled in his attempts to get in touch with the dancer, and it was not until the second night that he conceived that idea of trying the key of Carew's room in the lock of Melnotte's door.

As Melnotte, unfortunately for him, did not discover till afterwards, the three locks were identical, though, as Walker confessed before his death, he had tried the same dodge both on Mrs. van Dolen's room and the box-room in which he had hidden the spanner, and found that it did not work. It was sheer bad luck, from Melnotte's point of view, that the key should have opened all three doors, and he was only saved by the fact that, when Walker stealthily opened the door and slipped into the room, he was sitting up in bed trying to read, with his revolver on his knees.

The instinct for self-preservation must have given him sufficient courage to defy Walker. The fact remains that he held him covered all through their interview, and, apparently, succeeded in more or less convincing him that he knew nothing about the emeralds. Walker had been forced to confine himself to threats, and had evidently succeeded in terrifying Melnotte. The dancer was a little vague as to what had passed at their interview, but by dint of patient and tactful questioning Stuart elicited the fact that he had definitely given his promise to Walker not to breathe a word of what he had seen. Walker's last words, before he removed himself, were to the effect that, if Melnotte gave him away, he would never rest until he had tracked him down and taken his revenge. This was enough for Melnotte, who was already almost in a state of collapse, and whose vivid imagination pictured a life of menace and uncertainty before him should Walker escape the death penalty. There was no doubt in Stuart's mind that he had been only too eager to promise silence, and would undoubtedly have held his tongue to the end if the predicament of the Gearies had not weighed upon his conscience. As it was, when Constantine, awakened by the sound of the door closing, came to see if he was all right, he was hard put to it to invent a plausible story without giving Walker away. It was obvious that, even now, he was in terror of the man.

"Do you suppose they'll hang him?" he asked Stuart fearfully.

"I should think your evidence would be enough to convince any jury," answered Stuart. "Did he molest you again?"

Melnotte shook his head.

"He never had the chance," he answered. "After that I jammed a chair up against the door every night and sat on it."

Stuart stared at him in amazement.

"You don't mean to say that you sat up every night?"

"What else was I to do?" asked Melnotte drearily. "There was no bolt to the door, and I'd no guarantee that he wouldn't come back again. I wonder none of you noticed the amount of sleep I put in in the daytime. I had to be jolly careful, too, that there was some one else in the room, before I allowed myself to drift off. I've never gone through such agonies of sleepiness in my life as I have here."

"Why didn't you sit up with one of us?" demanded Stuart. "You knew we were watching, didn't you? You'd have been safe enough then."

Melnotte cast him a swift, sidelong glance.

"You'd have been pretty sick if I'd suggested it, wouldn't you?" he said. "You see, I had a sort of obsession that none of you liked me, and, towards the end, I was sure that I was under suspicion. Also, I didn't want Walker to get into his head that I was hobnobbing with any of you. I didn't know what construction he might place on it."

It was only too evident that the whole of Melnotte's energies had been concentrated on saving his skin, and it seemed useless to argue with him. In view of his state of mind it was to his credit that he had forced himself to come forward at the eleventh hour. Stuart was not surprised that he had not cared to face Arkwright with his story.

He read the notes he had made to Melnotte, who declared them to be correct.

"I suppose I'd better wait here," said Melnotte, looking the picture of misery.

Stuart reassured him as best he could, and went in search of Arkwright.

His training as a writer stood him in good stead. He was able to give the inspector a fairly vivid impression of the dancer's frame of mind, and get him to promise to let him down gently. As it happened, Arkwright was so elated at getting the evidence he needed that he was inclined to regard Melnotte with a certain contemptuous sympathy.

"Poor devil," was his comment. "He seems to have given himself such a thin time that there's no need for me to add to it."

In spite of which, Melnotte emerged from his interview with Arkwright badly shaken. He did not accept Stuart's offer of a lift to Redsands, but took himself off to London, and they saw no more of him until the Gearies and Walker came up for trial at the assizes.

Stuart's sympathy with Miss Amy Adderley persisted until he saw her and her mother in the dock. It was not till then that he realized to the full how clever their impersonation had been, and how thoroughly he had been deceived by it. The Miss Amy he had

known had vanished utterly. Belle Gearie's face was still ridiculously small and round, but she had exchanged her look of cloistered
innocence for one of youthful sophistication. Her closely shingled
brown hair gave her a misleading air of girlishness, and Stuart would
have put her down as being in the early twenties had he not known
that she would never see thirty again. In her mother it was easier
to trace the Miss Connie of the "Noah's Ark." Her hair, too, had
undergone a transformation, this time to a metallic and obviously artificial yellow, but the plumpness remained, though there was
hardness now about her eyes and lips that repelled him.

They took their sentence stoically, and never at any period during the trial attempted to incriminate Walker, though they obviously knew that he had killed Carew and would have had little
mercy on them if he had suspected they were in possession of the
emeralds.

Walker was the least interesting of the three prisoners, in spite
of the florid epithets bestowed on him by the Press. After his conviction he confessed, declaring that he had never intended to kill
Carew, but had hit him with the spanner in a moment of panic.
No doubt he hoped by this to escape the extreme penalty, but the
appeal made on the strength of his statement failed, and he was
hanged, just three months, to a day, after he had driven, in his role of
Grimes the chauffeur, into the yard of the "Noah's Ark."

The most interesting comment on the whole affair, from Stuart's point of view, was made by Constantine, who walked into the
little bunshop where he and Angela Ford were having tea on the
last day of the trial. He accepted their invitation to join them, and,
when they were leaving, drew Stuart on one side.

"I dined with Lord Romsey last night," he said in a low voice.
"It's astonishing how his son's marriage has taken the stuffing out
of him. But I expect you've heard all about that from Angela. It
took him some time to realize that it was a choice between losing
Geoffrey or accepting his wife, but he has given in at last, and gets
on amazingly well with his new daughter-in-law. I have an idea that
Angela will marry where she pleases."

Stuart looked him firmly in the eye.

"I hope so," he announced brazenly.

Constantine turned to go.

"Well, it's been an ugly business," he concluded. "But, as others have said before me, 'it's an ill wind that blows no one good.' One thing I can congratulate you on."

Stuart eyed him warily. He suspected the twinkle in the old man's eye.

"And that is?" he asked.

"You're not what Lord Romsey still calls 'a Papist,'" answered Constantine, as he made his escape.

THE END

CPSIA information can be obtained
at www.ICGtesting.com
Printed in the USA
LVOW01s2307200916

505527LV00012B/300/P